PUREFINDER

PUREFINDER

Ben Gwalchmai

COSMIC
EGG
BOOKS

Winchester, UK
Washington, USA

First published by Cosmic Egg Books, 2013
Cosmic Egg Books is an imprint of John Hunt Publishing Ltd., Laurel House, Station Approach,
Alresford, Hants, SO24 9JH, UK
office1@jhpbooks.net
www.johnhuntpublishing.com

For distributor details and how to order please visit the 'Ordering' section on our website.

ISBN: 978 1 78279 098 3

A CIP catalogue record for this book is available from the British Library.

Design: Stuart Davies

Printed and bound by CPI Group (UK) Ltd, Croydon, CR0 4YY

We operate a distinctive and ethical publishing philosophy in all
areas of our business, from our global network of authors to
production and worldwide distribution.

CHAPTER 1

He woke in a forest of people, or so it seemed to him at his ripe middle age of 30. A forest because each body in the room loomed over him. It was a room no bigger than ten feet square and 21 people were once asleep in there. 20, once he'd risen.

That time he didn't notice it at all but the first time he'd entered a room in a low lodging house, he'd retched. He was a man of 25 then, he'd seen enough to wizen him, but it was the stench that crept into the back of his throat and the stench that wouldn't let go of his windpipe. After five years, he was used to smells worse than that now. It was a fear of the cholera that made him exit a room quickly in the morning. *What are my perfumes? Stink and stench from slaughter-house and sewer. A fine start to Good Friday there*, he thought. The exact date was April 2, 1858.

At least I'm not in Ol' Nichol. His thought was remarkable for its odd optimism: he knew that today would bring uneasy conversations that…*might complicate matters.* After dressing he left the room, picked up his handle-basket from where he'd left it and, having paid the night before, exited the lodgings without word onto Union Street. It was barely dawn. Last night he'd paid for hot water and standing still – briefly – just outside the door, the cold sun pricked at his clean skin pleasantly. He smiled his usual, crooked smile and turned right to begin walking.

Where to walk, today? Where to pick? It's a Friday…but a Good Friday so many ladies, as well as ladies' walkers, will be out. In thinking these habitual thoughts, he'd already reached the end of Union Street and turned left onto Wells Street. Brighter, wider, Wells Street presented him with his first of the day so he removed his right glove, pocketed it, and picked up his find. Automatically his hand went to his basket and dropped it in. The pure was solid and a little greyed but not yet white, dropped late last night and picked too early for the orderlies to interfere with. He said aloud, 'A *Good* start,' and chuckled to himself. His tight-mouthed, high-pitched North Welsh accent had lost its whistle in the five years he'd been in London but his thoughts retained it: it gave him humour in any street, no matter how dark or how dark the looks he received. Though not considered an educated man, Bryn 'Purefoy' Lewis wasn't stupid – he knew now that for the rest of the day, unless he was able to obtain soap or lime, his right hand was for work and work only. He had survived well for five years in this way and in London, at that time, five years was a long time.

He'd decided to head in to St Paul's via as many fields and squares as was possible. *They'll be out in their masses for church today – if only to be seen at church.* But he knew he wouldn't get there without water. He knew water was dirty but…*better a bit of dirt than drunk at breakfast.*

As a purefinder, Purefoy had been a surprising success to himself: he'd expected to hate it, he didn't; he'd expected to get sick and die from picking up dog muck all day, he didn't; he'd expected even the costermongers to spit on him as he went by and they didn't – quite the opposite. Some of the other purefinders he'd encountered thought him mad because of his habit of taking off a glove to pick up but it was how he kept the smell at bay. Though no rich man and no local celebrity, his jacket pocket jangled to the sum of a florin. The easy air about his walk meant most considered him affable, harmless and, at worst, lazy. His BB, no matter how much she hated him, knew he wasn't lazy. With a florin's worth he knew he could get an orange for breakfast, bread and cheese for lunch, and soup for tea. He still hadn't lost the habit of calling dinner 'tea' and wouldn't anytime soon. If he felt the need for more, he could pick up a cup of tea from a street seller near Fleet Street come evening. With a florin, he'd still have spare enough for lodgings.

Already at the end of Wells and on Oxford Street, he paused and looked right. He flinched and looked away. Off Oxford, on Poland Street was the workhouse BB now lived in. He considered trying to see her on the pretence of asking for some water – it would be easy enough to get back on track to St Paul's if he just went by way of Broad and Berwick…he could get some water easily enough at Broad if they wouldn't give him any…

Within ten seconds he was at the top of Poland Street. Used to the Oxford Street adverts as he was, he didn't care to read them or care what wonders the rich were being sold that day. A small and slender man, his heart now pounded against his eyes and his pace quickened them to tears. He didn't mind, he hoped they'd help him get in. He reached number 49, walked in a little to take a deep breath, and knocked at the lodge with, 'Please, sir. Could I have some boiled water, please? I'm very thirsty.' The new porter at the lodge had a moustache that Purefoy had never seen before, it started close to the end of the lips and stuck out as cats whiskers do – there seemed no other hair on his face. His uniform was black with black boots but in London, nothing stays purely what it is for long – his jacket was spotted with marks of dirt. He'd been pacing even as Purefoy approached and now simply stared in answer. 'Please, sir. Just a drop.'

'Get out. Unless you've business here, go away.'

'As it so happens, sir, could I enquire as to the health of a Mrs B. Llewes.'

'I could check with Matron if you'll wait.' His gruff fronted voice calmed.

'Thank you, sir.'

'How do you spell that, please?' Purefoy had pronounced it the Welsh way and duly spelled it, adding that she might well be considered as Mrs B. Lewis. The porter took a note, walked to the back of the lodge, and opened a door; he then bent down and said something softly to a child dressed all in black sitting nearby; the child moved swiftly off.

'I imagine you'll not be needin' that water now then?'

'No. No thank you, sir.' The men smiled at each other. The porter resumed his pacing. Purefoy knew then that Banwen

Blodeuwedd Llewes might not be pleased to be called on at such an early hour, or to be called on at all by him, whether or not she was his wife.

He happily imagined her shouting from a window, impassioned in Welsh, and angry with him for embarrassing her only for him to taunt her back and end with a loud confession of his love – why should he care what the grand house thought – but his thoughts faltered when he realised he'd briefly forgotten how long she'd been in there. *A year and six...for her health.* In remembering, he realised then he did need water and something to eat. Before he could ask the porter, a gaunt woman had stepped into the lodge. Her nose long and her cheeks sallow, both were emphasised by her bustled curling mane of hair that held itself up; tired, she looked as though she'd cried more than Purefoy had that morning. She too was dressed all in black and, with control, said to him, 'Were you a relative of Mrs B. Lewis?'

'I am, I…' a knowing silence descended on the lodge.

'I'm sorry to inform you,' the matron continued but Purefoy wasn't listening. He took a step back. And another. He saw their faces twist into empathy, pity, and then look down. He felt his own becoming hot. He heard '…the north wing…' before his heart was at his eyes again. He turned on his heels. He walked in the direction of Broad Street trying very hard not to shout or yelp. For once, he wished that the brickfields had started earlier so the street ash might blur his face.

He could hardly breathe: he felt something filling his chest; his stomach had latched onto his spine, pulled his core downward – he was having trouble keeping his head upright; alternate sides of his head flashed hot then cold and he removed his Dai-cap to hold his face but stopped short of rubbing his eyes with his right hand. He slowed. He used his sleeve instead. It was no use: his breath came in faltering heaves as the mucous dripped from the end of his nose and his tears ran into his mouth. The back of his neck burned – the string holding his wedding ring around him itched. The ring itself felt lighter and more fragile on his chest than ever before. *Water; splash the face; water would help* – the only thoughts that came in words and not rushes.

He could see someone at the pump. He stopped on the corner to give them time to leave. Through his blurry eyes he saw a wolf of a woman rocking and flicking her head back and forth. He turned away in the vain hope of not being seen, but even through the loud, bloody sound of his chest he could hear her pining, howling. He turned and looked at her again. *A fur? Cotton reams?* She held something – something he couldn't make out – that she brought to her bared teeth each time she rocked. He took a couple of steps toward her. His breath finally escaped him: he saw then what she held. Empathy for the grime-lined wolf-woman filled him from his guts putting a stop to his tears briefly. He felt maybe, as both he and she felt as they did, he could help. He inched closer. Tears still silently gathered as he prepared to speak.

The woman snapped her head at him. He saw the dead child clearer now. It wasn't fur he saw before, but ragged clothes. It wasn't cloth but the dead-white legs of the child.

He tried to regulate his breath in order to speak but the wolf barked at him, 'You. *You*, purefinder, this is your fault – you muck-rakers, you shit-pickers. This is your fault.' She wailed then. *Enough to wake the dead.* The street had seemed bare before but he looked round once more and saw crossing-sweepers at either end, maidservants opening shades, and children emerging from all side streets. Panic struck him. A cold sweat. The woman again screamed at him, '*You*! You did this!' He retreated back up Poland Street, stepping back slowly. When enough distance meant he could turn without fear, he did so and quickened his pace. His eyes streamed again as his thoughts raced. *Had they seen my face? Would they think I did actually do it?* He ran. As he reached the workhouse, he looked back at Broad Street and imagined the porter, the sallow woman, and the wolf coming from it. His breath shortened. *My basket! My damned basket.* His eyes stung.

A sudden blow to the chest winded him entirely. He curled in on himself and coughed – his mouth was covered by a hand, he was grabbed by the chest and pulled onto Portland Street. An Irish accent told him quietly, 'I was like you once. Don't worry though, I'm here to deliver you from all evil.'

Chapter 2

Purefoy wept into the stranger's hand.

Parts of him he'd long forgotten twitched with each heaving lack of breath. He figured he'd soon be dead by this stranger's hand so didn't care to stop until it was all out. *Then I'll die – then I'll die or I'll be put out of my misery.*

'You should cry, Welshman.' The stranger's jocular tone reinforced the cruelty felt in Purefoy's winded chest. His nose was becoming blocked, his chest tight. Banwen's smell filled him; her wine-stained ankle birthmark and his hand touching it for the first time; the first time they wrote to each other; and the first word he learnt from her. These things left him unable to breathe properly, unable to care. His pain was unspeakable for him, he had only come close to this feeling once but BB had been there to soothe him. His memories of her flesh began to mingle with the sight of the dead child lying by the pump. Her ankle and the child's ankle; her laugh and the wolf mother's scream; each image pained the sharp sound of a train screeching louder and longer with each image – all he knew then was at some point, he vomited.

After a time unknown to him, Purefoy stopped crying. The stranger's grip was no longer around his mouth or chest but on his left shoulder. Purefoy had only consciously noticed the change as he leant against the wall with one hand, spitting and clearing his nose. 'Would you let go of me if I gave you half the money I have?'

'No.'

'I…I didn't murder that child, you know.'

'Yes you did. To that woman, everybody did.' Cold and clear, the famous Irish lilt was unfound.

'Look, I can't give you all my money but—'

'I don't want *your* money.'

'You can't take me to the beaks, I've done nothing wrong.'

7

'Oh can't I, now?'

Purefoy swung round and the two men looked each other over. Purefoy saw a wide-shouldered man, whose cheeks seemed redder than his lips but blotted with tiny freckles. Below the thick, orange moustache, the stranger was smiling. Purefoy realized there was something dandy about the man, no matter what parts were in the roughian style, his moustache and the way he held himself made Purefoy envious. The man's arms crossed. He stood with his legs almost shoulder width apart – firmly rooted to the ground. He dressed as costers were likely to – a good knee-length coat, thick black trousers, and a good waistcoat – but with a dustman's hat and a silk, green necktie. The stranger didn't like what he saw: an underdressed and underfed man, without any fine facial-hair, in the black and jacket-brown clothes of a nightman, with the glove of a purefinder but the hat of a country hand. He'd known what to expect; it didn't make it any less promising. They made a ragged, odd pair.

As they stood staring, Purefoy considered his options: *I could run...and attempt to outrun a man whose legs are one and a half times mine; fight – there's no fight here, only a beating.* At this, his mind scrambled slightly and he unconsciously breathed shorter breaths; his fear became a dripping ink at the back of his throat that he dared not attempt swallow down, until the thought, *Wait – slip away when I can...yes...or – or die, simply let the man do whatever he wants and be led to death...be led to...to Banwen. But wait...* This calmed him some. He inhaled heavily to steady himself. Purefoy's thoughts had always been able to calm him. He didn't know for certain whether they'd continue to do so.

'Come along then Bryn Prifardd Llewes.' Purefoy hadn't heard his name said properly by anyone but himself or Bran for years. How did this man know? How had he known how to pronounce it? A cold sweat started at the back of his head. 'Oh aye, taffy, I know *all* about you.'

Hormones pushed up his throat to choke his eyes and dry his

tongue. The smoke from the brickfields and the dirt from the dust-yards had begun to settle above the larger Soho streets and Purefoy was glad of it. Defeated, he asked, 'Where are we going?'

'To where I know a peeler who's gold.' The deep hush in the voice revelled in the 'gold'.

'I – I need some water and something to eat.'

'Oh you'll not need that where you're goin'.'

'And where, sir, are we going?'

'You needn't call me sir! Hah!' A laugh like a latch slamming.

'What then should I call you?'

'Think you'll get me that easily do you, Purefoy? You're more of a fool than she made out. Don't worry though, we're only headed to The City.' A flash of his teeth beneath the moustache and Purefoy saw rotted black stumps where you'd expect to see at least some shade of white.

'She, sir?'

'Don't call me sir, I said. Call me Murphy if ya must.' The snap in Murphy's pitch belied the strength of his anger.

'Well Mr Murphy —'

'Just Murphy.'

'You said, 'she' – who did you mean?' Murphy grabbed Purefoy by the neck and pushed him up against the wall. With one hand on his neck and the other holding his crotch, Purefoy could only think *Banwen. He'd gotten to Banwen.*

'Never you mind, taffy – this isn't a conversation. This is an arrest. Try to run away and I'll break your legs. Try to shout for help and I'll break your jaw. Do we have an understanding, *sir*?' With that, he dropped Purefoy who landed on his feet at first but slipped backward, backward until it felt as if the wall leant forward to hold him up. Purefoy stared at the ground trying to clear his head of the possibility of Banwen and Murphy having met in the workhouse, fallen for each other and fallen into sex…of Banwen being killed by this man.

At that thought, Purefoy stared Murphy in the eye. He knew he was steadying his breath now as he felt the anger uncurl from his groin to his gut to his sides to his clenched fists. He didn't think, he didn't want to think. An abyss spread behind his eyes – it grew darker the shorter his breath became.

'So there is some fire in you. Good, good. You'll need it.'

'Tell me who you meant by 'she' or you can kill me now and get it over with because I won't move until you tell me.' Purefoy expected a punch, a kick. Something.

'Fine. There's a haggard shitpicker who knows you from old livin' in Ol' Nichol and she said I should find you and take you in. She don't care if you know.' Murphy looked to his side then and spat.

The abyss seeped away from Purefoy and all fight fled. They were replaced by a poisonous acid wick standing straight up in his stomach, prodding his lungs. Attempting to stem the oncoming tears, he muttered, 'So you didn't…you never.' He laughed an exhausted laugh. The man known only as Murphy looked at him with suspicion. Purefoy continued to laugh a while.

* * *

Bryn Prifardd Llewes was the son of a dead man. His father was not yet physically dead in 1858 but he was a dead man – Mr Llwyn had returned from his part in Afghanistan thinner than his family had ever seen him and with far less to say. The once robust clerk, who had worked at every given opportunity on any work offered before, returned only to lie down in the day and drink at night, every night. Every night, that is, until he was challenged to prove he'd fought for queen and country – after all, he never spoke about what had happened, the men he was with, or where he was stationed.

'How could anyone in a pub believe a man who won't talk?'

Mr Llwyn beat the questioner close to death but stopped short when the man's face reminded him of a child he'd seen flailing half-dead toward him, asking – pleading – for something in a language he couldn't understand.

He ran from the pub then and ran out of Wrexham as far as he could get before his lungs betrayed him. The child he'd drank away was back and would never leave him. He knew that then. The drink had sluiced the start of the memory but nothing could take that final sight from him. Now it was all there – the image he had repressed enough to survive was now the only image he could recall. He replayed the memory in the cold, hoping his freezing limbs would calm him: *the boy approached, crying and pleading; the boy stretched out his little hand – he was lost, he... A command came from behind me but I didn't hear it – I! A private I knew stood over the boy with his foot on the shoulder and the barrel of his gun in the boy's skull...I should have helped, I should have — That private received a promotion; the boy approached with his hand...* and so the memory reeled over and over in his mind over the course of the cold night. Something simple inside him had lead him back to the family home by morning. After what happened on that day, Mr Llwyn was a dead man.

* * *

When Purefoy stopped laughing, he stood, wiped the tears from his face, and reached out his hand. Murphy looked at his hand and back at Purefoy. 'What the hell are you doin' that for?'

'Because I must.'

'I'll not shake your hand. I'll not shake the hand of a dead man.'

'That is exactly why you should – shake my hand and I'll go with you peaceably.'

Murphy looked at Purefoy again. A smile readied at the side of Purefoy's lips. Murphy remained bemused. 'You're an odd one alright, Purefoy.'

The men shook hands as the morning smoke reached their street. They had a few minutes before it would invade their noses, eventually their lungs, and Purefoy muttered to himself, 'Now I'm in arms with death, I am at peace.'

'What was that?'

'Nothing. Nothing of concern.' Purefoy smiled. 'In which direction would you like to go, Murphy?'

'East. From here on, you can stop asking so many questions concernin' our direction, d'ya understand?'

'Of course. You'll lead and I'll follow silently.'

'No. You'll walk by my side where I can see ya.'

'As you wish.' Murphy spat again and shoved Purefoy further along Portland Street. From somewhere just behind his eyes, a modicum of calm began to spread into Purefoy. His reptile back-brain still twinged with the desire to run but he ignored it, preferring to give himself up to death and thinking on the release of it.

Murphy didn't trust Purefoy. That much was evident in the way he walked and the way he kept close but more so in his thoughts. Murphy didn't like Purefoy's oddness but was thankful for his quietness; he didn't like the now half-dead expression on Purefoy's face but he could appreciate the quick gait of any purefinder; these contradictions in thought made Murphy dislike Purefoy more. Murphy wished he had better things to do with his time. Though the topic was a raw one to him, he thought he should've been getting work building the train lines, not fiddling around with some shitpicker but that would have meant leaving London a little. Murphy believed that London was where he was meant to be.

Five streets away on Greek Street, the relatively new Metropolitan Board of Works struggled to make themselves heard. A vestry away in Pall Mall and with mathematical precision, George Peacock's wife considered taking on one of her husband's students as a lover. Over the river and far to the south-east, the East Kent Railway had celebrated the opening of its Strood to Chatham line just three days ago. Were you to journey from Soho to Millwall, you could have heard the industrious sounds of Brunel's *Leviathan* before the day was out. In 1858, the engineers of the Isle of Dogs sought to make order.

CHAPTER 3

They walked for a spell, east on Portland Street. They were over Berwick before Purefoy began to think properly again. *This could be the last time I'm here.* Purefoy looked around him to take in what he could, while he could. To his left he saw a group of boys sitting, staring at the passers-by, *waiting for a rich man, no doubt.* To his right, he noticed the well-kept houses curtained with designed linen. He looked left again to see *ramshackles of what might as well be a rookery* leaning into and over each other. The stark contrast of what came from left and right – the desolate poor living opposite the luxuriously rich – had him reach for a penny to give to the boys. As the metal in his pocket clashed, a memory of a play he'd seen with BB flashed: *Two mirrors on stage, reflecting the other; one had its back to us but the other, bigger mirror could be seen and the reflection in the reflection made a tunnel headed by a medieval arch that confused the eyes and went on forever.* When he'd let the memory fall back, he'd walked by the boys but he purposefully dropped a threppenny bit so it'd make a decent sound and roll their way.

His head kinked backward a little, he hoped to catch a glimpse of the sky. He knew he'd be lucky at any time of the day.

The weather report in *The Times* would later state that the day had been 'dull', but the High Field Observatory hadn't taken into account the lives of the people beneath it or the extremity of the day for Purefoy.

Following his earlier moment of calm, Purefoy's mood had begun to change as the morning progressed and as he thought more on what was to come. His thoughts even remarked on the *...fleeting things* of emotional states. He wished now for some conversation but found himself perturbed by the notion of talking with his attacker and prison-keeper.

The streets had woken and the street peoples begun to set up their day – this was enough to keep Purefoy's thoughts busy for a while. Since being swallowed by London, Soho's always had a pull for the lost, the wild, and those willing to try their luck. The crossing sweepers seemed omnipresent with brooms on every corner and coster boys – calling any unwilling, unfortunate woman-sweeper a witch – as present. Purefoy couldn't focus properly on them or any of the other early-starters but knew they were there just as he knew what business he was missing out on at his feet. Business thoughts led to the complicated conversations he was supposed to have today – he had left two whole pounds with his man at the tanners in Bermondsey and a guinea at a specialist, way out in Deptford. *Today was meant to be the day I had those conversations; today I got my money back; today the day I told B—* He cut his thoughts short. The heat once in his chest didn't burn immediately back but remained an ember, pulsating, an ache. Around it came only a cold understanding of the space between each rib. Most of him grew cold. On feeling it, the city withdrew and let him be as they walked a little on.

On Dean Street, Murphy indicated they should veer right. The small road they took became Soho Square. Even on a dull morning, Soho Square is impressive. When BB still lived with him, Purefoy and she would picnic there when they could. *In church, they tell you about the calm death brings, but they never tell you about the nervous throes that follow. I hope BB didn't suffer—*

'She was with child, you know.'

Murphy had broken Purefoy's thoughts with – what he'd attempted to be – an effect of disinterest. Purefoy's flushed, angry face looked up but saw that Murphy hadn't looked to him at all and was indicating a woman on the square. The thought that Murphy had ever known BB screwed further into him. 'But look at her now. Back out and thin. You can't expect anything less, I suppose – not from an old-hat like her. "Abandon hope, all yee who enter" there, I say. Know what I mean, Llewes? ...No, of course you don't.' Murphy's voice was exceptional in that its accent gave it nothing of the usual colour, instead only a gravelly monotone with the slightest variations. Purefoy knew the quote and ignored the insinuation. He tried to remember where he'd read it but by Murphy's prompt, the city and all its stimuli came rushing at him. It was the stench of the square that came back first. He thought he'd desensitized himself to any smell over the last five years but with the smoke gathering, the dust settling, the people and their animals coming out in throngs, and his nerves fraying, Purefoy's nose was overwhelmed. He coughed. Murphy turned. He coughed again and so loudly, so painfully, he stopped. Murphy laughed. Tears began to gather in Purefoy's eyes as he continued to cough but it didn't help clear the smell sitting in his nose – it was shit: the sticky tang of it was everywhere; the mud of the park mingled with dog pure, human cesspits buried beneath the surrounding street, a great rotting smell worse than any pure he'd ever—

'Have no doubt, Purefoy, you're mine now.'

'What?' Purefoy coughed the word through.

'I'm here to keep you well into the end of your days.' Murphy laughed then and slapped him in the centre of his back. Purefoy's stomach was an acidic reflection of the cold viciousness in Murphy's laugh. Somehow, the coughing had stopped. He looked directly down and saw a moth struggling in the mud and some clear, sticky fluid. He picked it up, stood properly, and began blowing on it to raise its wings. The moth quickly flew.

'Come on then.' Murphy's hand was back on Purefoy's shoulder. Murphy stood to his right, a finger touching Purefoy's neck that made Purefoy flinch inwardly. 'I've got to introduce you to my associates.' They entered the main green of the square.

Purefoy knew he'd been here before but he'd never seen it so populated. Though you couldn't see it, the sun had only been out for an hour yet people stood at all sides animated by conversation. On entering, there was a rush of stimuli to his ears: screeches, sighs and heart-rending cries resounded; the loudness of it made tears begin to gather in his eyes—

16

'Welcome to my world, Purefoy.'

'I imagine this is only a small part of your day, Murphy. After all, you've got to walk me to your sergeant yet.'

'He speaks. So your cowardice is dead – good. You shouldn't be too afraid of me but I couldn't say how much you should be afraid now.'

Murphy turned and an old man making his way from the southern side to the eastern met his eyes. They nodded and the old man cried, 'Woe, woe betide you, you guilty souls what owes me—' loudly across the entire tumult of the square. A horrible discourse rose then – some words of despair, some fierce accents of spite, and striking of hands with curses deep and hoarse – raised the crowd into a noticeably uniform buzz.

'Are all of these people your associates?'

'By God Bryn, no: just the ones without shoes. The rest of 'em are as lucky as you.'

Purefoy noticed their naked feet: though some were white, most were red, pink, and purple; scabbed, scarred, and bleeding. A woman just four feet away who alternately looked at the old man and at Murphy in darting blackbird-lucidity had a small pool of blood at her feet from where her ankle, her toes and her soles had been cut.

Purefoy looked away, not knowing what else he could do. 'And why are they here, now?'

No response.

'Sorry, Murphy, why are they here?'

'Spurned by justice and pity, where else can they go? So degraded but with little hope of a good death or a good life, they stick to where they can.'

'Is there no work for them anywhere?'

'Work? Haah! You tell me, shitpicker – what work is there for a woman with child and no father? What work is there for the lame and anyone with scabbed feet-heels? You've been right lucky and you know it.'

'Yes, I have. I know.'

'So you know there's no charity either.'

'Charity starts at home.'

'And every man in this country is his own home.'

Purefoy was silent then. Usually, through any subject, any company kept, or any amount of ale, he was an optimist – one of those fortunate few who believe in the goodness of progress and the progression of goodness, but at that exact point he had no rebuttal. He thought on Banwen to bolster him and thought, *soon*.

The old man clapped his hands and the entire square fell silent. Purefoy closed his eyes to study the silence. Roads away, horses' feet hit the floor in front of their carriages. Behind him flies, gnats, and wasps buzzed over the crossing sweepers morning-talk but in the square not a sound but breath was heard. Eyes open again, he studied the cause of this new silence: he studied the old man. As he did so, the old man sat on his heels at the corner of where the square met Sutton Street. He lifted his right hand up as if begging and rested on a thick, short stick with his left. His long white unadorned hair looked clean by comparison to the rest of him. Under his eyes, black lines and grey skin met his purple nose, his cheeks too were lined but his complexion sat so unhealthily that the lines ran and disappeared into his white stubble. He sat, slowly eyeing the inhabitants of the square for a short while, then he fixed his gaze ahead of him – suddenly the crowd ran to get past him, but with an alarming sleight, he struck each one with the thick stick in his hand. Purefoy couldn't understand why they didn't choose another exit.

'Come on. Our turn.' Murphy walked ahead a step.

Purefoy waited. *Perhaps Murphy will walk too far and I can simply run back the way we came.* But Murphy turned and looked and waited. Purefoy followed.

'How are we this fine morn, Old Man Sharron?'

'Well enough.' It seemed Old Man Sharron didn't like Murphy, or words either, this morning.

'Well, I'm glad to hear it. Can we pass?'

'You don't owes me nothing, but by other ways, by other roads, and not by this passage you can go.' Though old, his voice had an authoritative strength.

'Pay the man halfpence, Purefoy.'

'I'll not take 'is tin and you knows why, navvy.'

'And you know I ain't a navvy so keep yourself to yourself then.'

'Well enough.' Murphy turned, walked away from the old man and took Purefoy with him.

On looking back, Purefoy thought how kindly the old man looked and must be if he did something for all those people to then receive no payment. *Lonely, too.*

Their strides took them a little north and through the passage to Oxford Street. Here the multitude of sounds and smells that had arrived since Purefoy was last there were an earthquake around him from which he had no shelter but submission. He folded his desire to break free into the rank and file of the walkers. The gentlemen on their fresh-scented walks to work, the sweaty omnibuses that he'd never used, the face-washed street sellers, the downy sweepers, the out of work flue fakers, the squeaky zealots, and the board men – all walked or gawped and hoped that today would bring something better as people would for a hundred and fifty, two hundred and fifty, years. Oxford Street is a river cutting the north from the south with old men – some kindly, most lonely – its keepers. They walked its banks east as Purefoy's hunger and thirst grew.

CHAPTER 4

They took the right, east onto Oxford Street. Here Purefoy was presented with an opportunity to buy something to eat. The woman selling wore a shawl and had a pleasant demeanour. She didn't shout or call like so many orange sellers, simply held an orange out to whoever would pass her by. Purefoy signalled her from a few yards away and got tuppence in his fingers. 'Good day to you bucks. One orange is sixpence.'

'Sixpence? Really?'

'Alright, fourpence but I'll go no lower.'

'Fourpence is still expensive.'

'Well this is Oxford Street, luvvy. We're going up in the world, don't ya know?'

The orange he'd planned on at three times the cost. Before he could pay, Murphy moved him on. Pleasant as her demeanour was before, her voice became as shrilling. She shouted abuses at Murphy and wailed. Purefoy half expected, half hoped, to feel an orange hit the back of his head. He smiled. A glimmer of warmth reddened his cheeks.

'Come on. Walk quicker.'

'I must eat something, Murphy. I will not make it through the day if you push me so.'

'You will. There are devout men who go weeks without food. They trust in their betters, don't you?' The resignation in 'will' told him that Murphy couldn't care.

Murphy stopped at the head of Crown Street. 'Look down there. Tell me who you see.' Purefoy looked south. The spring damp had begun to rise and meet the dust that caused even ladies to grind their teeth. The wind wasn't as strong as Purefoy had seen it but it was playful. He would have laughed had the sorrow at the back of every thought not kept his mouth in check. There were coffee-stalls and puffed up patterers nearby, there were a few eccentrics who were probably showmen, there were more about but there was no one he recognised. 'I can't definitely say that I know anyone that I see.'

'None of us can.'

'Sorry?'

'So you don't recognise anyone on that street?'

'No. No one at all.'

'Good.'

As they walked down it, Purefoy tried to view the end of Crown Street. He couldn't. He couldn't tell what was ash and dust, smoke and mist or building. So deep was the road and so dense its tails atmosphere that he hoped they would turn off. Something hit his right leg. He looked down and back: lost in looking down the road, he hadn't seen the hand of a beggar rise up to meet his leg. The forest of people from earlier flashed in his thoughts again. Then a forest from when he was a boy.

Murphy mumbled something. Purefoy heard a '…damned city' and noticed Murphy's face had turned pale. There was a look of disgust. Purefoy looked away, unable to understand how one caste of rough man could look down on another…

A whisper at his ear, 'Behold the Valley of Woe.'

Murphy had leaned in close; his hand on Purefoy's upper arm. 'If you were to run from here and attempt to cross the river, you'd regret it.'

Purefoy didn't dare move his arm for fear of Murphy ripping it out. They crossed the street taking an alley he didn't recognise but on to New Compton Street; another shift and they entered the top of Seven Dials. Purefoy wondered, if he shouted would anyone asleep in the Little White Lion help him. *Not unless I made it worth their while.*

Here though, Murphy stopped again. The abrupt end to their pace brought them close and Purefoy could feel Murphy's breath on his forehead. It didn't have a discernible smell. 'You see those swell coves?'

'The well-dressed in the centre of the dial?'

'Aye. Listen to 'em.'

Purefoy tried. In the rush of being pushed around, his nerves had calmed but focusing was still difficult. The clatter of the waking was around him and workers still sloped by. Nothing. They weren't speaking as far as he could tell. 'They're quiet.'

'Aye. That fella with the long front-beard and the bow-choker, that's The Inimitable. His Scot full-bearded friend is Halliday. I bet a hundred and fifty years from now, they'll be heroes. They'll pay ya to walk 'em around a few doss-kens and talk to 'em. As if they've no voice of their own. Brick fools—' Purefoy couldn't fathom Murphy's meaning, '—all in good time, aye. All in time. Come on, we've a way to go yet.' To Purefoy, 'brick' had always meant 'good' or 'good at' so how could someone be a 'brick fool'? He couldn't fathom Murphy's words.

They crossed Seven Dials. Murphy let go of Purefoy's arm as they did. The gentlemen appeared to smile at Murphy. He gave them a dismissive wave back and not a word was uttered. Purefoy tried to get their attention with his eyes but they were only observing, distantly.

Murphy continued, 'They told me once this Prussian cove said he'd "never seen a class so incurably debased by selfishness and so corroded within as the English bourgeoisie". What they didn't tell him of course was that they're not the only ones.'

Is he being friendly? Should I laugh? Would its falseness annoy him? Bemused, Purefoy walked.

How should we respond to aggression when it's couched in benevolence? Thirteen years before, Engels had written a diatribe; a year before, The Inimitable finished serialising his anger at his father's keepers; and on April 2, 1858, Purefoy stomped on Murphy's foot, elbowed him in the ribs, and stepped once.

He looked back to see Murphy fall forward: relieved, he looked ahead. He felt a pain in his ankle. He was falling. His gut didn't have time to clench.

Nothing he saw as he fell felt slowed or different, just flawed and painful. His right side hit the ground followed by his head; landing on his shoulder meant the right but the top-right of his head hit. He heard a high-pitched ringing. The pain dizzied him and he moved to get up but a sharp tug on his ankle meant only a low growl came up before he stopped moving. He felt a wide, deep pain hit his chest twice, three-times. He curled in on himself. His eyes watered and his chest wound.

A fierce, gravelly shout came, 'Ya nicky shitwort! Ya damned Molly-Ann muck snipe – ya try that again and I'll break your fookin' legs an' carry ya there meself.' Murphy's monotone was gone. So too the hope that the two would separate and Purefoy could grieve alone.

Though his eyes were closed, his gut felt the change in orientation. From lying down to stood with one arm over Murphy.

Grief leaves and returns unexpectedly when you've just received it; Purefoy inwardly cursed Murphy but called to BB, wishing he could be with her wherever she was; he lapsed into unthinking then. His head lolled and he let his muscles loosen – a tight grip on his neck opened his eyes. In front of him was Murphy's face. The sun had wrestled through the clouds and the street weather enough to illuminate both their faces. Purefoy first saw green irises in wholly white, wide eyes, so close to him the pink sockets glistened. Moving his head back some he realised Murphy's skin was smooth, smooth and his shallow cheekbones were pink like a freshly burnt baby whereas his cheeks were milk-white; he was dotted with freckles all under his eyes, at his temples and on his forehead. He was hardly lined at all, with only two crow's feet. The lines he saw weren't from life's work on the face but from Murphy's brows crowding together over his nose to pinch the skin to a ridge. Purefoy could see Murphy had taken care of his health and his skin. Beneath that nose, an orange brush of hair made into the popular navy style was supported by a thickly stubbled, hard-set chin. A half-open mouth breathed hot, moist air and reddened each time it did. His neck seemed taut and inflamed but the longer Purefoy stared, the slower their breathing became. Purefoy questioned, *If I'd known him before all this, might I have liked his face? He has a child's face under that thicket. I might have liked the look of him...but I wouldn't have trusted him.*

Murphy saw bloodshot, brown eyes surrounded by olive skin, ruddy on the cheeks; between sat a bulbous nose with out of control capillaries; below, a pale-pink mouth with laughter lines either side that ran back up to the nose. The skin on his face was taught from hunger but his high, olive cheekbones gave the look of survival; lines mapped his face – from cheeks to eyes to crows nests – most noticeably on his forehead where lived a line for every year he'd lived and a deeper set for every decade. Shaven a couple or a few days ago, small silver dots flecked with black grew slowly. Murphy released his grip, a finger at a time.

The two men leaned aside one another and both put their hands on their knees as they got their breath back. Purefoy saw a beetle beneath him, pushing his way through the dirt. The glimmer of light passed. All was dull again.

Murphy stood and coughed. They looked at each other and Murphy smiled. Purefoy lowered his head with the ugly realisation that Murphy really was twice his size.

CHAPTER 5

The irony of walking down the regal Crown Street, through the infamous The Dials, to Castle Street wasn't entirely lost on Purefoy but in the face of his day so far and what he knew was to come, it failed to raise a smile. He tongued his mouth and felt a newly loose tooth, *Pigswill for jewels*. The Castle Street they walked on then would become Shelton Street. In a place near where Purefoy grew, the word 'Shelton' would be associated with asylums.

Murphy and Purefoy walked slowly, abated from fighting. Still on Castle Street, they crossed Endell and the pedlars, fish-women, and news criers bayed in preparation for the 9 o'clock rush. Before they stepped out into Drury Lane, Murphy slowed and removed his hat. Neither of them wished to talk but he'd signalled something. As the hat was removed, his hair stood out as another beguiling feature to him: its red was long but tightly fashioned back, slick over his head and he'd a full head of it. A thick line of dirt had sat under the hat on the top of Murphy's forehead and he rubbed it once with his left arm before using his hat to signal the shop behind Purefoy. Purefoy turned and removed his Dai-cap, not knowing entirely why but that it was fitting for hats to be removed. Earlier this morning, he would have chuckled lightly at the oddness of these social rituals.

Had he looked as they walked, Purefoy would have seen the shop-board but after a while of living in London, you stop seeing the signs. It was a photography specialist – he hadn't yet found out how that new magic worked and hadn't ever had the time or inclination to do so. Now the men stared in through the window. Their fascination in the images made them cut a strange look – beggar children peering in at the sugared treats in a confec-tioner's window.

'As a lad, I was told about the last Great Frost Fayre – me Da said he wished he could have taken the memory and kept it

exactly as it was until he died. That's what this is, it's—' Murphy
stopped speaking and cleared his throat. Purefoy waited for him
to start again but that start never came. He returned his focus to
the photographs.

Purefoy noted the ones with tags: 'The Microscope' showed a
white-shawled woman peering with her eyes closed into a metal
tube, his immediate thought was, *Gammy nonsense; why are we
looking at this? Why is he doing this?* His annoyance belied his
anxiety. He moved his gaze from 'The Microscope' to 'The
Mourning Bracelet of Harold Flyton' and found a photograph set
in a clasp that made the centrepiece of a bracelet woven from
human hair – he knew that the hair had been cut from the dead
woman in the picture. The thought pained him – to cut anything
from a dead body seemed…he didn't know where Banwen's body
was. *Why hadn't I asked? I – I should have asked – I…I was too scared,
too hurt.* He stayed outwardly quiet but his eyes burned as the
tears escaped them. He looked away from Murphy to another
photograph, 'In memory of Elizabeth Jane Sparring – before
burial': its eyes closed, a lifeless child was held up by two adults
and its mouth sat in a grim contortion.

'In we go.' Murphy had clasped his hand down on Purefoy's
shoulder as he said it; a small, strong reminder of his position
between them. Purefoy was happy to leave the window display.
Murphy knocked on the door. A few seconds later, a face
appeared at the small glass panel in the door, its nose twitched in
a snarl and its jaw chewed. The door opened and the thin man
ceremoniously motioned with his arm for them to enter. The shop
was dark and bare, it had only one other door. The products
themselves hung mostly on walls or stood in patterned frames on
tables near the walls. One high counter stood half covering the
other door and running parallel with the wall making a small box
of a shop. It seemed it had only one other room but a thick lime
and chemical odour so Purefoy presumed a hole to a cesspool or
small sewer. In this case, he was wrong – he smelt only the

photographer's essential tools – and his nose was only beginning to truly get used to defining smells properly, to being sensitized, again.

The thin man was as tall as Murphy and it wasn't a snarl that Purefoy had seen in his nose before – it was his nose. A long nose with the muscles of his nostrils so tightly packed toward his eyes, it was no surprise they had the strength to hold up a thin pair of spectacles. After closing the door, he'd moved back to behind the counter and pushed his grey hair behind his ears. 'Good day to you. What would you like today?' His speech was clipped and proper but had none of the usual patronising tone shop clerks reserve for the poor.

'Nothin' really, M. We're just seein' if anythin' might be judged to take our fancy.'

Purefoy watched the clerk in case he'd want them to leave but no judgement came. 'And will I find out any more about you today, Murphy? Like your real name for instance?'

'Like *your* real name you mean, M?' The two men smiled at each other.

'Well, will your company and I receive an introduction?'

'No. There's no need. We'll be gone just as soon as he's seen what we need to see.'

'And have you?' A calm, quiet question.

'You know we haven't. It's why you let us in before you're even properly open. Show us what's under the counter.'

'I warn you Murphy, this isn't for the faint of heart and – if you'll excuse me for asking – how do I know the company you keep has the necessary discretion?'

'There's more here than you know. After today, my company here won't even be a shade of his former self. I'd be surprised if he ever speaks again.'

They looked at Purefoy then. A chill ran down his side and he moved his gloved, left hand to hold his right side. He nodded. Purefoy didn't know how much they toyed with him. This was enough for M.

M reached down. Four photographs were placed on the counter top. A quick glance told Purefoy that all of the people in them were naked or nearly naked. He'd heard about this but never seen it. 'This one is a master of the art – a Frenchman by the name of Auguste Belloc.' The photograph M indicated had a woman standing with her back to the camera, set in a faux-woodland scene with only a white veil covering her right lower-leg. She had healthy, wide hips and round buttocks, her left breast was visible as she had raised her left arm toward her turned head. You could see her face in profile and, though her eyes were closed, there could have been a smile on her face. Her hair had been tucked in front of her. Purefoy thought, *She has BB's shape. Would Banwen have…she might've…if it paid enough. I might.*

The photograph next to the woman was of two naked men. It was framed and titled 'Cain: A Mystery'. One man stood furcated over the other. Half bent over and holding the other from the floor, he looked at the man in his arms imploringly. Muscled as they both were, the other simply lay beneath him with his head turned away. There was a dark mark on the shoulder he rested his limp head on and the standing man held the other's arm over him. Both men's penises stood fully erect.

The clerk watched the progress of Purefoy's eyes. As they moved from the men to the next, he interjected with, 'This piece is a regal one. Notice the grace her majesty displays in receiving the prince's arbor vitae into her commodity. The veracity of the likeness is unparalleled in other specialists' products, I'm told.'

Purefoy ignored the genitalia the clerk indicated and looked to their faces. The likeness to the Queen and Prince Albert was incredible: the roundness of the Queen's cheeks, the design of his moustache, and thickness of the Prince's sideburns but *It has to be a fake.* The picture disagreed. The more Purefoy kept that thought and the more he looked, the more he couldn't understand. *Why would anyone so known show off so much?* He looked then at their joined sex. He remembered Banwen and him, not the first time they'd had sex but, when they stayed together until she was red-faced, shaking, and happy. He hadn't spent until she was happy and tired. As a reward, he felt, she swallowed his mettle and they lay on the grass in dappled shade, beneath the trees.

'This last example I took myself and am quite pleased with the rarity of the result.' M had only now shown a definite interest in the photographs – as if the three previous were nothing, just other portraits in the hundreds he'd seen and had no interest in. This last, he pushed for Murphy and Purefoy to examine. 'I call it 'Francesca: The Rigged Double Velvet'.'

Purefoy couldn't make it out at first. *Two black vases opposite? No...* He looked closer. The vases he'd seen were corseted Oriental women stood with their backs to each other. Though a yard apart, they held hands crossed at the wrists. Between them stretched their corset laces in webs of ties and nine-tailed knots. They stood naked but for the corsets in an empty white room. Their skin was only visible against the white of the background by the profile shadows. Their breasts sat atop the corsets bonded by lace and their thin pubic hair, matching in size, was visible. They seemed twins but the closer he looked, the more variation he noticed on their skin. Their necks were marked underneath their long hair; each had small cuts on their legs; one's eyes smiled, one's face was fixed in concentration. Purefoy couldn't tell whether they were happy. There was a grace in their calm. There was a beauty in their poise.

Purefoy felt eyes watching him and turned his head right but Murphy still looked at the photographs. Though disregarding judgement before, M now wished to be judged. He looked to Purefoy and slowly to Murphy. Purefoy didn't know what to say. Murphy stared at the photograph in an animal stupor. When M cleared his throat, Murphy looked up, nodded, and said, 'Rarefied. Quite rarefied.'

'Could I interest you in my Francesca?'

'Though they're new, M, you know I'm rarely here to buy unless I'm with the most pleasant of companies.' M smiled lightly then looked down and began to put away the photographs. Murphy had already stepped back to leave but offered, 'I'll see ya round The Castle sometime, M.'

'Perhaps so, Murphy. Thank you both for your interest in our specializations. Good day to you.' Murphy laughed a hard, forced 'Hah' and opened the door.

Chapter 6

To their right, Drury Lane.

Purefoy heard stories about the place even before he'd gotten the train to London with BB. The women, the palaces, the shows – all were considered scandalous and brilliant by the good and the fun in Wrexham. Now with the road next to him, now with five years of knowing the place, he inhaled a short, sharp breath in preparation.

He looked away. Back to where they'd walked, then back to the north-west. There was nothing left for him there; only nostalgia told him to return. In looking, he'd felt a sharp tug in a muscle at the back of his neck. He tried to tease out the muscles but twisting his head in any way hurt after stooping to see the photography. Some small fever gathered at the base of where his brain met his spine. He reached up and rubbed it.

'No one ever suffers but you and you've shit on your neck, ya know.' Murphy was smiling again.

'We call it 'pure' in the business.' Attempting to cover his mistake, unsuccessfully.

'And how is the pure business?'

'Harder to come by since—'

'Since what? Since my lot came in? Is that what you were gointa say?' Quicker, louder.

'Since winter.' After Murphy's first words, the two men hadn't looked at each other but both their hearts were beating a little quicker. Stood aside him, Murphy punched Purefoy on the left arm with ease and a laugh, catching him just below the shoulder with his knuckles. Purefoy's upper arm went dead. None of the pins and needles he'd expected came for another 15 minutes. He held his left arm with his right and looked down. He didn't know where to look and hoped they'd cross over Drury. 'By the right flank, soldier. March.'

A drill command; Purefoy recognised it from his father. *Was*

Murphy a soldier once? What time is it? I can't tell...

Murphy's identity reared its head only to be hooded by the city again: a rotund, big-red-nosed man held his arm in their path. A Hounslow, deep-pitched accent followed with, 'The poet returns!'

'Morning Albert.'

'Morning to you, Murphy. I see you've company. Can I tempt you gentlemen into my palace a while?' Albert indicated his gin house, thinly disguised as a crockery shop, behind him and smiled. He refrained from showing his teeth but his eyes smiled wider for it. He had a pleasant smile that made Purefoy think, *How easily people are fooled when there's money to be made.*

'I don't see why not, Albert – my taffy friend here is flush today.'

'Ah, a Welshman. Well, my mother was Welsh and we welcome all in my palace, don't you fret.'

Down the steps into his basement shop, Albert wore sizeable scuffed-grey boots under his black, lined trousers and cream shirt. His most notable fashion was how white his apron was – spotted at the corners and folds, of course, but on his chest there wasn't a speck of dirt. Later when his shop became a pit for The Fancy, he would change into something 'respectable' so as to take their bets with the visage of a businessman. His palace was cramped and had no seats but for the steps outside. Three white plates in the window, indistinguishable from porcelain, gathered dust at their backs. The single room they entered had nine doors coming into it – Purefoy thought, *What makes a palace a Palace? When is a palace not a palace?...It's thoughts like that that lost you your—*' His vestibular balance had been thrown on entering but on that thought his insides lurched to his left. He moved his left foot out to balance himself. He found only gravity encouraging him down. He lowered his core and clenched his jaw. There was something about the room that threw him. The lines of its walls, doors, its fire inspired vertigo – something he couldn't see but knew was there, knew was wrong.

The only company at that hour was a woman crumpled asleep in the corner and an English Bulldog. A yard in front of them, it stood to the left of the counter. This bulldog wasn't handsome, even by The Fancy's standards – the fat folds in his neck gave him three chins, chins large enough to be faces. Purefoy stared. He had grown to observe dogs and predict their ways – their owners' ways – but this one threw him. Its belly lay scraping the ground even as it stood, panted, and drooled; its breath was short but its underbite gave the impression of being able to tear throats energetically; it was white all over but for a black spot on its chest. Purefoy knew its pure would be small but richly concentrated. *It can't get out much so it could be a regular profit, if…*

The dog caught Purefoy's eye and began to growl. He'd a calm understanding of dogs. Glad of the opportunity, he knelt.

The growl grew louder.

Albert and Murphy looked at each other with something akin to mirth. Purefoy noted the red growths at the sides of the dog's eyes.

The dog yipped.

Albert and Murphy did nothing. Purefoy raised his open hands slowly and spread them by his shoulders.

The dog lurched and bit his shin.

The pain was instant. A shock, arching his spine.

Purefoy sucked in through his teeth. The underbite had gotten into his stringy flesh. Pressure from the dog's top jaw cut the bone. The dog sucked in through its wet cheeks and small teeth attempting to increase pressure. Its greedy spittle covered the trouser end and bubbled the sound of wet mud being boiled.

The pain increased, shooting through him. He controlled the noise he made as much as he could but that too sounded painful.

Murphy brought round a small glass of gin and the dog immediately let go, releasing droplets of blood onto Purefoy's trousers.

Resigned, Murphy let the dog lap from the glass in his hand and said, 'Dogs eat needy dogs, Prifardd. He can smell you're hungry.' Smiling, he continued, 'Have a drop – you're buying after all.' Albert poured a glass.

'No thank you, Mr Albert.' Albert looked to Murphy but said nothing.

'Oh I insist, taffy. We've a long day ahead of us, you and I – you especially.'

Purefoy stood and drank the gin in one. The vertigo he'd sensed earlier hit him now. He felt a large weight resting on the forefront of his head and he pushed down on the makeshift bar to ensure his head stayed up. He was not a man used to alcohol in any form. Without food, the alcohol would eat him.

'Have you got any water please, Mr Albert?'

'It's just Albert, old son but, come along, no one drinks water – you never know what's in it. I makes this myself and I can promise it's all good, clean stuff. 'Ave another?'

'Better not, Albert,' Murphy interjected. 'Our little friend here likes to take his time with the old Ruin…and any other mother for that matter. Still, he's a profligate entrepreneur; he's a right killer when he needs to be…'

'Ah – a businessman then, eh?' Murphy stood and came to the makeshift bar.

'I'll wet the other eye though; aye, a businessman.'

'A proper brick. '

'Aye; he'd sink well.'

'Hah. What…ah…tell me Murphy, what's the opposite of glocky?'

'A wit. A slang cove with slang…but—'

'That's you then.'

'That would make me a part of your usual mob who play the crooked cross with innocents.'

'Oh no, we 'aves no pettifoggers mollyin' mooncalves in 'ere. No, sir.'

'At least not in the day. Right, Prince Albert?'

'Now now, I'll not have you offend our sovereign's husband. I don't care if you are a learned man, I'll not have you—'

'At least not 'til I buy you a drop?'

'Well…well, that might go some way to undoing the damage…'

'Pour one for yourself; Purefoy here'll pay when we're done.' The two men went on like that for a while. Purefoy didn't want to say anything so listened instead. Firstly to the bite on his leg as it hissed a steady stream of pain signals to him but secondly to how Murphy's tone had changed. In a few minutes, Murphy had gone from prison guard to jovial. Purefoy lowered his head and let it hang over his chest, resting.

'Will we be seeing you this evening then, good wit?'

'Not tonight, Albert. Tonight I've something special planned.'

'Ah! Say no more, sir. It was good meeting you, Mr Preefhard.'

Purefoy realised Albert was talking to him. He raised his head from his chest and mumbled, 'You too, Mr…just Albert.'

'Come on then, taffy. Time we were away. Pay up.'

Purefoy looked at Murphy. Murphy smiled wide enough to show his teeth-stumps. At this, Purefoy pulled change amounting to sixpence and put it on the makeshift bar.

'That's very kind of you, sir! Let me give you a word of advice in exchange for your generosity: be careful on the lane now. It's opening time for The Laced Mutton and you'll find many an establishment on this lane, with that name, waiting to receive you gentlemen.' Murphy laughed softly.

'Thanks Albert, but I'm no Mussulman and—'

'No Catholic either.' Murphy laughed again.

'Aye. See ya again.'

'Goodbye now.' The woman in the corner woke as Murphy and Purefoy left.

Albert was right. The street had come alive and all the doors that could be open had opened. There seemed to Purefoy a *Wash of colour – so much so soon so early.* Hoards of women stood on the street dressed in flashes of extraordinary colour on their necks and around their waists. One struck Purefoy as bird-like: her sharp, red cheeks, her long, slow arms, her distant gaze; the red scarf at her chest and the magenta ruche at her waist contrasting with the black-crosshatched grey dress and the black of her flat shoes. *Not a robin – too elegant for a robin – a tall bird with a red chest. A crane from warmer parts, if such a thing exists.*

Considering Murphy's previous tone, Purefoy felt an attempted request might work, 'Murphy…'

'Mmm?'

'Could we – could we go to talk to that woman with the red scarf? I just want to see a – I just want to tell her that she looks beautiful so I can see a proper smile before…'

'Before the day's out.' Murphy laughed again, far less softly.

'Mmm.'

'A last request then? Hmm. Sure. Why not.' He didn't sound pleased but it had worked and, though a small thing, Purefoy felt a shiver of reprieve run down his spine as he lowered his head. The road was still not too busy. They crossed.

The closer they got, the more of the woman's pallor was revealed to Purefoy. The red he'd noticed first was entirely distinct from the tulip white of most of her skin. From across the street she was graceful and closer, she was fragile. Her hands were as white as her face. It wasn't cosmetic. The black around the eyes was thick soot, not black oil or paint. He saw that she wasn't wearing stockings and the red scarf slightly covered a low-cut dress. Her stillness belied the goosebumps on her legs. If she did, she pretended not to see him and remained still. When close, he noticed how half-closed her eyes were. He couldn't tell whether it was an affectation of gentile disinterest or if she really didn't see him. A yard away, she was thin, thinner than expected; the carmine rouge on her cheeks wholly distinct because they were squares with corners just touching her eyes. Their frank, childish form made him pity her.

He couldn't do it.

He couldn't do it when he realised her grace was illness, not poise. He stopped short and Murphy stopped with him. With a flash of anger, Murphy demanded, 'What are you doing, Bryn? We're in the road, here.'

'I – I can't do it. I—'

'Not what you were expectin'? Aye. Then the right flank it is. Quick march.'

With a shame spreading to his own cheeks, Purefoy turned. They headed to the pavement. He craned his painful neck round just to see her from the front: she couldn't have seen him – her eyes were glazed and one pointed up while the other stayed true.

Purefoy felt a firm jolt to his front and stumbled quickly backward.

He faced the front. 'Can I in'erest you two gen'eeles in a buttered bun?' Murphy had slowed and stopped. The man speaking was of great girth, so much so Purefoy's thought was *Prinny. Fat fat Prinny.* Only his overworked braces seemed to hold him up. He was taller than Purefoy, an insurmountable obstacle. He wasn't holding any food but Purefoy was too confused by the size of the man to consider anything else.

Murphy spoke for them, 'No. No, thanks.'

'P'rhaps a quick dab up in Hair Court for *one* of you then? I noticed you lookin' at my girl and I can tell ya, her graceful ways is disguisin' – she's a rampun' bi'er.' After each sentence, he was short of breath and sweat mingled with his wiry sideburns as it leaked from his stovepipe hat. 'No, no thank you. We'll be on our way.' Murphy spoke for them again and stepped forward; Purefoy was fixed to the spot. Transfixed by the man's size and its contrast with the way he spoke, Purefoy couldn't equate the two. *How could a man afford to get to such a size?* was his next thought. *Why would a man, a man so rich as to get to such a size in an austere time, need to sell a woman? Or give a woman up instead of working the time needed himself?*

An ekstasis came over Purefoy, a sense of not knowing where he was or how to act; the feeling of losing all control over your directions, your actions, and not struggling against it but giving yourself up to it totally. After the man's talk of a rampant biter, Purefoy suffered cognitive dissonance. In his mind there was the woman, a graceful and pitiable fragile thing who wouldn't touch or be touched in case of being broken; there was also the great giant in front of him, claiming ownership over the woman and offering her up as a sacrifice.

Purefoy stuttered something and the giant pounced on it. 'Ah, so there's in'erest arf'er'all. I knew it, when I saw you gen'eels I knew you knew a fine actress when you saw one.' He spread out his hands in a figure of welcome but Purefoy saw only the massive span of his hands and the greased lines on them.

'Listen, bully, you're no pimp or pander – I can tell that – so leave us be as we ain't touched the girl. Alright?' Murphy's volume had raised a little.

'Whass your rush then, eh? I never said I was a bully and I never said you was bilkin', did I?' The giant's hands lowered and clenched once.

'Aye but you're no pimp either—'

'No, I'm not. The name's Huhne, I'm simply a represen'a'ive of my girl there. I'm a producer.'

'Well, that's a new one.'

'She's a brick actress with a fine show, you'll see: lady-like bleached mor' with no hin' of a bobtail until you gets 'er; then when you does unrig,' he coughed then and breathed excitedly, 'she becomes a cleavin' puzzle for dockin'.' He was leaning into them now and Purefoy took a step back; the workers, late for their nine o clock start, were rushing around them; the dizziness made Purefoy's mouth dry.

Murphy raised his voice again. 'Listen, neither of us are interested – thank you. I'm sure she *is* a fine actress and you're an excellent producer but we've business that keeps us from theatrical endeavours. Do you understand?' He'd billowed his chest, grown an inch, and lowered the focus of his gaze, all while saying this.

'I do understand, guv, I do, but I'm not sure your friend 'ere agrees.' Purefoy looked to Murphy.

'Let me put it in terms you'll understand: we're not brother starlings, there'll be no grinding beasts and we're no goats; in a while's time, this man…' he punched Purefoy on the right arm, '…this man will be a capon; it's too early for any theatre of *any* kind so we've no interest in your bloody lane.'

Murphy had grown taller, redder, and fiercer with each sentence. His fists clenched.

The giant, thinking twice about speaking again, stepped out of the way. They walked past and the giant retreated into a doorway.

'Murphy…I don't feel quite well, what – what just happened exactly?'

'A double-act. What happened to you then? Lose your nib around pretty girls do ya?'

'No, I – I've not felt right since Albert's palace with its doors and dog and—'

'It didn't have that many doors, ya know.' Murphy's quietened monotone had returned.

'Sorry?'

'It had three doors. The one we came in, the one behind Albert, and another.'

'No, it had nine doors. I saw it. It—'

'No, you saw what you thought you saw. It's three with six painted. Albert likes to give it the feel of somewhere grander than it is. The dog was real enough but your woman's smile wouldn't have come until you and your pocket did. My fault; I shouldn't have let ya.'

Purefoy was still puzzled – the ekstasis he'd felt had derailed his thoughts. He hadn't realised that he lived in a hallucinatory age until then – only a few ever do. The giant he'd seen was only a giant to anyone of his size. Murphy had seen him only as an overweight annoyance. They walked further south on Drury Lane.

'And that man, how was he so big? Was I seeing some – some – something that was another trick?'

'No tricks necessary there. The man was that big because he's the capacity to grow that big. He probably eats four times as much as you do on most days.'

'Four times?'

'There are men who woke up within a mile of you who earn and spend four times what Ireland makes every year.'

'But that, that's just—'

'Greed's never greed to the individual, we only see it in comparison. Hush up now. I need to think.'

They walked past King, Parker, Great Queen, and Princes Street in silence. They walked slower than before, Murphy thought and Purefoy bemused. He felt the gin seeping away but sparks of nervous adrenaline remained.

A memory of BB singing played in his head, she sang the slowest and softest he'd heard anyone sing 'The Muffin Man'. As it played, it distorted: the notes shifted from her voice to that of children – the children he'd seen earlier; from her slowness, it played faster and louder with each repetition; the rhythm shifted from melodic to Mayday celebrations; a memory of children in Wrexham playing 'ring a ring o roses' ran itself alongside the song and entered the song with its song. His eyes felt dry as his head began to feel heavy again. He rubbed his eyes with his left hand. His skin felt coarse but lined with a pickled sweat. 'Did he ever live here?'

'*What*?!' Murphy's burst of anger made Purefoy flinch.

'I – I was…nothing. Sorry.'

'All you grubbers'll get your wort dues. Don't you worry,

taffy.'

Murphy's thoughts weren't on Drury Lane or even on the situation. He'd let himself become angry with Huhne and he knew it did him no good. He was annoyed at himself but annoyed at his brother and annoyed at the way his day had gone so far. Losing his temper meant something could slip out that shouldn't. He'd successfully kept Purefoy distracted, scared, and confused enough to not give anything away but he knew he'd have to calm down. He decided on a show of strength to detract from his bitterness.

Maintaining a quiet, calm, monotone, he spoke, 'Do you know what you're guilty of Purefoy?'

'I – I'm not guilty of any —'

'You're guilty of envy, avarice, and arrogance. Those are just some of the reasons why you're where you are now. They're tied together those three but you came to London wanting more, didn't ya?' A brief, unwelcome silence.

'...don't we all?'

'You had the arrogance to go about business even as you failed, your woman failed, and you failed your woman because of envy – all in the name of avarice. In the name of money.'

'I just – I only wanted...' Words failed because a fever had been planted in him. Murphy let it.

Beneath their feet the dried horse manure of yesterday began to flake and the horses – more in number every year – gave freely to the supply. Though they called it mud, everyone in London knew what they were treading on. There were children who remained barefoot throughout the day so they could get it in between their toes. Their only sand was manure.

Purefoy attempted to process all that Murphy had said in a sensible way. He hoped for some calm to steady him. He hadn't found it. The thought of *Prinny was a giant who ate four times what I do* stuck in him. *Giants crush things simply by living, whether they intend to or not. It's in their nature.*

'What will happen to me at the end of today, Murphy?'

'How should I know? You'll probably be in a local lock or on their ship. With any luck, you'll be drowned in the Monster Soup.'

Only a few of the greatest minds at that time realised the potential and the danger in what sat beneath their feet. Only a few in London believed John Snow when he published *On the adulteration of bread as a cause of rickets* and told them that it wasn't the smell that was dangerous but instead something living inside, something you couldn't see, that was deadly. Rickets have always been a problem for Britain. If it was too early for physicians, it was too early for a public conception. It takes a critical mass to reveal a layer unseen. John Snow would die just two months later being known at that time for his treatment of the Queen's birthing pains with ether. Only years later would he be recognised as the great British physician.

Chapter 7

The silence between them was preferred by both parties once fully awake. London gave them no such silence. Drury Lane quickly became Wych Street and on each street corner, more joined the crossing-sweepers. Flat capped, sooted children sat at the corner, waiting for work or the opportunity to make work; coal-heavers chatted; Chinamen begged and duffed behind them; Hindu tract-sellers stood near; nearer to them, so too did the long-song sellers. All vied for the charitable and the buyers.

Purefoy noticed their pace had slowed considerably once past St Clements. He looked at Murphy as Murphy looked ahead with a briefly knotted brow. More people filled the streets, the roads heaved with traffic and the reckless. Ladies of the town, their menagerie of servant girls in tow, attempted to get to where they needed to be before other such ladies crowded around; more ladies followed; more tops than bonnets became populous; though board men and muffin men were more here than on Drury Lane, the jackets and boots became densely blacker, the closer to Fleet Street they got.

Once on Fleet Street, they could hear two voices in argument above all other sounds. One sounded a plea, the other a threat. Though there were only two voices, they repeated the same phrases over and over in incantation – simultaneously, each iteration sounded different from the last. Each plea had a different timbre and each threat a different exclamatory growl. With each iteration the meaning seemed to shift. However close they got, the words were always clear but the context of the situation remained unclear. *The bird in the cage on the spinning disk; the bird wasn't in the cage.* Purefoy's thaumatrope thoughts would prove more fitting than he'd know – the voices grew hoarse, blended, but the volume swung down then up and continued to alternate.

'Father…'

'Satan—'

'Father...' The plea came from a sandwich-board man advertising the end of the world.

'Satan!' The exclamation came from a priest who held a book and a cross at arm's length, thrusting them toward the boardman with each shout. There was a similarity in the lines of their faces – more in their bone structure. Both men were wiry and seemed tired, both sets of shoulders stooped, and the boardman was only a little taller than the aged priest. Their eye colour, the same; the compassion, opposite. Where the boardman empathised, the priest feared what he saw but stood his ground for fear of giving in to weakness. They were two sides of the same line mistaken by their linearity.

Once past them, Purefoy imagined them as the same voice in the same body arguing with itself; never showing externally its exact meaning but knowing, in its utterance of each twisted syllable, the intention it meant at that time; though it didn't know what intention it meant before it was said, only as it was said – a line turning in on itself within the voice box of the body of the line that it was part of.

They were stuck in morning street traffic.

The exact kind of traffic Purefoy'd learned to avoid. Had he taken the route to St. Paul's he'd thought of earlier – before meeting Murphy, before all this – he'd never have approached Fleet Street. He'd have gone over it or under it but to go on it, at any time but nighttime, is worse than a slow tramp. He knew that not far away, on Ludgate Hill, hordes of people would block the way. He chuckled lightly to himself.

Murphy and Purefoy looked at each other. Both smiled but neither knew why the other did.

The denser the crowds, the wider Murphy's smile. Purefoy felt the pressure of the crowd closing in. He stood elbow to elbow with Murphy and another man to his right – decorum stopped him looking at anyone but Murphy. He began to sweat and looked over at Murphy. Murphy had already removed his hat and held it with two hands in front of him. There is a mutter of sighs that comes from a crowd so pressed in such a small space. It starts as a mutter, becomes an irritation, and is followed by the release of either progress or conversation. There was no progress.

A ruckus of noise emerged from the streets. The sound of horse hooves had stopped only to be replaced by shouts, grunts, and horns. Purefoy's head felt tight, unable to think on anything but controlling the sounds reverberating in him. He began to wince with each increase in volume. Once the busmen, cartmen, and rickshaws had upped, so too did the street crowd. Purefoy knew the volume would only increase. To stop the pain in his head growing into his spine, he buried it and focused only on his immediate surrounds. The man to his right wore clean, polished, black long-boots whereas the man in front had straps under his shoes keeping his trousers firmly in place.

Purefoy let those items, and what they meant, sink in. He tried to block out all else to calm him. Before further cataloguing calmed him, the men in front of him spoke. 'Tell me Flashman, will this street ever move?'

'I should hope not. Then we'd have to go to work.' The men smiled but neither laughed.

'How are your babes, Flash?'

'Well enough, old man – people must look to themselves first, after all.'

'Indeed just the other day I was saying there's no such thing as society.'

'What's on the cards today?'

'Same as it was yesterday, Gideon. The bloody Greece question.'

'Do those filthy beggars still want more loans?'

'You're the head banker, Gideon, you tell me.'

'Well of course they bloody do. Who doesn't want them from

us? The problem with Greece is that we'll never get it back.'

'How do you figure that?'

'Well, I'm sorry to bear the message to you, Flash, but though the founder of civilization, Greece has never been very civilized in its accounting. It—'

'Who says? I've not heard a thing about it apart from the Germans complaining.'

'Well I'm getting to that. *I've* not researched it but our continental friends tell me that some Frenchie wrote about it ten and a bit years ago. Get this, his name was 'Ed About'.'

'And did he have his 'ed about him?'

'My, you're funny this morning. It seems he did. He did his research and figured that the Greek finances have been up the windward passage for so long – and the people have gotten so used to it – that there's no hope for them.'

'So what are we going to do?'

'What do you think we should do, Flash?'

'Well I'm not the chief banker, Gideon, you are. I do whatever you tell me to.'

'Let mother hen take care of it, eh? Quite right, old cock. We're going to help them – we'll let them have a loan at our usual rate—' At this, both men sniggered.

'And when they don't pay, we'll take what we can or they'll starve.'

'The old rules are the best then.'

'Ah, but this one has a new face. Here we're doing them a kindness and we'll even tell them they've got to be more careful, to pull their hats down and weather out the bad times with more production.' Both men laughed riotously.

At this, they realised their loudness and continued, quieter.

'Any other news, mother hen?'

'Well, there's a dip in trade with France and old Nippy likes us—'

'He likes us, does he? He always came at me as a tiny, sweaty horse of a man.'

'Let's just say they like to keep us in their pocket so that's not so grave. The army, however, will continue to complain and die in their numbers while their generals ask for more money.'

'Will we give it to them?'

'Maybe. It all depends on what news your coves bring in. What's the gas, Flash?'

'Well the big three are the big problems—'

'Bubes, crinkums, and toffers, you mean?' A guffaw from both.

'Close. Naples, India and China, respectively.'

'Mmm, go on.'

'The minor concern is that the King of Naples has captured one of our ships.'

'Bloody wops.'

'Yes, exactly – we think it's probably only political and will blow over fairly easily but they're obviously desperate and in need of money. My lot are more worried about what might happen if it crashes or sinks due to a drunk captain.'

'A comedy of errors that might put an end to their touted unification, with any luck.' The two men laughed again. In the span of their conversation, they'd all moved three yards forward. Purefoy's head had stopped hurting quite so much but now the men's flippant tones and porcine laughs made his neck tight. Murphy continued smiling.

'The front bench wants us to rule India now—'

'Good. Show those dirty wogs how to do it.'

'Yes…but that does mean a whole lot of problems for you and a whole new title for old Vicky.'

'Bloody good show, Flash!' The man Gideon slapped the other's shoulder. 'Can you imagine the coffers?'

'A lot like your father's, I'd imagine.'

'And yours…good show, though. Could you quantify and correlate a good show for the packs?'

'The message is never a problem – it's the administration—'

'Oh, my tackle to all that. So long as they know we're in charge and the surplus keeps fighting over there, we'll be most comfortable.'

'I agree but do you think her majesty will?'

'I know so, Flash. Who wouldn't like to be empress?'
'Careful, they'll set their sights on China next.'

'Yes…that is another problem.'

'They're getting stronger, you know. Canton won't hold, Choosan won't stick, and Hong Kong won't budge – if we stay too long we'll certainly have to press our welcome and that's something I'm afraid of.'

'Getting our Nebuchadnezzar wet?'

'Getting it chopped off, Gideon.'

'Ah, well, yes – that's something the entirety of the West is afraid of. America's just as afraid of China as we are but with an empress on side, we'll certainly give them a good show should we need.' A lull then; as if mention of a true 'show' was enough to erase the shared illusion.

Purefoy attempted to get a fix on the men's faces. He wanted to see how they looked. Their clothes were indistinguishable from the crowds suits and had he not been so close, he was sure he wouldn't have been able to spot them. Positioned as he was, he could only see the face of the one named Flash – like his voice, it was porcine with rubbery red cheeks and a putty-like forehead that spoke of brandies and partridges. The face said he'd never suffered a day without food, nor worked in a factory, nor chased pure, nor ploughed a field, nor spent a day without boiled water. His grey-green eyes reflected the stone and steel he saw in the balance books his father had given him. Wealth lines spread from his eyes to his temples. His bend was rounded from chest to waist.

'But how do you propose we'd pay for that kind of heightened presence, Gideon? Establishing rule means more men, more women, and more bloody soldiers.'

'In lieu of the push we'll get from India, we'll just need to tell the vestries that we'll have to cut back. We'll cut back, then the same – if not more – contributions will come in, we'll take rule and then the real treasures will come in. Simple economics.'

'So we'll all be in it together.'

'Well, of course. There might be ways around paying those contributions for those in the know but I'd be utterly shocked if the richest were to do so.'

'Shocked?'

'Utterly. Entirely. Oh yes.'

'But you'll be doing it, yourself—'

'What a thing to say.' Both men laughed until they felt the need to hold their stomachs and clear their throats.

'Have you seen the hunt recently, Flash?'

'Ah yes, our other bother.'

'I'd say it's rather more than a *sport* of bother. Wouldn't you?'

'If only it was sport he knew how to do, Gideon. If only he was his name's sport, it'd be a damn sight easier to make him legal. It seems any games with him involved are certain to play out with a certain docking, churching, and clocking.'

'So no reprieve from his troubles, then? Not even a bull? *Could* a good bull here or there fix it?'

'I'm afraid not, mother hen. We can deny questions for some time to come but eventually we'll have to give up on the hunt as we have to with all our unnecessary alliances.'

'Ah yes, the Legg and the cable. I've said that we should ignore their business for some time now—'

'Don't worry, mother hen. So long as we're *seen* to do something with them, we get all the benefits of any business partnership without any of the losses.'

'Well, you certainly are better at framing partnerships than I am.' Another guffaw from each.

'How's the slanty getting on, Gideon?'

'Oh, exceptionally. He's gutting what he should as efficiently as we could. We'll do more but, for the moment, he's done an almost regal job. He's also a bit more of a rock-breaker than we initially gave him credit for – he's entirely happy to carry on working, no matter how much he's under fire. And how's your old post's replacement?'

'Hmm?'

'You know, that…cove.'

'Cove?'

'Perhaps—'

'Ah, yes, splendidly. He's done as I told him and then some. I'm sure he'll make upstarts think twice about getting above themselves.'

Purefoy couldn't listen to the two men anymore. They talked of jobs and wealth easily while he only hoped to find water. It was the conversation, not his thirst, which made him stop listening. It went on, incessantly on, with how to spin things as if their matters were all illusions and tricks. *What was that thought from earlier…I hadn't realised I lived in an hallucinatory age.*

The street had become less blocked, the men walked ahead. When Purefoy looked for them again, he couldn't spot them in the crowd. They were unremarkable amidst their peers. Purefoy looked at Murphy as the noise lowered to a hum. Murphy'd replaced his hat and still smiled.

'Murphy, could we stop for some water, please?'

'No.' He continued to smile.

'Well, can I ask why it is that you're smiling?'

'I thought ya never would. The cove ahead of me in that crush may have just lost his reader, his billy, his jerry and I may have just found 'em.'

Purefoy considered, *Does Murphy need a new pocket-book, handkerchief, and watch? That's a lot for a man who already has a swell necktie…but he might sell them…as he might do with my clothes.*

Luck had never been kind to Purefoy. He'd tried his and found it wanting. Inimitably, he carried on trying and carried on hoping for happiness. He hadn't thought to turn to theft – not for any moral reason but – because he knew the eventual, incarcerated, outcome and that he feared.

'Will ya try ya luck, Prifardd?'

'Don't call me that, please.'

'I'll call ya whatever I like. Why not, anyway?'

'I don't...'

'What? Like it? Well, you—'

'I don't deserve it.'

'Why? What does it mean then?' Purefoy turned his head slowly to inspect Murphy. Murphy'd stopped smiling. He too had turned. Murphy's unlined face didn't give anything away. Purefoy thought Murphy was ...*a blowhard and a pothook, leading strings his whole life – he lies. He's lying now – there is no nooluck woman who knows me...but what if there is? It would be just my luck that it would be...Lady Luck herself waiting for me.*

'It means nothing. It's not important. What should I try?'

'Hah. Oh Bryn, a quick filch. Or are you only a bleater?'

'Sheep jokes?'

'So?'

'No. No thank you.'

'You'd do well to remember that it's your last day on the outside. They say a man should try everything once.'

Purefoy didn't respond in speech but his brow knitted itself together in lines.

'Ah, come on – I know a jeweller near here we could easily do a spot of mornin' anglin' and make you a star for your last day. I'd go easier on ya if ya did.'

'But you wouldn't let me go?'

'I can't do that...but I could go easier on ya for the rest of the day. Ya know, not be so rough with ya.' Temptation's so pretty, even for the smallest of rewards. Temptation didn't seem urgent to him – he had under twenty hours to live but it didn't cause shivers he associated with urgency; it simply sat as a possible, pleasurable endeavour waiting for him— 'Gesshuffuckounnameeway.'

Both men were pushed passed by an early drunk.

The drunk wheeled round and made them stop where they were on Ludgate Hill. Though two yards ahead, they could smell him and – full as all smells were – this overpowered them. Murphy looked briefly away; Purefoy was used to similar so looked at the drunk but then up as a pigeon flew overhead and back again at the drunk. The man's head fell onto his chest but he looked up with his left eye so his head tilted onto his right breast. He carried a bottle in his right hand that he swung at them and up to his lips occasionally. When he did swig, he knocked his whole head back and gulped, only to flop his head back down. With each taste he grew less coherent and angrier. His face flushed red. 'Youuu. Youuu ball o' waxes and yuh warm dukes – don't you come closer or I'll 'ev ya.' Morning drunks can usually be walked past with a nod but this man was fierce. 'I maayy be three sheets but I know when I've 'ad to up Styx and thish—' The man drank again. 'This is it!' Another man suddenly pushed past them and punched the drunk directly on his right shoulder, sending him spinning around. The two drunks ran off in the direction of St Paul's.

Murphy spoke quietly then, 'What a noddy file.' The two men could still be seen by St Paul's.

Murphy shouted, 'Bastards!'

Murphy grabbed Purefoy by the arm, he dragged him along as he ran to the drunks. Purefoy had to keep up or be dragged under. Murphy weaved them around oncoming walkers – often through. The men had stopped at the steps to St Paul's, drinking. Purefoy's heart began to race though he didn't know why they were running. Murphy had let him go. They raced and the towering architecture of St Paul's loomed. Murphy ran ahead. The two drunks finally looked up, they saw Murphy running at them. They turned and attempted to run – it was too late, Murphy was on them. His biceps broke their noses. He knocked them down with his arms outstretched.

'Purefoy! You move and you're next.'

Murphy knew Purefoy's thought of escape. After the threat, Purefoy walked up to them. Murphy kicked each man in the side and each man was slow to rise – too sodden, too heavy inside. Murphy kicked repeatedly, grunting as he did. The two men had no wind in them to shout, only to whimper. When one of them managed to get onto his knees, Murphy smacked the heel of his palm into the man's chin. From kicking their sides to kicking their heads, Murphy progressed easily. He stomped on both heads, one after the other – blood began to fleck the pavement. Purefoy tried to take in what he saw but, for the moment, the only thing was the blood spread around them, St Paul's tower, and the thick lines of blood that ran slowly across the pavement and pooled at his feet.

CHAPTER 8

After the noise and the flesh had stopped, Purefoy stepped back but the blood on his boots followed.

After looking at the now half-open heads of the men, the sounds around him hid in fear of his beating chest – it was in his throat again but now thick with a mercury saliva, filling his mouth.

The urge to vomit came and he retched. There was nothing to give but a shove in the mouth. *I never knew there was such a smell to a man's death.* Uncontrolled, he breathed deep and quick. He stabilised himself but not the London around him – it felt oddly quiet. His head wouldn't move quickly but he looked around and saw so many people not-looking at him, Murphy, and the now dead men that he knew they'd seen it all.

The front of St Paul's is always busy. It's where we gather when there's an attack on liberty, where we camp and protest, where we occupy, where we grumble over the taxes demanded for a war, or we jeer at some poor wretch nailed by his ears in the pillory. Here the news-heralds proclaim our victories of economy – here the public-relations men read out their budgets; vendors of infallible nostrums wax eloquent on the virtues of their wares; and everyone looks at everyone seeing all of it. All of it on the steps of St Paul's Cathedral. *More madness,* Purefoy thought before he bowed his head and waited.

* * *

The morning of Mr Llwyn's return from a night spent in the cold did not alert their neighbours. It would not have alerted anyone but Mrs Llwyn had the young Purefoy not been awake early. The sun and the son had only just risen, in tandem, to reach the larder. When they did, Mr Llwyn did. He thought, *It is the boy. The boy – he's alive! I should bandage his skull, I should check his shoulder.*

Purefoy heard something at the edge of the larder and started at the sight of his father. Mr Llwyn whispered, 'Dewch yma, bachgen. Dewch yma.' [*Come here, boy. Come here.*]

'Da? Mae ddrwg gen i, Da ond—' [*Dad? I'm sorry, Dad but—*]

'Pa de poeni, dwi'n un ffrind.' [*Don't worry, I'm a friend.*]

'Da…? Dach chi'n—' [*Dad? Are you—*]

'Dewch yma, bachgen. Dewch.' [*Come here, boy. Come.*]

So Purefoy went to his father and his father inspected him. Mr Llwyn cried silently as he did so.

Mr Llwyn knelt down and whimpered, 'Chi'n iawn, yn awr, fach un. Chi'n iawn.' [*You're fine, now, little one. You're fine.*] They held each other and rocked back and forth then. Purefoy couldn't understand why his father was crying but rocked to make him feel better.

Mrs Llwyn came into the kitchen dressed only in her calico chemise and petticoat, both males looked quickly up at her but the older spoke first, 'Is this your child ma'am? Don't worry, he's safe now. He can go back to you now.'

Mrs Llwyn looked over her husband. He was sweating and she saw he had a fever; his eyes were wide. His muscles involuntarily twitched as he stood. She recognised the form but not the man. She told her son in as calm a voice as she could, 'Bryn, dewch yma. Dewch i fi, nawr.' [*Bryn. Come here. Come to me, now.*]

'Ond Ma—' [*But Ma—*]

'Nawr, Bryn Prifardd Llewes ap Llwyn. Nawr.' [*Now, Bryn Prifardd Llewes ap Llwyn. Now.*]

Purefoy knew never to ask again after his mother had used his true name. He left his father's embrace to go to his mother's side. Mr Llwyn's eyes darted, obviously confused – he took a step forward with 'Ma'am, I—' but fell under the weight of his confusion and hit his head. A drop of blood later dripped onto Purefoy's shoe as he, his mother, and his sister carried Mr Llwyn to the doctor. There Mr Llwyn woke screaming. He punched the doctor and Mrs Llwyn restrained him. 'Sshh, Rhys. Sshh.' He stopped moving and they whispered to each other until he slept and she cried. After that day, Bryn Prifardd Llewes ap Llwyn was the son of a dead man.

He would see him once more.

* * *

Murphy still stood with the bodies, cursing and searching them. Purefoy raised his head, unknowing how much time had passed. Purefoy approached as Murphy took off their shoes and tied them into pairs. 'Want a pair?'

'Murphy, we should leave. Now.'

Purefoy rarely needed to be steely; he put one hand on Murphy's shoulder, another on his arm, and pulled him slowly but forcefully away from the bodies. Murphy tugged and kicked a little but was so surprised he didn't put up much of a fight. 'Murphy, we need to leave before any real police get here. Do you understand?'

'Aye. I suppose I do.' They walked quickly around St Paul's and north onto Cheapside. Purefoy looked back at it. He realised what it was that often drew him there, it wasn't the startling amounts of pure; it wasn't the proximity of any particular park, circus, or field but in his free hours he would stare at the length, the top, and the masonry of St Paul's. To him, the shape from the outside seemed like an elaborate maze. The top seemed exactly that now, a spinning top placed upside down and called a roof. *But spinning tops always stop...* He knew that out of sight stood the Royal Exchange, the place to trade in Britain, and its own towering tops.

Coming over the mud behind them, under the guidance of a single driver, was an omnibus. Over the oncoming noise, Murphy gleefully shouted, 'Now art thou arrived, fell soul.' He smiled his black smile and spots of blood appeared darker in the cracks of his cheeks. He motioned Purefoy on. Murphy jumped onto the omnibus with ease and held out his hand. Purefoy took it and landed heavily on the step – it broke beneath him and his feet dragged on the floor. He cried a sharp animal noise. The pain was excruciating. Murphy pulled him up. Away from the towers of St Paul's and the Royal Exchange, they were safer.

A perturbed passenger rose up. 'Excuse me but surely you two shouldn't be on here?' Murphy laughed.

Purefoy was no longer in a mood to be kind or soft with people, he spoke quietly but visibly contained himself, 'I suggest you sit back down now, sir, before the blood on my boots becomes yours. What we do is none of your business.' Purefoy and the man held each other's gaze. The man's gaze slowly moved to Purefoy's feet. When he looked back up, Purefoy nodded. The man sat back down.

Murphy had taken a seat on the entrance, his feet dangled where the broken step flapped. Purefoy moved and stood behind him, looking out at passing Cheapside. Buses are always a time to reflect. Purefoy couldn't immediately fathom why he'd chosen to help Murphy but knew that once he had, his temper had risen. Now he flushed with anger, adrenaline, and shame— *I should apologize to that man but…no. There's no need. It's done now. It would only be made worse.* His stomach pained him but he remained intent on restoring calm. He'd never been on an omnibus before. There seemed to him a reprieve for all his senses. The continuous sound of the horses, the bus, and the surrounds were enough to let him forget the pains in his body and focus solely on thought or, in this particular moment, enjoying thinking how he had no thoughts and seeing how long he wouldn't think for. It wasn't long; the thought of the Royal Exchange came back to him. He thought, *One day it too will be occupied as St Paul's is.*

The conductor had made his way from the top deck. He stood to Purefoy's right, unnoticed. He coughed. He remained unnoticed. He touched Murphy's shoulder.

Murphy sprang up and hit the conductor's arm away. His Irish growl came back with, 'Away there with the other dogs!'

The conductor remained. A little redder in the face, he remained. Obviously used to it, he spoke loudly and comfortably, 'Where're you two goin', then?' Purefoy detected a slight Yorkshire accent.

'As far as we like.' Murphy's retort still didn't faze the Yorkshireman.

'That'll be a penny each, please.'

'A penny? You're on the cross, northe'ner. Pike off before I break you and this bus in two.'

The Yorkshireman stood still. His hat hid his eyes but his cheeks grew redder while he stuck his chin out, ever-so-slightly.

'Tuppence for us both, you said, sir?' His adrenaline drained, Purefoy simply wanted to eat or drink and be done with the violence. He didn't yet think that The City is a muscular system that breeds casual violence. The only way to understand it, anatomical dissection. The conductor nodded and Purefoy handed him tuppence. A murmur went through the passengers. Murphy moved to the top deck, Purefoy followed. They sat apart, in silence, and their angers calmed.

'Even now, Bryn, the place draws near and it's there we'll meet the person I need to take you to.' Quietened, collected, Purefoy strained to hear him.

'We're coming to the Queen's Bank. Is that where you mean?' His pitch higher through shouting.

'No – Commercial Road. Though it's queer you should mention The Reserve. Aye—'

'Queer?'

'Aye, you'll see.' Murphy had spoken too early.

At the junction of Poultry and Corn Hill, they still had Corn hill, Leadenh All Street, Aldgate High Street, and Whitechapel Road to ride until they got off. Purefoy absorbed as much detail of each street as he could. *This is my last day. I'll never come this way again*. But his blood sugars lowered. By Aldgate, he couldn't focus. As he drifted out of consciousness an image slowly formed in his mind of Murphy kicking to death the nameless bankers they'd walked behind on Ludgate Hill, kicking them to death in front of St Paul's, in front of The Royal Exchange. He didn't know if he slept.

Murphy nudged him. The sound of the conductor's voice meant they had to get off. Once off, Purefoy wasn't sure where they were. They were still on Whitechapel Road. He'd rarely ventured into the East End in the whole time he'd been in London, not for any particular reason, but because he'd spent so much time south and west that the east hadn't seemed regularly necessary. He didn't believe the rumours and before BB had gone to the workhouse, they'd considered moving there for the cheaper rent.

'Come on, there's the entrance.' Murphy had pointed to a church Purefoy recognised. Purefoy sleepwalked to the door. Murphy knocked. The door opened a little and a face appeared. Murphy whispered to it and it to Murphy. The door slammed shut.

St Mary's Church stood at the halfway mark of Whitechapel Road connecting to Commercial Road. It wouldn't open again for Murphy. Not without aid.

Chapter 9

Purefoy attempted waking. By the lightened grey of the sky, he knew it was just before midday. Murphy's face was neither light nor morning-like. For the first time that day, Purefoy saw Murphy confused. He started to pace in front of the door as the big cats in The Zoo did. Purefoy's haze of yawns didn't affect Murphy but he occasionally glanced sideways. Purefoy was weaker now than when they first met – Murphy didn't know but Purefoy was finding it harder to think of escape or think clearly at all.

'Perhaps they—'

'Shut up, Purefoy. You don't know a jack from jack. She's meant to be here.'

'She?'

'Aye. Now stow it. I'm tryin' a think.'

Purefoy considered that Murphy could have been lying about what he intended for him: he'd heard about people being taken for the labour test without knowing and then breaking rocks for 10 years after...*but how had he known my name? Most of my proper name? How had he got it?*

Three women – one old, one maid, one miss – walked by; they stared silently at Murphy and interrupted any train of thought Purefoy had. They walked with locked arms and a muff each over the entirety of the path. Purefoy saw a glint of sharp metal in the hands of the miss as he stepped backward, out of the way. As they passed, their bustles curled up to a point, like the tales he'd heard of African scorpions. Neither Murphy nor Purefoy met their eyes nor the eyes of the woman they waved to going in the opposite direction.

The noise of the street came to be a constant that Purefoy balanced himself on. As was Murphy's pacing, the tightening of his gut, as were his often-closing eyes. When he heard a lull in the passing traffic and footsteps traversing the mud, he woke a little.

He looked again. There he saw a woman whose hooped skirts never touched the ground and whose small bonnet crowned her head brightly. She, with ease, made her way directly over the road as if all parties cleared and stopped before her. She seemed disdainful to Purefoy as she passed him, passed Murphy, and glided to the door.

She unlocked the door. She looked back over her shoulder at Murphy. He'd realised what was happening as soon as she'd walked past. He'd stopped pacing and relaxed. She nodded and then entered. Murphy looked back to ensure Purefoy followed.

'You're late, ma'am.'

'You're early.' She spoke without looking back. Purefoy thought it might have been to give him less chance of recognition. They paced down the middle of the small church. She shouted, 'Wherever you are, I *told* you to let this man—'

'This gentleman, ma—'

'This man and his associate in so that they could sit and wait. Where are you?! Where are you, hmm?' Whoever had appeared at the door wouldn't appear again.

The sculptures and the stained glass windows noticed Purefoy. The way the light of the latter shaped the lines of the former surprised him. In his dehydrated state, his tiredness, he saw an ample plain full of distress and torments. Wraith-like, robed men in the windows speared creatures in the windows next to them. Not even the few lit candles near the sculptures of proud saints could cauterize their zeal and the danger in their eyes. The everyday horror of it struck him most. He imagined someone buried inside or below the church in their own sepulchre. Though in his state, he didn't remember it well, this was not how he remembered it.

'Purefoy.'

Murphy had called him back. 'Come along man.'

'Are you the Brin Pryfard Lewes—'

'It's Preevardd Shllewes—'

'Stow your whid, Irish, or you'll get nothing from me.' *So this is the woman.* Purefoy didn't know her but had enough small sense about him to know that this was it; that this was the woman Murphy had to take him to before he could be taken to the police. *What did Murphy mean when he said she was nooluck? And if she knows me, as he said she does, why is she asking if I'm...*

He tried to examine her in the light of his memories of this place. Her nose was thin and sharp, her cheeks tight against her face and her mouth small; she had brown eyes and, though tied and under a bonnet, long brown hair; her skin was smooth and unmarked as far as he could see though she had no signs of health and he worried that she would fall ill easily. He didn't know her. 'Are you the man that married a Banwen Kath in this church in 1854?'

'I – I am.'

'Then this letter is for you and you have...well...you have your letter. Irish, with me.'

'Don't think about going anywhere, Prifardd, the doors are locked.' The woman and Murphy walked on through a door to the side of Purefoy.

Purefoy had been a fortunate child in many ways. He'd had the opportunity to learn to read unlike so many others. His mother said he was naturally gifted. She'd always told him he'd go far. She'd ensured that he continued to read and write even as they aged and took on jobs. He thanked her before reading the letter.

Dear Mr Llewes ap Llwyn,

It is with deepest sympathy that we must inform you of your sister and your mother's death. We hope you receive this news via a suitable parish where they can offer you such condolences as you will need and we trust in the Lord's will to make it so.

Before her untimely passing we had had word from your mother of your marriage to Miss Kath in St. Mary Matfelon, London and with this…

Purefoy read no more. The ground didn't feel solid beneath him, he reached out to a pew with his left hand and sat quickly.

The same burning he'd felt that morning was in him but doubled. He felt betrayed by time. Though he'd thought all his cares dead with BB, the inkwell of his fears flowed back up: his compassion mixed with it and lost all colour; memories of his simple Wrexham clashed with The illusory City. *Banwen…of course, Banwen*; his mother's worn face smiling and crying as he told her he was leaving for London; a rushing piano song he'd heard near an institute that made him walk swifter; he tried to stem the flow of thought, of acid, in him with breath but it wouldn't stop; he thought he heard grunting; he listened again but wheezed – each breath out was making a high-pitched sound deep in the back of his throat; he was sobbing and attempting to contain it but the attempt only made it more so; his throat hurt; the first time he was really scared for his sister – the first time he realised he really cared for her – came to him and moved on; an image from when he was very young of his mam and dad sat in the kitchen, crying into each other's shoulders and him being hugged between them after they saw him; Bristol George, Jemmy the Rake, Corporal Casey all, one by one, wishing him well with a great, unavoidable pity in their faces; a clear thought, *This can't last. It won't last* that got lost in the swell in his stomach, in the burn in his chest; his spine trembled; the hair on the back of his neck itched; and the once certain weight of his wedding ring, melted into air. He tried to stop thinking.

He slowed his breathing.

He attempted to steady, to right himself. He heard grunting again – his failure to control himself caused the brief reprieve to shatter. He dropped the letter and buried his head into the space between his knees, his hands folded together over the medial malleolus muscle of his ankle; he rocked back and forth in his seat. He was quieter, certainly; the burning once in his chest contained itself in his head and his cheeks. He no longer let himself make noticeable sound but for an occasional mucous-heavy inhalation. His tears ran straight from his eyes to the sides of his knees. Still he heard grunting. Confusion stopped his rocking. He listened again, the grunting grew in volume.

With a blow of his nose, his pain receded to the back of his mind. *Like a child's feeling...BB always said she hoped I'd never grow up too much.* The grunting became rhythmic. Purefoy stood and turned his head; it came from the door Murphy had gone through. *What if he's killing her? In a church...* He took a step toward the door when he heard an accompanying sound, in rhythm. He recognised the call. It must have been the woman. The sound was similar to one he'd known. She wasn't hurt, they were having sex.

When Purefoy realised, he sat back down and picked up the letter. The thought, *As two lie in the grave, two lie to join...* tasted bitter. His right hand covered some words and a corner in dark pure. He folded it carefully, attempting to not write on it in pure again. He had to keep it, if only for the rest of the day. The grunting and the panting became hums and coos; with one deep vocal sound they stopped – followed by a long, breathy release. The silence of the church enveloped them.

In the clean church, Purefoy could smell his hands, his feet, his clothes. He looked at where his tears had marked his trousers, there was pure there too. The sounds of steps made him look up, Murphy had returned with the woman. 'Got ya letter alright then, Purefoy?' He smiled wide before continuing, 'Come on then. We've places to be.'

'Give the man a moment, Irish, he's...well he's no doubt in need of a little rest.'

'I'm willing to hedge that, after all he—'

'Why you – why even savages need time to grieve.'

'Don't tell me, you'd wager ya soul on it?'

'I'd wager something, yes. I'd say everyone needs a time to or…or your name's not Murphy.'

'It's not.' Murphy smiled and looked up at the woman from a head tilted forward, his doffed hat covering darkening eyes.

'Well at least give the man some of your earnings if you two must be on your way.'

'I never thought you a *socialiste*, Angie.'

'And I never thought you a demon before.'

'You should think more often.' The two stared at each other in the cold silence. She spoke again in defiance of his stare, 'I should imagine that you Irish, of all people, would want a fairer Britain and a fairer Europe.'

'You mean a better place for Ireland?' His monotone reasserted itself.

'I mean a Europe that includes everyone, even Britain—' Murphy laughed. 'And, you may laugh, but if we don't stop in-fighting there'll be no place for good men willing to travel to where the work is and no place for men like you either. Look at the railways.' She was incensed.

'I'd rather not.'

'…what say you, Mr Lewes?'

'I…I don't know, ma'am.' His throat was raw. He tasted iron.

'There. Purefoy can't conceive of it and we savage Celtic types would do well to stick together. Come along Purefoy, we're leaving.' With that, Murphy took Purefoy's arm and they stood. They walked to the back of the church and exited on the opposite side to their entrance. 'Let's get you to a part of The real City.'

'Who was that woman, Murphy?'

'It doesn't matter. The only thing that matters about her is that she's the dumb glutton that holds the key to commercial street and I just made a profit.' He laughed.

Before Purefoy knew where they were, he saw a sign for Commercial Street.

CHAPTER 10

BB and Purefoy were married in St Mary Metfalon, behind them. Purefoy considered his wedding day: there were no great masses, BB wore no great trail, but to them and to the light in them it was the brightest day they'd ever known. He cut his thoughts short – there are few greater sorrows than to recall our times of joy in wretchedness.

Commercial Road was vast and dizzying. Wide and long. It and its constituent parts stretched out in front of them. Once on it, Murphy stood gazing down it. They stood. Purefoy could make no decisions nor think any clear thoughts without fear of breaking down on the street and staying where he'd broken or being dragged – he maintained one clear thought, *Walk. Follow. End it.* His family and his wife, lost to him now, frenzied in thoughts at the back of his mind with a constant, dull ache that he couldn't permit to come to the fore. He asked,

'Murphy, do you know that woman well?'

'Well? I hardly know her, but I know her.'

'Do you...do you love her?'

'What? Come now, Purefoy – where's this from? And what business is it of yours?'

'I – I heard you and her...in the church...'

'Ah. Well. Wapping's different from love – the two aren't connected. Everyone does it but everyone pretends not to. There are infinite philosophical minutiae to understanding the pleasant relationships of humans with each other. Wait, are you—'

Purefoy's head had unconsciously begun to loll onto his chest. Purefoy swayed. The frenzy in him had been uncontrollable without water and he had succumb. He could feel his internal functions switching off, one by one, starting at the neck, going to his knees.

Murphy put his arm underneath Purefoy's arm, around his back, and lifted him upright. 'Alright sweet, we'll get you some sugar. That'll keep you. We're the perfect place for it.'

He didn't know Commercial Road as well as he'd like but he knew it well enough. He knew where to get anything, anything at all. He hadn't expected Purefoy to be this weak. He was glad of the time to think. He didn't know what was in the letter and hadn't inferred it from what Angela said. She'd said 'time to grieve', he'd simply played blue devils to keep her skirts up but she must have meant Purefoy had lost someone. The severity showed in his collapse. He knew he'd need to read the letter. He'd walked them 20 yards on Commercial, a twirler he knew was another 20 away. He knew he wouldn't get another chance. Murphy propped Purefoy against a shopfront. Purefoy felt nothing. 'Sir. You cannot put this man here, sir.'

'Hush up, Chinaman.' Murphy felt Purefoy's pockets.

'Sir. You bring shame on this shop and you will bring shame on yourself.'

'Knife it, Chinaman, before I knife you.' Murphy had found it. He read quickly.

'…may you live in interesting times, sir.'

The man re-entered his shop and closed the door. Murphy felt a bead of sweat drip down the side of his neck. He couldn't make out whether it was from carrying Purefoy or knowing he'd just been cursed by a Chinaman.

After reading the letter, he was surprised to feel sympathy for Purefoy. He knew what it was to lose family. He thought on the extremes of the past hour, from sex to curses – he laughed internally and knew them both intertwined, he then thought how it was his extremities that were most affected by the last hour.

Murphy was sharper than Purefoy in thought, in wit, and in understanding his place but he knew he often let it get the better of him; his wit could become arrogance and arrogance led to cursing. He tucked Purefoy's letter firmly back where he'd found it, put his arm under him again, and lifted. The twirler he knew was now just two yards from him. 'Alright, Murphy?'

'Alright, Twirler.'

'Need any rags? Or any rags twirlin', patchin' an' a like?'

'I need a grocer nearby who sells fruit peels and who won't mind a bung-eyed cove.'

'Found a new knight of the brush and moon to booze with, have you? Hah, well, you've a gonoff's luck today. 'Bout forty yards behin' me is one but you're lucky iss there, mos' of 'em been replaced by Chinaman's stores 'ese days – chains and chains of 'em. They all wants stretchin', you ars' me.'

'Thankin ye kindly, Twirler. I'll see you at The Duck anon.' Both sets began walking.

'No, sir Murphy, you won't. I'm with the temperance ladies now.'

Murphy was already two yards away when this was said but the twirler kept mumbling until he met a potential customer.

The grocer's was well stocked and its proprietor keen to help them through the door. Murphy propped Purefoy on the counter and looked around, it too had obviously seen better days. The grocer brought round a high chair. The two men gently lowered Purefoy onto it – civility established, Murphy moved to business. 'Very kind of you, sir.'

'Not at all, sir.' The man's accent wasn't plummy but its clipped nature told Murphy only a certain level of extremity would be acceptable. 'How can I help you gents, today? Something for your friend's head perhaps?'

'Perhaps, yes. I thought a fruit peel or a halfpenny treat to wake him up.'

'Hmm. May I ask what the cause of his head is, sir? Would it be hunger or…something else? I only ask because I'd rather give a fair recommendation.'

'Hunger, he's not much of a drinker.'

'Yes. Yes I see. Well we've sugar plums that—'

'That have lead in 'em. Don't think me rude, grocer, but he needs clean food if he is to wake.'

'Right you are, sir. Well, we do have fruit peels but we also have preserved apricots that will last you all day should you care to—'

'The fruit peel, please.' The two men knew this game very well.

'Yessir. How many would you like?'

'One.'

'Just one, sir? I should say there may not be enough food there to wake a man entirely.'

'Fine; two then, please.'

'Very good, sir.' The grocer took two dried, wound peels from a jar and placed them in a paper bag. As he span the bag by its edges, he said 'That'll be tuppence, please.'

'Tuppence? For two peels.' The crux of the game.

'Yessir.' Murphy knew how to make peels, how much they really cost.

'I've only one and a half to my name.'

'I could put one back…' One back.

'Aye. Please do.' One forth.

'Or if you'll be returning, I could take one and a half now with a guarantee that I'll see you again.' One rejoinder.

'Certainly. You've been a civil gentleman in this and I'd recommend this grocer over any other on Commercial Road.' One display.

'Very good, sir. Thank you for your custom.'

'Thank you, good sir grocer.' The finish.

CHAPTER 11

The two men emerged from the grocers, unscathed, but Murphy's newly aware nose turned up at the stench of The City. Inured as he usually was to it, today it overwhelmed his olfactory senses. He put Purefoy down against the shopfront so he could cough and blow into one of his newly acquired handkerchiefs. There he fed Purefoy.

At first it was a struggle to keep his head up, open his mouth long enough and get the peel in. With a readjustment of Purefoy's spine and his head tilted back, his mouth opened slightly. With a little guidance, the peel stimulated Purefoy's submandible salivary gland. With a little of Murphy's help, Purefoy's masseter muscle began to pull his jaw into a chewing motion.

Purefoy's eyes opened slightly. He didn't want to open them. He saw Murphy bent down in front of him with, for what he once might have might mistaken for a look of concern but now knew to be, a look of examination, of ensuring his profit was not lost. He closed his eyes. He couldn't feel a reason, a real reason, to keep them open. He chewed knowing the hunger would get the better of him if he didn't. His innards shivered in delight and the extremity of how necessary the fruit sugars were. In his violent hunger, he'd rushed and swallowed before getting the most out of the peel. He opened his eyes. His mouth lolled open but he found himself unable to speak properly.

'If ya want more, you're going to have to stand.' Murphy held out his hand. Purefoy took it, raised, and stood. He stepped from the shopfront and to Murphy.

Each limb felt fragile, each breath difficult – the stench tempted him to sit back down, to stay down. Hunger has its own logic. This feeling was what he and BB had feared: the clamour for survival, the destroyed sense that you'd eat and do anything to stay alive. Murphy handed Purefoy the bag. Purefoy ate again. The layer over his thoughts was no longer a dazed one. Euphoric acceptance of his end, yes, but despair at knowing it would not end soon enough.

'Now we walk. We'll take our time. You eat, I'll talk.' They walked east on Commercial Road. 'Ya see, Bryn, ya can't trust anyone, not a single cove who hasn't already given you their trust – you can't rely on anyone or anything. Everyone is lying to themselves all the time just to get through the day, d'ya think they're gonna *not* lie to you? Everyone lies to everyone, Bryn. This is what you have to expect, accept, and keep going through. Fraud is man's peculiar vice but violence is the easiest, closest to it – even intelligent men are violent in their intelligence. Hypocrisy, flattery, so called 'magic' – they're falsities, theft, and simony; d'you understand Prifardd? The more we walk in The City, in the commerce, on Commercial Road, the more we'll see all a' these. You can't trust me but now ya know that I know that you can't trust me and so I'm helping you. I'm offering a weak man a hand before I hand him over...everything dies, Bryn. Everything turns to mud and meat again. That's all there is. We need to be the frumper that cuts through it. Commercial Road is long and we've a hell of a way to go. In a hundred and fifty years' time all of this will be in the shadow of steel towers and this road will take the life blood of one commercial heart to another, whispering promises of splendour to itself, not knowing it's lying to itself...

'You...you probably think I'm drawing a long bow because you feel like hell. You might be labouring under the false impression that I'm trying to make you game...well, that's the thing about going through hell: once you've done it – it doesn't seem like hell anymore, it seems normal...and *that*, that's what you need.'

Purefoy had finished the fruit peel, gone on walking, but not listened to Murphy. As Murphy talked, Purefoy had tried to establish – not what he needed but – what he wanted. His head was sunk low, his shoulders hunched over, his spine leant forward from his hips slightly and his hands were firmly in his pockets.

Though he salivated and knew he needed more food, he wanted a royal purl or a humpty dumpty – the last time he'd drank either of those drinks, he'd forgotten any doubt or worry he'd felt before. He wanted oblivion. He tried to remember the area from the one time he'd been. He couldn't. He looked South; small plumes of smoke floated up as bubbles in water rise and disperse; but each plume was accompanied by a loud chatter. *More blab and blabbering nabs. Is Murphy still talking? He is. I suppose I should listen a little.*

'…but first we conquer violence. Then we move onto fraud. Finally, treachery – those three are bulging with concentric circles of possibilities but only at the end do we rid ourselves of them. Ya need to do them, to commit them, to conquer them.'

'And how am I to conquer anything without food, Murphy?'

'Oh, you'll survive. It's what we do. Anyway, ya've already broached violence – I saw the way you handled that noddle on the bus – ya just need to conquer it.'

'And again I ask, how am I to do that without food?'

'English Burgundy, that's how.'

'Booze?'

'Aye.'

'I've the money. Lead the way to the boozing-ken then.'

'I thought ya'd never ask. I've just a little somethin' to do first.'

'Constable, excuse me. I think I might've just been cursed by a Chinaman and – not wanting to cause any offence of any kind – can you tell me which areas I'd need to be careful around, please? If it's not too much trouble, that is.' Purefoy hadn't noticed the approaching policeman until Murphy stopped him. Again Murphy's switch in tone was pitch perfect and immediately polite. Aridity filled Purefoy's throat as he looked down at the bronzing red blood on the tips of his boots.

'No trouble, sah,' the policeman obliged. 'They don't care for no drink so you can go near the Prussians a bit north though don't be confused by the Jews, there's Prussians around. And Chinamen seem to live without eating so far as I know so you can settle in a good coffee house – that is if you can find a good one 'round here!' All three men smiled and rocked on their heels, only Purefoy showed unease.

'No, it's their Opium at night they likes; and you'll find half-a-dozen of 'em in one bed a-smoking and sleeping away. No, sah, it wouldn't be at all safe for you to venture down Butcher Row alone if you've offended 'em. I should also tell you to keep away from the docks this season: it ain't the Chinamen so much, nor the Lascars, nor yet the Bengalees as would hurt you; but there is an uncommon rough crew of English nationalists hangin' in and about there, and it would be better for you to have a constable with you, much better; I could assist you if you need to get to somewhere in partic'lar...?'

'That's very kind of you, constable, but we'll be fine with the Prussians, as you said. Thank you for your help.'

'You're welcome, sah. One final warning, a great many chimney sweep come down to these parts when their working days is done and may make themselves into unfortunate debtors. You would do well to stay afar from them. You can usually smell them a good deal away! Good day.'

'Haha. Thank you again constable, good day.' Purefoy knew this could be his chance, the chance, to escape Murphy. If he spoke to the constable first, spoke quickly, he could jump behind him and plead for protection ...*but then...but then Murphy could tell him what happened this morning and Murphy's good with words. He might...he might...* Purefoy said nothing.

Later he'd think that it wasn't just Murphy's intelligence that stopped him from talking to the police but an unconscious knowledge that he clung to Murphy. Despair clings to company.

The oblivious policeman walked west and they, east. Purefoy was annoyed at Murphy for approaching the police in the first place but, mostly, for not warning him. He let his head sink further down into his shoulders and watched Murphy's feet.

Before that day, Purefoy'd enjoyed watching the gait of a person before looking up at what they were wearing or carrying. He'd try to guess at what they did by their gait. If they owned a dog, he'd ask himself, *What relation are they to the dog? Maid? Master?* —

'Don't mope, Bryn, we're almost there.' Purefoy hadn't noticed an emotion but grief consumes. They took a left onto Jubilee Place. Purefoy felt his eyes closing again, the tiredness in him returning. *How quickly sweetness is forgotten.* He knew he needed more food but could hear the occasional blab from before and ignored his gut. Murphy stopped and turned to Purefoy. They hadn't taken two yards onto Jubilee Place and both stopped. 'Right flank, taffy.' Purefoy looked right and there was The George Tavern. They entered as soon as they could cross.

Even now, in the middle of the day, the pub was full. The atmosphere was, of course, smoky but both men knew what to expect and savoured it. The smell of a pub full of smoke is a delicious thing. When even the air is a stimulant, pubs are social cohesion and frisson.

At the bar stood a short, drunk, Chinaman. Murphy attempted small talk but the man interrupted Murphy saying, 'May you come to the attention of the authorities.'

Murphy moved away. Visibly annoyed, Murphy was losing his calm veneer in the midday smoke's warmth. 'Inn-keeper, two Royal Purls pl—'

'Make that one Royal Purl and one Humpty Dumpty, please sir.'

The innkeeper did his work silently and pointed at the large-type price list. A good innkeeper knows when to listen and when to add his voice. Purefoy reached to pay for both drinks but Murphy had already put cash on the table. Purefoy looked enquiringly at Murphy, Murphy ignored it. Paid, both men gulped of their tankards.

'When was the last time you were in the East End, Purefoy?'

'When…when I was married, four years ago.'

'So ya'll not be familiar with the local flavour then. One of the reasons I asked that blue bottle back there about this spot was to give ya a taste. That's not to say there's anything wrong with it so much…it's just a little queer.' Purefoy could hear that Murphy wanted to show off his patter talk for a while so drank, enjoyed the warmth of the drink, and half-listened. 'That's not to say they're a bad lot round 'ere – I heard a member of the Stock Exchange keeps a public-house in Clapham now. This shows ya the class of men who think it no disgrace to take taverns nowadays.' He paused then, waiting for a response.

Getting none, he continued, 'On the inside of these rocks you'll find ethics but not ethics ya've ever dreamed of: wild, brilliant, distorted ethics. Philosophies so different from what most of us would call human, they've practically a life of their own. Thoughts that breed thoughts – not all things in hell are justifiably so, Bryn. Take our friend here.' Murphy moved up to the Chinaman again and put his arm round him. 'Some of us are good men here, aren't we sir?'

The man stared at Murphy before speaking. 'May you find what you're looking for.' The man got up and left The George.

'Maybe the Chinese economy of words doesn't mix so well with the Irish.' Purefoy laughed. A snort of disbelief at Murphy's patter. He drank more. 'I've figured it out, Purefoy; you're an insect. That's just one of the reasons I don't like you. I can talk to ya, for sure, but I don't like ya.'

'And how am I an insect now?'

'Well men like me, we'll dig and we'll fag for whatever so long as it pays but not you – what you do is like what an ant does. London's the mud and you're the ant. Ya live on the back of this great beast and you pick off bits of it – I've heard Lascars talk about fish that swam along the bigger beast-fish eating things off the side of the big fish's back. That's what you do.'

'I just use what no one else is using – I don't bite anyone's back and if—' Purefoy could feel the brandy burning into him, giving him a Dutchman's courage.

'No, no – you don't understand; the fish don't bite the back of the big fish, they clean it. They protect it. You're a cleaner, Purefoy, and that's what I don't like about ya – it demeans a man to pick up after others.'

Purefoy didn't know what to say to Murphy's remark. Before it, he'd been prepared to argue for himself but now he realized that to debate with a man who doesn't understand the importance of cleaners, or of insects, is pointless.

'Murphy, why have we stopped here? Why are you sidling now?'

'I'm gonna go easy on ya for a bit because…because we both know what's comin'.' With this, Murphy looked into his tankard briefly, then drank the last.

Chapter 12

Murphy tired of Purefoy's silence. Both men had finished their drinks. Purefoy lifted his up, looked at Murphy and asked, 'Gut a quart pot, Irish?' Purefoy knew the gallows were on him, he figured he'd take some of their humour with him.

Murphy flashed his black stump-teeth. He put his tankard next to Purefoy's. 'A Hot Flannel and a Royal Purl, please sir.'

'That's cheatin', Purefoy – a Hot Flannel's proper fodder. Can't allow that or we might end up here all day.'

'So I cheated. So kill me'. Purefoy looked at Murphy, smiled, and put all his money on the bar. Murphy laughed, they received their drinks. Purefoy received a little of his money back but didn't care enough to count it. Murphy said, 'I think I see some friends o' mine. 'S go over.'

Murphy stepped slowly over to the loudest table in the pub. He seemed trepidatious. With each step it was as if the floor could crack and swallow him whole. He turned back to Purefoy and signalled for him to follow then raised his finger to his lips.

The man Murphy tapped on the shoulder turned to them and Purefoy instinctively looked away. He didn't know where to look. The man's skin was patterned half-black and half-white with a wave of diagonal colour across his face, like the new Friesian bulls that had started to appear in the markets at Wrexham. 'Alright 'Sterios, how are ya, ya Greek bastard ya?!'

'Murphy! You scared me for second…arr, not dead yet?' There was a round of exclamations from the table.

'Not for a long time. Though this old cove could do with a seat.'

'I'll move. I'll die a while over in the pisser.'

'Good man, 'Sterios. This here's Purefoy. Say hello, boys.'

'Hello boys!' The occupants of the table were already cup-hot and laughed at their own joke. Purefoy found another chair. The chair was barely able to stand. Purefoy sat gingerly on it. 'The last time I came hereabouts, you boys were in ruins and I believe you had to sponge to me.' At this the men's chatter fell and they looked at each other. 'Ah, don't trouble yourselves – thanks to Purefoy here, I've been paid today. Purefoy, this is Neshus, Shearon, and Phillis—'

'Phil—'

'He's a philistine. Don't listen to 'im. They're good, healthy Prussians and—'

'We're Polish, Murphy.' Phil spoke again.

'And I was just about to say that.' They were all well-built men, as big as Murphy or bigger.

'What line of work you do, Purefoy?'

'I'm a—'

'He's retired. He's even leaving London soon.' Purefoy nodded and settled into the motions of reaching the bottom of his drink. The Poles cooed in honest admiration then tutted in begrudged respect. Murphy had turned jovial again; this could have indicated that Purefoy could relax a little, were it not for the violent changes in Murphy's tone. He observed the men in their sometimes English, sometimes Polish chatter; he noticed the strong muscle density, the relaxed straightness of their posture; he knew the last time he'd noticed that combination of things was in horses.

They were loud but not angry men. They drank quickly and bought everyone at the table drinks when they went for more. Purefoy thanked them and accepted as many more as he could. 'We have day, night, but tomorrow away from docks. Today we drink. Tomorrow we suffer.' At this all the men laughed. Purefoy had begun to relax some, to accept his fate again. He attempted to be in the conversation.

Shearon spoke directly to him, 'How are you, friend? You look like sea and green – a dead man maybe.' He laughed and hit the table.

'He's right, Bryn, but then you've always looked a bit green to me.'

'I'm fine, thank you gentlemen – I think – I think I'll just use the facilities.' Purefoy smiled.

'Aye, me too.' The thought, *Murphy would hound me down the pit.*

'Yes and I.' Neshus joined them.

'Did you boys ever use the urinals on Cheapside when they created that stink four years ago?' Murphy, seemingly happy, continued conversation even in the toilet – Purefoy sat in the nearby privy. 'No, I am not here long and will stay until work done.'

'Aye but work's never done for men like us, no?' Neshus laughed. Purefoy remained as quiet as physically possible. The smell from under him was as incredible as anytime he'd sat above a cesspit. He could hear their urine streams against the urinal wall.

Neshus sucked in through his teeth suddenly. 'Y'alright Neshus? Are you feelin' alright?'

'Yes – ah, no. I – I piss pins and arrows for a week now.'

'Can you remember the wasp's – the ah – the woman's name?'

'Francisca, Francisca Maude, she—'

'D'ya meet 'er in here?'

'Here? Yes, of course. She—'

'Shouldn't be trusted. You'll need to go to a doctor—'

'Nie, no. It is only—' Murphy'd stopped urinating and gesticulated.

'Trust me, go to a doctor. You need to. After that, find someone who'll sell you a 'capote' – they're a lot, *a lot,* of money: capote is *dużo pieniędzy,* yes? But they stop you getting burnt.'

'Doctor then 'capote'? Yes, 'capote'. Purchase 'capote'.'

'Good man.' A slap on Neshus' back and the two men were done. Murphy, loud then, 'Purefoy, don't die in there, will ya?' A silence.

During the conversation, Purefoy had been attempting to control his stomach: he'd breathed slowly in through his mouth and exhaled through his nose; he'd pushed and squeezed his core muscles to silence the gasses he was emitting; he knew he needed to shit but felt as if a cork stopped him – he considered that the alcohol, his only proper food for that day, might be the thing stopping him. Now that he was alone, he could take the necessary measures. He wanted to put his hands on the walls either side of him but didn't trust them not to fall; he laughed a little at the thought of destroying the privy and the pub; he stopped laughing when he thought he might fall into the pit beneath him; he continued to breathe deeply but quickened the pace from before; he pushed inwardly a little; he raised one arm above his head and felt his face flush red; he pushed more; he held his breath; unconsciously grunted; he breathed out and in and pushed as much as he could – nothing happened.

He stopped, breathed out and felt a small, grotesque pain in his sphincter ani externus.

He thought, *Damn all. Four times what I eat? They don't do this...* and groaned. He attempted again – nothing again. He attempted a final time: raising both hands above him and then pushing down on his head with them while continuing to push inwardly down – something. An emergence; he couldn't let this opportunity go so breathed rapidly in and, holding his breath, pushed again until his face was red. An unsatisfactory drop of stool hit the water, he knew there was more. He didn't let his sphincter close but breathed out slowly and in again slowly – he stifled a laugh at his situation. He pushed hard again and a great release came – everything in him flushed out.

He thought a bubble had popped in him and purged all of the walls of his insides. He laughed. Then he knew that it would be the last shit he ever took. He abruptly stopped laughing. He looked into the black below him. 'My life's work.' He laughed.

Back at the table, Neshus' blood boiled. More drinks had been ordered but there was a woman present. Though she acted aloof, Neshus was gesticulating at her. She sat letting him. However affected she was, she didn't show it – this must have been Francisca Maude. She had destroyed Neshus' health but didn't care. *She looks like she could destroy every man's health.* Murphy and the others were translating what they could but they needn't have. Before Purefoy returned, she'd asked if any of them would like to spend time with her. She sat, shameless.

Neshus' voice rose. Murphy looked at the innkeeper; the keeper was aware of the situation and observing. Purefoy thought, *How easily we hurt each other; how animal-like it is; how unintended, how…how natural.* He was refreshed now and warmly drunk again.

After preening her hair, her hand, she stood – Neshus stood with her, almost shouting as each sentence ended – and she walked out. Purefoy remained stood, unsure; Neshus' nostrils flared, a horse again. He pushed past and Purefoy stepped aside. Murphy followed Neshus, grabbing Purefoy on the way out. Being grabbed, moved, and thrown about was something Purefoy was getting used to.

Neshus was galloping back and forth in front of The George. The woman was nowhere to be seen – a carriage, a cabriolet, an omnibus perhaps. Neshus brayed and whinnied. His nostrils flared again each time he tried to speak and only breath came. 'Neshus, come on man – calm yourself.'

'You do not know – you not – I…it was woman who betrayed me before and now again, even here.'

'Aye. People betray people everywhere, my friend. I'm sorry.' Murphy truly did sound sorry. 'Come walk with us and maybe we'll walk away this boiling blood. A walk, yes?'

'No! I – I...yes. Perhaps I...yes. Yes. A Walk.'

Purefoy observed Murphy with, he felt, more accuracy. It was possible Murphy wasn't simply always lying or acting; it was possible that he really did care for these Polish men, *As much as he cared to care for anything.* Was he one of the uncaring, unthinking 'underclass' *The Times* had written about? Or was it that *The Times* didn't understand what people had to do to live, to live with themselves, and survive amongst others?

Purefoy looked back at The George Tavern, its external features were in the revival Gothic and even Purefoy knew that Gothic was considered a good, Christian style. Before today, he'd heard the Gothic talked about as a 'morally superior time'. He laughed. He was unaware of the conversation Murphy and Neshus were having ahead of him. They were briefly unaware of him. Murphy looked back at the same time Purefoy looked forward. Murphy jerked his head at Purefoy, Purefoy walked quicker.

'Women, they are tyrants. No?'

'Aye, sure they are but for every man that sees a tyrant, another man sees a heroine.'

'I – no – I do not know what you say, exactly…'

'Well, sir, there are always two ways to see something.' Purefoy held up a coin when saying this, turning it. 'And in people – especially in people – there are usually more.'

'A whore is a whore and maybe a…mother?'

'Exactly and a whore needs a drink, a bed, and food as much as the rest of us—'

'If not more.' Purefoy's little additions to the conversation calmed Neshus. Purefoy too.

'Do they come back, the women here?'

'Ya mean…'

'I mean after you shout, after you angry.'

'Not to me, they don't. Purefoy?'

'Not unless you're married.'

'Good.' The three walked east in silence as Neshus visibly calmed. He rubbed the sweat on his shaven head back and breathed longer breaths – Purefoy felt sympathy though he only knew him briefly; even then through the man that he knew would lead him to his end. Purefoy laughed at himself. Neshus and Murphy quickly turned to him in surprise. Purefoy couldn't help smiling. Neshus laughed then: it was a small, considered laugh, an agreement; he laughed again, longer; he looked back at the horizon ahead of them and laughed loudly; Murphy laughed and shook his head; Purefoy laughed; they laughed at each other laughing. They had reached the point at where they could cross the boiling blood.

'I think you will see more anger and drunk men, later, yes?' Neshus cheered.

'I should hope. Wouldn't be much fun otherwise.' The men had stopped walking.

'Good luck then, Murphy, and Mr Purefoy – you are lucky to know Murphy, he is as we say 'a true poet'. *Powodzenia. Do widzenia.*' Neshus turned back toward The George.

'*Do widzenia*, Neshus.'

London has always been a polyglot. London is where we run to hear new, fantastical imaginings of language; where we wrap ourselves in foreign matter in the knowledge that a cocoon of experience will enable us to lose and warm ourselves until we've wings enough to take our newly communicative selves elsewhere. The City speaks only one language, London speaks with infinite variations. That day was the first time Purefoy had been near enough to Polish to understand some of its obvious words, he'd remember it for as long as he lived.

CHAPTER 13

Their time with Neshus had relaxed Purefoy and revealed another side to Murphy; they'd walked with him to where Commercial Road briefly became Mercer Place and now Albert Square stood to their right. People sat eating lunch. There was no sun but there was no rain and the cloud had taken on its typical post-meridian, depression-threatening, London-ash. 'Shall we sit a while, Murphy?'

'What?'

'In the square – shall we sit a while? It's a garden of sorts, almost a forest.' Purefoy was still in high spirits from the men's shared laughter.

'And why would I do that?' Murphy, evidently, no longer cared for laughter.

'Because you're going easy on me for a while and because...because I've always loved forests. Could I have one last one before I go?'

'...you had your last request with that biter back on Drury, remember? And look how that turned out.'

'Yes, yes, I know but this time, all I want to do is sit.'

Murphy looked over at Albert Square; there were people but no one he knew; a couple of sellers made their way around but not too loudly; and there were no patterers pestering so they wouldn't be too bothered. '...alright, we're making good progress anyway.'

'Yes, I'm sure we are, wherever we're going. Could I be privy to that information, by any chance?'

'No chance.'

'I thought not.' The men looked at each other and saw that they smiled; they stayed looking at each other for a second, surprised that they seemed to have come to a status quo. Purefoy thought silence best for a while. They crossed over the road into the square.

Their time slowed. As soon as they sat, Purefoy studied the surrounding bushes. He loved the feel of leaves and bark. Their leaves weren't foliage green but of a dusky hue; their texture an ashen cover to rubber; no polished boughs but knotted, course and rude; rose bushes, perhaps… He pricked his finger and a droplet of blood came. He put it into his mouth. He spat it out as soon as he tasted it was his right hand. The beer had made him reckless as he feared it might …*but then, what is there to fear at the end*? He laughed and looked to Murphy. Murphy was stretched out, dozing with his eyes half closed and struggling to stay awake.

'Excuse us, sir – I'm just partaking of my lunch over there when I noticed that you two gents look affable and might be interested in a talk.' The man who spoke to them was young, wiry, he wore a top hat and a necktie in the roughian style.

'We're not.' Murphy wasn't quite asleep; he yawned as he said, 'Leave now, harpie.'

'I'm no harpie, sir, I'm a Occupation Installment Consultant. I—'

'Aye, you're a crimp. Get on with ya, snatcher. We're both gainfully employed now leave us enjoy our lunch.' With the words 'crimp' and 'snatcher', the man had already started moving away. 'Are you, Murphy?'

'Am I what?'

'Gainfully employed?'

'I make money, I survive. That's gainful enough.' Purefoy got the distinct impression Murphy wouldn't sleep in this forest if he could help it.

Their time was briefly freed. So many of his memories were in a forest it seemed only natural that he'd be in three on his final day. This one, as close to a forest as he thought he could get in London, he liked; he wished BB had seen it and had sat with him; he felt that anyone could claim this spot, this action of being, as their own and choose that they wanted to be in the forest; he thought clearly, *It could be a refuge for the lost and the lonely*; he watched insects crawl over stubborn tufts of grass then leap up, as a swarm, and fly off. He hummed a song his grandfather had taught him. There were pigeons but no other birds he could see. 'What do you think, Murphy? Was it worth it?'

'What's that?'

'The sit in this forest?'

'Ahhh. Oh I'm not really one for your forest, Bryn – I say struggle on against it, struggle against the need to lie down.'

'I would say to lie down in your own place, in your own way, is a beautiful thing.'

'Aye, we'll never see eye to eye.' Murphy smiled and, turning his head from his lying position, opened his eye and winked at Purefoy. 'Come on then, you've had your forest and I've had a rest.' They left the square as quietly as they'd entered. Back onto Mercer place and east. It became Commercial Road again after a few yards. Half-day workers populated the street now, some rushed to other jobs. The jostle of places on paths became close to dippers.

A group of eight men stood ahead, working at a job Purefoy couldn't see. From afar, there seemed to be two gentlemen clerks and six workers in uniform. The men in uniform regularly knelt at the side of the road and stepped back. The clerks observed.

Once within fifteen yards, the smell and the men's leather uniforms made it obvious they were nightmen – probably with a few cesspits to handle and maybe some of them were flushers today too – and the clerks made notes at the men's actions. Purefoy could see an open cesspit by the side but it was odd because he couldn't smell it. The men were discussing it with the clerks, talking over how '...it makes it much easier.' Murphy instinctively slowed their pace, intrigued as much as Purefoy was confused. In their observations, the clerks' eyes were wide and pink; they salivated excessively out the corners of their mouths and down their cheeks, down their pencils; mastiffs, they sniffed the air.

The men were taking it in turns to inspect the nightsoil in the cesspit. One by one they moved by the clerks to the cesspit, picked up some of its contents, and stepping backward they released it from their fingers onto the road. It fell on the floor, in between them all, and didn't smell. Each man continued the ritual but some with more vigour than others. Though less frightening than the last, Purefoy felt a sever cognitive dissonance for the second time that day. He couldn't equate what he saw with what he knew; no smell and a cesspit; what flushers called nightsoil was the same soil he'd pushed out of himself with great effort earlier. Everyone knew. 'So why is there no smell?'

'What d'ya think, Purefoy? D'ya think your shit don't stink?' Though he said it quietly, Murphy laughed after saying this.

'I think it's very odd. What are they doing, exactly?'

'Could be an official thing – miasma, ya know.'

Sensing a professional interest above curiosity, Murphy slowed their walk to an amble. He whistled as Purefoy watched. The nightmen weren't simply testing the shit's effect on the road, they were teasing out its textures and cleaning anything they found. There was a small pile of bones near the cesspit opening. A clerk said something and the next man to go up put his hands together as if to collect water, he knelt, he dipped his hands into the faeces and stood – he looked to the clerk and the clerk nodded. The man moved his cupped hands up to his face and rubbed the soil into his face and into his half-open eyes. The same man did this again and the clerk asked him a question or two until the next nightman stepped up.

Further miscomprehension came to Purefoy. This wasn't a dizziness as it had been with fat Prinny the giant but an immediate flinch of disgust. It happened simultaneously in his stomach and his throat. When he saw the nightman bury his face in his hands, Murphy's whistle spluttered into a laugh but he

continued whistling as soon as he'd recovered. They were next to
the men. This would be their last chance to observe.

The last man to approach the pit looked serenely at one clerk.
That clerk nodded with a smile while the other said something to
the nightman who nodded in reply. Without word, the man
moved to the pit as the man before him did and took up a handful
of shit; he brought it up to his nose to smell it at close quarters.
What came next, Purefoy could never have expected.

The man moved his hand to his mouth and slowly but surely
took a bite of the shit. As he did, some fell out of his hand and hit
the ground – Purefoy observed this piece as it hit and knew that
it was exactly as all the excrement he'd worked with. Purefoy ran
the image of the man biting into the shit through his mind again:
the shit coming into contact with the man's tongue became the
shit coming into contact with his own tongue.

Chapter 14

Being on a Commercial Road is unavoidable if you enter London. It's a long road, easily found and easily followed. It can take you from docks to the centre, from having nothing to having too much. It will promise you the earth but it's an unknown place, dangerous and depraved. Its features can make you forget why you came. Murphy and Purefoy had regained their pace after observing the nightmen.

Purefoy had wanted to stop the nightmen, to run to them and tell them what they were doing – whatever they were doing – they need to stop. He'd heard the tales of new purefinders going blind. All it takes is carelessness, tiredness, and a rub of the eyes after a hard day's work – maybe you could escape it once if you washed your hands and face quickly afterward but *...who has money enough to wash their face every night?* He hadn't been able to swallow down the disgust in his stomach to get close enough to the nightmen nor did he think the clerks would let him.

They past shops but Purefoy didn't care to look what they were and Murphy may have already known. Murphy whistled. After a while in The City you stop looking for the signs.

Men stood wall-walking, waiting on advertisers to buy up some of the prime Commercial estate but much of the space was occupied with dummy placards. Many of them drank, Purefoy considered asking if they'd spare a quart.

The status-quo between Murphy and Purefoy was comfortably established, Purefoy was mollified in alcohol. Though he'd only known him for half a day, Purefoy thought he'd like to know his executioner; to know his real name, at least. He questioned to himself how much Murphy really knew about him. *Had he or had he not known the actual contents of the letter?* Purefoy's earlier collapse and his drunk dried his judgement. He put the thoughts to one side, telling himself to remember them and ask them again when sober. He didn't know whether he'd let himself become sober again. He didn't tell himself to remember to become sober.

A soft breeze came down the road bringing mud dancing in the air; anyone that was walking stopped smiling and made their mouths as small as possible; they squinted knowing that if the mud were to touch, they'd have a fire in their eyes. The afternoon air had dried. Purefoy felt his thirst again. It started slowly as something that required simply a movement of his tongue.

Spread across the road ahead of them were multiple gatherings. They all seemed to be moving into the side of the road that Murphy and Purefoy walked on. Murphy gave no indication of changing sides. They blocked the whole road until a carriage came through and they'd disperse, only then to circle back onto the road. The dry, fly-like gathered would swarm out of the road and into the road.

The closer they got, the crowds were less made up of one homogenous folk or definable tribe but a mix of every skin-colour, religious denomination, gender, and class swarming around each other. They were swarming into and out of a square. Every language Purefoy had heard, he heard then.

Murphy walked them into the throng and into the square. 'Here we go, Purefoy – your last chance to get a feel for women. Welcome to Ratcliff Square.' Murphy's insensitive remark dried Purefoy's throat further. Inside, Purefoy could see a priest stood, elevated, on the right and a Hindu man stood, elevated also, on the left; there were people in between them, some listened intently to one side and some moved from one to the other – there were even more people gathered further on. There weren't only Christian and Hindu elevated either, there was a Rabi, a Chinaman, a Protestant, a Catholic, an Ethiopian, a Muslim who everyone called Mussulmen, a Quaker, a spiritualist and more stood above everyone.

Now near the elevated men, Purefoy heard them answer questions put to them but they did not answer only to the person who asked the question and, instead, answered loudly to everyone – they delivered short sermons in the name of their Gods. Many finished their short delivery with a reminder that all their words could be purchased. There were also decriers in the crowd: well-dressed men who scoffed and loudly explained how the previous speaker was wrong. These men offered no alternative answer but were righteous in their belief that the preachers were wrong.

In comparison, the forest of Albert Square seemed peaceful and very far away. The swarm tired Purefoy with their dry heat. Murphy held onto Purefoy's arm as he forged a pathway through the crowd. They had to squint more here as the many people dried the mud beneath them and threw more of it up into the breeze, the more they trod.

Soon the preachers were answering each other's questions with remonstrations. The mass goaded them on. Murphy laughed increasingly loudly, Purefoy's throat dried – the two ambled on and Purefoy was sure he could see Murphy's spare hand moving carefully in and out of other people's pockets to his jacket. Partly to stop him, mostly to know, Purefoy asked, 'Are you a Papist, Murphy?'

'Why Bryn, I never woulda thought you knew such hurtful terms.'

'I – I – I don't mean to off —'

'Ah, I'm just takin' ya down a peg or two. It's none of your business…but I will say this, I don't agree with any o'these blasphemous bastards.'

'But they're not blasphemous, they're preaching the word of God. I mean, yes, they're all preaching a different word of God but they've got it mostly right.'

'The sweatin' quim they have. Your God isn't up there, Bryn – he doesn't care. If ever he was, he's gone now and he likes his foreign parts, ya know? So he shouted 'chaos', gave it us in the cooler, and left us to our own devices. This lot were just too deaf to hear it and too brick stupid to feel it – poor fools.'

The silence after Murphy's last two words trailed into Purefoy pitying him. Murphy looked ahead into the crowd and gave no signs of disheartening but Purefoy felt Murphy needed reassuring. 'I think you're wrong, Murphy, but I think that these preachers are probably wrong as well. I've not had much education but I do think this: the Tower of Babel wasn't a story about why the people of the world speak differently but why they believe in God differently. To me, they're all wrong because they divide people. Scripture should bring us together.' *All literatures should, if only by highlighting how apart we are.*

'So he's listening to all our prayers, is he?' Droll, Murphy could well have rolled his eyes.

'I think it's us who need to listen.' Murphy smiled a full, impish smile at Purefoy. They moved further on.

'Now, sir, I believe I've told you before that it costs to touch my pocket.' Murphy had been caught.

His eyes darted quickly as he looked for immediate escape, he found none. A brief panic spread over his face as he turned to his accuser.

'Charlotte! Crikey you made me start.'

'And I can see you're starting early.'

'Aye, well, a man should make hay while the sun shines.'

'And you're an especially good man.'

'As you're a good lady. How's the trade?'

'I read in *The Times* just the other day that women of my trade are all 'unfortunates' now and we've all fallen into 'shame' – as if we ever had any to begin with. I was as frustrated with that as I have been with anything so yesterday I ensured trade was especially good. Thank you for enquiring. And you?'

'Aye, can't complain. Had a customer today – in a church of all places.'

'Well you do have a certain way with woman, Ma—'

'Why thank you dear but there's no need for honorifics today,

ya can just call me Murphy. This is Mr Bryn Purefoy Llewes.'
Murphy gave a small bow as he indicated Purefoy.

Charlotte and Purefoy looked the other over – Charlotte
looked and Purefoy shied from looking. He did so because he
saw that she was a well-dressed, well-held woman and he'd
already heard her intelligence. 'You needn't look away,
purefinder. I find your class no better or worse than my own and
you should know that I am of the same class of people as
Murphy is. Only I know how to dress.' All three laughed then.
Purefoy noticed subtle warmth in her laugh. Her smile was such
a natural warmth, he wondered if she'd been a nurse before she
came to London. Though there is little in poverty, there's warmth
in struggle.

'The males of our profession are entitled to dress however we
well please.'

'Perhaps. You do have a silver tongue.'

'Tongue enough to convince you to come see me soon?'

'Few have the tongue for that. Though you've the
cheek…we'll see. Until then, it'll have to be monetary remuner-
ation.' They smiled at each other; Purefoy noticed their gaze held
for longer than was usual.

'Ya know, Charlotte, in a hundred and fifty years, they'll have
the good sense to make the trade legal then I'll have to wear a
suit.'

'I'm afraid I don't think they will, good Murphy.'

'No?' Quiet, serious.

'No.'

'Will you walk with us a while, Lady Charlotte?'

''Lady.' I like this one, Murphy, wherever did you find him? I
would walk with you, purefinder, but today I cannot. If we meet
again, you needn't call me Lady or goodlady – simply Charlotte,
thank you. Where are you two going?'

'We're headed to Butcher's Row.' Murphy answered, of
course. Calmly, he put his hand on Puerfoy's shoulder and

squeezed. They still had the crowd and more preachers to get through.

'If ya don't mind me askin', what are ya in Ratcliff Square for, Charlotte?'

'To defend our trade.' With that, Charlotte turned and walked into the crowd. Purefoy didn't know why but Murphy kept them there, watching as Charlotte disappeared.

'Butcher's Row, Murphy? But didn't that policem—'

'Hush up, Bryn. Listen. You said we're not listening enough, so listen.'

Purefoy tried. He closed his eyes. He attempted to hear something out of the ordinary but nothing came. He opened them again. He followed Murphy's gaze and saw Charlotte rise above the crowd. She spoke loudly and clearly, 'My good ladies and men – I would call you gentlemen but I have known far too many men and far too few of them have been anything like gentle.' This elicited laughter from the women. 'They're working men and built for work.' A small cheer came from the men. 'These other speakers here would tell you of the temptations that will lead you to hell, to Jahannum, gaol, and gehinnom. However there is one area that none of them can agree on and none that the scientific or atheists amongst you can agree on either, that delicate question of what many call The Great Evil – prostitution.

'I will now put forward a few arguments from perspectives I have taken from so-called 'unfortunate' women and try to defend against the main arguments against these women.

'Let us say I am a prostitute, what business has society to abuse me? Have I received any favours at the hands of society? If I am a hideous cancer in society, are not the causes of the disease to be sought in the rottenness of the carcass of society? Am I not its legitimate child – no bastard, sir? Why does my unnatural parent repudiate me, and what has society ever done for me, that I should do anything for it, and what have I ever done against society that it should drive me into a corner and crush me to the earth? I have neither stolen, nor murdered, nor defrauded. I earn my money and pay my way.' She was a passionate, convincing speaker. Though he'd never thought about it at length, Purefoy agreed with her. She continued, 'That is but one perspective I have heard and taken record of, here is another. I was told, "We come from the dregs of society, as our so-called betters term it. What business has society to have dregs – such dregs as we? You railers of the Society for the Suppression of Vice, you the pious, the moral, the respectable, as you call yourselves, who stand on your smooth and pleasant side of the great gulf you have dug and keep between yourselves and the dregs, why don't you bridge it over, or fill it up, and by some humane and generous process absorb us into your leavened mass, until we become interpenetrated with goodness like yourselves? What have we to be ashamed of, we who do not know what shame is?"

'To deprive humanity of proper and harmless amusements, to subject us *en masse* to the pressure of force – of force wielded, for the most part, by ignorant, and often by brutal men – is only to add the cruelty of active persecution to *the cruelty of passive indifference* which made us as we are.'

Charlotte had reached a passionate moment in her speech and breathed deeply, growing redder. She let the silence sit a moment and continued, 'I put it to you good people of the streets, and especially to those elevated above you, that there is but one outcome that can ensure fairness for all – make legal prostitution and make safe the prostitutes.'

Of all the speakers, Charlotte's short time had received the most cheer. Purefoy stood dumbfounded. He didn't understand prostitution – the business, the politics, the people – but he was faintly happy that someone did. When she stepped down, Murphy was whistling and clapping. The whole crowd cheered. Murphy cheered the loudest. They clapped out the sound of other preachers trying – failing – to argue against.

Murphy wanted her then. They'd danced before but never the

dance that led to them lay next to each other. In the past he'd wanted them to dally through streets like a pair of doves, earning their keep, however they may, but loving only each other and flying the coop together. He saw that all that was behind them. They both had gone too far down their separate paths – his, the casual street merchant and hers, the professional business model – to ever go together but he wanted her then. He whistled and clapped in appreciation of everything he knew of her, in appreciation of how she understood them.

Chapter 15

Purefoy finally knew something definite about Murphy. It connected them. He knew Murphy didn't want one – they both knew some fledgling thing was inevitable.

'Murphy…' Murphy turned his head to listen. 'When I asked if you had gainful employment you could have told me what you do and I—'

'Like I've said, it's none of your business.'

'No, I know, I know. I have a question though, do you – now please don't get offended – do you lie with men as well?' This was pushing his luck but he was too curious not to.

'Why? Have ya money enough?' Murphy smiled another of his surprising smiles.

'I – I didn't mean – I was—'

'Ah don't trouble yaself, Purefoy. I don't lie with men, no. I'm no Mary-Ann but I do know a good few and they're just as good as the rest of us – some o'them, some o'them make a pretty penny.'

'Yes. Yes, I've heard about certain gentlemen's clubs.'

'Exactly. In those places, so long as you've togs swell enough and tongue enough, you can make in a minute what the rest of us make all week but I…well I don't and that's all.' So even Murphy had rules. We all set ourselves lies [sic] we won't cross. They walked.

They'd advanced far enough to be almost clear of the Ratcliff Square hoard. Murphy stopped, looked back. The crowd still swarmed but the speakers stepped down and the mass became formless greyed-ghost-outlines. Nothing is permanent in The City but the city and that too burns. They were nearer the river now than they had been all day – they could smell it. Purefoy's tongue was dry and rough on the roof of his mouth; he felt his lips, they too were cracked. Salts gathered at the corners of his mouth and he attempted to lick them. His tongue felt bovine, detached. He felt small painful lumps under his tongue. He laughed a little and Murphy looked back at him. They walked south to the end of the road.

Across Brook Street, Purefoy noticed a sign for Butcher's Row. A remark, or a question, from earlier tried to come back to him but stopped; he could tell it wasn't only his thoughts that slowed. He yawned. They crossed.

On Butcher's Row, a cavalcade of scents came toward him. The sharp, sweet mix of lemon, sage and spices that some butchers throw on their steps; the dry, rusting smell of meat; occasional wafts of smoke; all progressed toward him and woke him a little. Looking into the shop windows for only the second time that day made him salivate. The hanging fowl, the great slabs of red and cream, even the brown of the cheap-meats made him want to stop and offer anything he had for the food. Two feelings struck him: hunger and the urge to piss. *'Thirst' and 'piss'...my least two favourite names for beer.* Murphy walked them further south.

They didn't get far along Butcher's when Murphy stopped and knocked on a door. Though red, the door was like any other not belonging to a shop; Murphy had given it an odd number of knocks and waited. Purefoy's bladder increased its pressure.

The door opened after a short wait. A small, bald Chinaman opened the door and bowed his head giving them entrance. There was a thin corridor ahead of them. Once inside, Purefoy sensed something he'd never smelt before. The Chinaman led them silently down the corridor. Murphy's step became perceptibly lighter. Purefoy tried to tread lightly but found the effort on his drunken body made more noise than if he simply walked. At the end of the corridor, steps took them down into a cellar.

There, people lay sleeping in numbers Purefoy had only heard wild tales about. *The tales are true.* Low as the ceiling was, the room's length forgave it – the cellar must have occupied the space beneath a few buildings. Not a forest but a desert of sleeping pilgrims walking opiate dreams. Mostly Chinese and mostly male, there were people in the beds whose gender and colour couldn't be ascertained. Purefoy knew that the air was starting to affect him. He wouldn't find his way back to the forest. That scent that he didn't know, he realized what it was now; he'd never smelt opium before. Like tobacco, it held no immediate interest for him. His skin began to feel clammy and smudge the dirt gathered there.

They were led past numerous dreamers and fires. A hand shot up out of the dark and grabbed Purefoy by the arm.

It held Purefoy's wrist tightly. He let out a startled sound and turned to see what mad dreamer had mistaken him for a dream. Purefoy's bladder winced; he controlled it, it calmed. 'What a marvel!' The dreamer spoke and Purefoy recognised the voice.

'Is that you…Bristol George?'

'Ark at 'ee – Bristol George, hah! Jus' George, laaad jus' George. Am I dead, Purefoy, or in some quiet 'eaven?' He was sleepy but his smile and tone portrayed contentment.

'You're in neither, George. You're in a…a den. I should think you're enjoying yourself if you're in heaven.' Purefoy attempted to be as friendly and quiet as he could; he looked to Murphy who nodded.

'If it don't displease you, lad, I'd 'voker with thee in this 'eavenly den. Are you still purefindin'?'

'I was George but…but I think I'll be doing something different after today.'

'Change me lad, tha's bone. Tha's bone. Is the only fly. You get my word, don't you?'

'I do, George, I do and you're right. We shouldn't be cooper'd by change.'

'Is bone you still 'voker romany.'

'I dropped with you for the word and we thank God for small things.'

'Is a bone thing you're small then, taffy!' With this they laughed and Bristol George coughed.

'George, why are you here? In this place?'

'Ah, Purefoy, is – is —' with this, George became visibly anxious. His hands searched for something as he began to breathe rapidly. Purefoy's Chinese guide came to him and handed him a pipe. George quickly gave the guide a coin, lit the pipe, and wiped his eyes with the heel of his hands. 'The day you dropped off the back drum, lad, tha's the day I met my mot, my nug but she—' he sucked again on the pipe and his face relaxed, 'Tha's the day it began.'

'So she brought you here?'

'No, laard, she's with some city flatty now…'

'Oh, I see. George, you—'

'No, is not the flatty – Devil take 'im – is what she did before.' He propped himself on one elbow and brought Purefoy's arm a little closer. He didn't look at Purefoy or at anything but the ember in his pipe and he sang quietly,

'She leaned her back against an oak,
it was all alone and alo-one.
First it bent and then it broke
down by the Greenwood kingdom.

She leaned her back against a thorn
and there those two pretty babes were born,
she took her penknife out of her pocket –
she cut our babes, she took their docket…'

The understanding dawned on Purefoy as George sucked on his pipe. The patterer Purefoy had known was one of the respectable street-sellers; he was a happy man back then. He looked at George's face. The once well-rounded cheeks were flat now, the red under his eyes had turned to grey circles. His beardless face was stubbled with grey and his once fox-brown hair was grey too. George lay back down and closed his eyes. He drew smoke from his pipe and smiled. '*My nug cut our babes but I've the Chinee bug to help me.*' He smoked again and smiled again, he turned from Purefoy.

'Come on, Purefoy. He's gone for a while now.'

Murphy's hand on Purefoy's shoulder did little to comfort him. It had been George who'd welcomed him and BB; it had been George who'd taught him the few tricks of language that had worked. For a while they even walked together. Without George, he'd never have sold half as many literature-scraps in those first few years as a patterer. George was Purefoy's guide, a patterer's patterer – a generous man.

'…the opium's taken him.' Purefoy hadn't meant to say it aloud.

'It ain't the opiates, Bryn, it's life that's taken him.'

'But if he wasn't here—'

'He'd be in the boozing-ken, as you and he'd call it.' Murphy knew Purefoy's first London occupation now.

'It's always happened, it always will happen; sorry, Purefoy.'

'You're wrong, Murphy. In a hundred and fifty years—'

'It'll still happen and men'll still turn to somethin'. The difference bein' that this'll all be gone. The peace of the poppy won't be peaceful…what was George's full name?'

'George Donnison.'

'May peace find ya George Donnison.'

Sat on a small bed, Purefoy and Murphy were brought opium and a pipe – Murphy paid without question. Purefoy's bladder sounded again and with a shudder made its needs clear.

'Murphy, are there men's facilities in here?'

'There's a pan under the bed. That'll do.'

Purefoy stood quickly. He went to the other side of the bed. Though he knew there'd be someone a foot away from him, he tried to use the pan directly in the space between the beds. He ignored the encouragement from his insides and controlled his urine's flow. The shadow on the next bed didn't stir at all. He was thirsty again just as soon as the last drop hit the pan.

Murphy had already lit the pipe. The smell struck Purefoy again, its faint nut aroma. Murphy motioned the pipe to Purefoy. Purefoy shook his head lightly in answer. Murphy didn't move his hand. 'You need to Purefoy. We're not leaving until you do.'

'Can I get some water?'

'Here? No. Here you get one thing, the pipe. The pipe can give you a lot more but here you get the pipe.'

Murphy motioned again. Purefoy took it and inhaled slowly. He'd tried a pipe at his second job when he was fourteen, it had been overwhelming: the taste was disgusting but he'd inhaled too quickly then and coughed painfully after. With the opium pipe, he inhaled slowly and took a little. He swallowed it, as he'd been taught, and quickly let it come out. He quickly salivated. Happy of the moisture, he swallowed that too. He was surprised he didn't cough. Murphy motioned that he should repeat the action. He did so.

Like tobacco for Purefoy, the drug's effect wasn't instant. This time, the smoke hadn't tasted unpleasant. Murphy had taken the pipe back and continued to smoke. 'I've never smoked opium before. What should I – is it similar to the feeling of drink?'

'No. It's the opposite.'

'Oh.'

'Aye.'

'You, er, you hear rumours that people see things that aren't there. Is it – is that true?'

'Only if you've an over-active mind. It's more like a feeling of...of calm. If you're tired, it can make you sleep or if you're in pain, it can make the pain less for a while.'

'So...so what did you mean when you...when you said the poppy won't be peaceful?'

'D'ya remember the group Charlotte talked about? The Society for the Suppression of Vice? Those capons'll see to it. They'll see to it because they don't understand themselves or any humans for that matter.'

'Oh well.'

'Aye.'

The drug had taken its effect on Purefoy. He didn't feel a need to talk. He hoped Murphy wouldn't want to go anywhere. He salivated enough to keep his mouth happy. His thoughts were absent again and he was pleased. He didn't consciously think 'I'm pleased', he felt it then knew again that he'd felt out whether he was consciously thinking it. He smiled. He knew these thoughts unnecessary but he enjoyed them. His stomach rumbled. He smiled. A feeling in his skull tapped under the top of it. The feeling of rubbing his palm along a red brick wall fizzed under there in the space of a sugar cube. His stomach gawped. Murphy looked over at him, smiling. Purefoy looked at Murphy. They looked at Purefoy's stomach and smiled wider. They returned to their individual thoughts.

Purefoy thought on BB – for the first time that day, it didn't immediately stir discontent; he thought the thought at a distance from himself; he remained calm for a full 15 seconds before he stopped himself thinking of her. *So that's what it's for*. Without words, he felt out whether it was also for forgetting and he looked back to where they'd walked, back to George. He rubbed his wrist and the initial strength then the quick dissipation of George's grip came to him. *Is it a waste to forget? Perhaps...but perhaps not when it is too terrible to remember.* His mother's and his sister's face then; a tear came to his eye without warning or knowing until it wet his cheek. He looked briefly at Murphy to see if there was still a pipe glow. There was none. He felt it coming back then, all of it: his mother's tired smile when he told her about his first job; his sister's first fever and his young, desperate fear of losing her; the last time he saw BB as she entered the workhouse, smiling through her tears and waving him goodbye. He couldn't stop it. His mouth was drying and the alcohol was slowing. He tried to control it – in the dark, his face felt like an ember of its own; he felt his cheeks inflame and his trembling lips but hoped he wouldn't disturb the dreamers; they had theirs to forget without his burdening them further. He breathed quietly, rapidly through his mouth. He knew then that it couldn't make you forget, only hold you at a distance. Murphy put his hand on his shoulder. 'Come on Bryn. It's time we got a gage.'

Murphy stood and Purefoy followed. *A drink, yes,* a drink was what he needed. Purefoy controlled his breath and inhaled deeper with each stride. He wanted more opium, he wanted to see them at a distance; he wanted his moods to steady, for this day to steady; he inhaled deeply and held his diaphragm in place. He felt one day China would have a part in everyone's lives. The tears stopped and he breathed slowly again as he followed Murphy past the dreamers, up the stairs, down the corridor, and out onto the street.

Gustave Doré began his L'Enfer in 1857 but didn't know he would make the same work 15 years later under a different name – London: A Pilgrimage. One of his illustrations was named 'Ludgate Hill – A Block in the Street'. Doré wasn't only linked to Purefoy by the time they lived but in capturing The City. As Doré would unconsciously repeat his work, so too did Purefoy on his last day.

Chapter 16

Drinking was the only recourse.

Not fighting, not distraction, not women, not opium – drink and drink alone would help. The thought of food had left him. Murphy began humming as soon as they were on the street.

Purefoy walked behind Murphy ignoring the smells of the butcher shops and the cries of how cheap their meats were. For the first time, Murphy didn't turn back or check on him at all. They went left onto Queen Street. Still Murphy didn't look back. Still Purefoy followed. Murphy began singing, not in tomfoolery and not proudly but still loudly,

> 'I likes a drop of good beer, I do.
> I'm fond of a drop of good beer.
> Let gentleman fine
> sink down to their wine
> but I will stick to me beer.
>
> Along with malt if they'd give us less salt,
> and all their finings queer,
> we'd thank them chaps that keep the taps,
> and swallow a deal more beer;
> but still our London fear,
> they can't beat far nor near.
> There's very few, I think that do
> adulterate the beer.
>
> I likes a drop of good beer, I do.
> I'm fond of a drop of good beer.
> Let gentleman fine
> sink down to their wine
> but I will stick to me beer.

Well, wars will come, and therefore some
must pay the shot, 'tis clear,
and for the fray, we'll cheerfully pay
a half-penny on the fear;
though they might have exempted beer,
and put it on luxuries dear;
but, while we've the chink we Britons will drink,
Success to the war in fear!

I likes a drop of good beer, I do.
I'm fond of a drop of good beer.
Let gentleman fine
sink down to their wine
but I will stick to me beer.'

Murphy stopped walking at the end of his song. He didn't laugh as Purefoy had expected but instead turned around. The men looked at each other. To both it seemed the other had visibly aged that day. Their faces were of two very different reds. A pigeon flew too close to them. They both looked as it swerved their shoulders and their gaze. The sky had taken on its sulphurous late afternoon yellow.

'Bryn...I've only a bandy to my name.'

'I've some.' He checked. It felt like very little.

'We'll need to see a lender.'

'No, I've tuppence. That's—'

'Eight whole pennies. Two ales each or the blue ruin.' They looked about them, not wishing to look at each other. Not wishing to answer. Purefoy saw signs for a 'Bank of Deposit', a 'Credit Union', and a 'Pawnbrokers'. He remembered why he rarely looked at the signs. The thirst, actual and alcohol, sounded so loud in him, it offended his ears. His stomach growled. Both of the men looked down. A silence rose.

Purefoy thought over what he had of worth. He let out a little sigh – it rubbed against his chest. He felt the string around his neck. No. He thought he might sell most of his clothes – this was his last day, why not? Then he considered that he might not be given anything to wear in prison or wherever he'd be. He rubbed his neck. The string caught his finger. His cap? Sure, it was a gift but he might make a penny. His gloves? Who would want a purefinder's gloves? It had to be – he cut his thoughts off and looked up.

* * *

Their first visit to the workhouse, Purefoy's Ma had told him his father might not act like his father that day; that he might be lost. He didn't care, today he saw his Da. They were dressed in their best clothes. Purefoy was confused but didn't say so because he knew his Ma and his *chwaer* were upset. The workhouse was only a little west of Wrexham and they walked easily enough. Their Ma told them the story of how she and their Da met. How he had the best voice in town and wooed her with charm but the most gentile charm she'd ever known. How he had waited for her parents to agree. How they didn't agree; how he gave them a month to accept and she felt how much he truly loved her. She assured her children there'd be no milk spilt by that family anymore. She was right. They arrived and the Master, Mr Kemp, was informed. They were expected. Mr Llwyn lay on his bed with his legs crossed, idly swinging his feet. On their entry, he calmly sat up – he was clean-shaven and looked well – and smiled as he looked at them. Mr Kemp suggested they not look directly into his eyes. They sat on small chairs in the box room. Mrs Llwyn had instructed the children to stay by her side. Mr Llwyn looked at the Master, smiling, and said, 'You'll not crack me, Devil.'

'Mr Llwyn, your family are here to see you.' Mr Kemp spoke as softly as his baritone allowed.

'A good attempt, Devil – a very good torture – but these aren't my family. They wouldn't be here.'

Mr Llwyn stood. He walked over to Purefoy. He knelt down and took his hand. 'I'm glad to see you've recovered, young one, but not so glad that you're here...or are you another trick? It's not your fault...even if you are.' Mr Llwyn inspected Purefoy's head.

'You must be the boy's mother. I'm glad to see he has recovered and I can only offer my company's sincerest apologies, ma'am – I've a boy of my own and I'd never let any boy purposefully come to harm.' He extended his hand to Mrs Llwyn. She took it.

'Rhys, mae'n fi. Edrychwch.' [*Rhys, it's me. Look.*]

'Ah, I see you're a very good actress...I won't be speaking to you again and I suppose the little girl is my girl, is she? A very fine trick, Devil. Were I a weaker man you might have cracked me.'

He turned back to Purefoy and knelt again. He whispered, 'Listen boy, you must escape this place – run from here, you understand? Convince your other actors. Here they will keep you and grind you into nothing – it's how they make their money, their trade, their...fun. It is an economy – an economy of souls – in this hell and you must never return to hell once you've seen inside it. Do you understand? Go, lad. Go.'

Mr Llwyn put his forehead on Purefoy's and they looked down. Purefoy saw a tear fall from his father's cheek. Mr Llwyn stood and spoke loudly,

'Go! All of you, you can go. Don't come back here or you will be damned. Take whatever he's paying you and leave – woman, do not bring children into hell again or I will kill you myself.'

Mr Llwyn ushered them out of the room and closed the door. As soon as it was closed, his legs gave way beneath him. He sobbed for his lost family he thought a country and a world away. He sobbed for his destitution and he couldn't stop. He didn't stop until the sun set. On their way out, Purefoy looked back up at the window to his father's room. Their first visit to the workhouse – their only visit – was the last time they would see Mr Llwyn. Bryn Prifardd Llewes ap Llwyn was the son of a dead man.

* * *

The silence between them thickened. We are all, always, carving through silences. Murphy wanted a drink. Purefoy wanted oblivion.

'What'll it be, Bryn?'

Purefoy looked at Murphy and pursed his lips. Purefoy looked down, chewed his cheeks. The grey of his surroundings filled the spaces in his thoughts. A cold, heavy grey – not a black or a burning red, as he'd been told of hell, but – an unyielding grey. People had often told him to 'live everyday like it's your last' – if that had ever truly been the case, he might have destroyed himself every day. We cannot live everyday like it would be our last – if we did, we'd never make anything lasting.

When he closed his eyes he saw his father's workhouse window but now someone stood in it, waving. A woman – a beautiful woman; when the window fell away, there stood BB looking her best. Her auburn hair, parted on her left side and swept over, highlighted the round-health in her features; her cheeks were still naturally red; her inquisitive green eyes happy to see him; her black dress had new, small frills on the lower arms with a white neckline. She looked finer and happier than any music-hall artiste they'd ever seen; her hands didn't show the years of hard work that time would bring them; she placed her right hand on his chest, lifted his head with her left, and kissed him. Her forehead rested on his, she whispered, 'Ti fydd cartref yn fuan.' ['*You'll be home soon.*'] The image was moving back, she waved. Only a black void was left. He preferred the black to the grey. The black gave everything definition.

He opened his eyes and looked up. They'd only been down

for a second. Murphy pursed his lips. He raised his eyebrows quickly and smiled. Purefoy laughed, they both smiled wider – were a gentleman to find himself in Butcher's Row, he would have thought them stupefied but at that exact moment, Purefoy had more clarity than he had had all day. He thought, *Give it all away. For once you'll deserve your name, Prifardd. Give it away. Walk. Follow. End it all and be with her.*

'I'm told there used to be a river here,' Murphy said absently, '— there are loads of lost rivers – but I'm told that this one ran backwards, into the land, to become what's now Commercial Road and Cheapside. There's another, somewhere, that feeds the one underneath us but I don't think you'd get to see that unless you lived another hundred and fifty years.' They smiled again. Purefoy saw the beauty and the humanity in his executioner's black smile.

'If I lived to that age, I'd have forgotten all this and forgotten you. You wouldn't mind if I claimed the discovery as my own, Would you?'

'How d'ya know I wouldn't be there with ya, Purefoy?' Murphy's familiarity retreated. Purefoy looked at the pawnbrokers again. How easily, how quickly we turn.

'I've something of value, Murphy. Something we can sell.'

'Show us then.'

Purefoy blinked and BB waved him on, letting him know that it's fine, it's what has to be done for him to survive that day, her wave told him they'd be together sooner for the trade. He reached inside his shirt. With one flick, the ring rested on his chest.

Instantly Murphy's hand grabbed it. He stood close. Purefoy felt a pressure on his neck. Murphy inspected the ring and smiled. A sharp tug and the string snapped.

'Needs must, eh?'

'Needs must.'

'Soon there will upward come what I await; and what thy thought is dreaming must soon reveal itself unto thy sight.'

Purefoy didn't understand but knew it better to stay quiet than to speak and make the situation worse. In the brief silence, he heard the running waters of the Regent's Basin.

They walked over to the pawnbrokers.

In the window, the detritus of a collection of lives sat wanting.

CHAPTER 17

Before entering the pawnbrokers, Murphy paused. Purefoy looked in the window at all the left treasures of other people's lives. Murphy hesitated. He moved as if he'd forgotten something.

'I need'ta think for a bit. We gotta get a good price, ya know? Let's walk ta the end an' back.' Purefoy's response was a simple nod. He felt slightly more awake but still didn't know his standing with Murphy. Murphy didn't watch him now but treated him as a drinking grig. Perhaps it was Murphy's control over him; perhaps it was that Purefoy had relinquished all hope of survival and replaced it with hope of death; or perhaps it was because his body ached and he cramped with hunger; but Purefoy followed Murphy and left whatever balance they had intact. Under his breath, Murphy sang,

'I likes a drop of good fear, I do.
I'm fond of a drop of good fear.'

Just a few doors down from the pawnbrokers, the Credit Union sat. Its front was no more imposing than any other shop front but defined itself by four large windows that covered the entire breadth of it. Everyone outside could see inside and vice versa. Murphy stopped outside and asked, 'D'ya think we should try this in there?' and before Purefoy could answer, Murphy was singing quietly,

'Let gentleman fine
sink down to peacetime...'

Purefoy looked again. Inside, a woman held her child in her arms next to signs that declared 'FAIRER MONEY LENDING FOR ALL'. The woman rocked the child but even Purefoy, with his limited knowledge, could see it was crying. A man sat behind a barred window. No seat was provided for the woman. Purefoy noticed that the woman was crying too. Her eyes were red raw. Between the woman and the man sat a wall with the barred window and a door. As he watched, the door in the wall opened and the man from behind the window extended his arms. The woman placed the child in them. The man closed door and reappeared at the barred window with the child. He pushed bank notes under the bars. The woman took them. Purefoy turned away. 'Let's not, eh Murphy?'

'...but I will stick to me fear.'

The end of Queen Street neared and Murphy was still acting strangely. He wasn't drunk but he didn't respond in any way he had before. Still quiet but a little louder than before, he sang,

'Along with malt if they'd give us less salt,
and all their finings queer,
we'd thank them chaps that keep the tax,
and swallow a deal more beer;
but still our London fear,
they can't beat far nor near.
There's very few, I think that do
adulterate the fear.'

Purefoy was unnerved. He was giving up everything he had, he'd embraced oblivion, and now Murphy sang?

He didn't say anything but felt his neck tighten a little as he tried to move it slowly enough to see Murphy's face without Murphy noticing. Murphy didn't notice. Murphy hardly looked away from his entranced stare forward.

They were soon outside the Bank of Deposit. Murphy put his hand on the door, blocking the way in. He turned to Purefoy. The whites of his eyes were pink. His forehead creased, he sang forcefully at Purefoy,

'Well, wars will come, and therefore some
must pay the shot, 'tis clear,
and for the fray, we'll cheerfully pay
a half-penny on the fear;
though they might have exempted beer,
and put it on luxuries dear;
but, while we've the chink we Britons will drink,
Success to the war in fear!

I likes a drop of good fear, I do.
I'm fond of a drop of good fear.
Let gentleman fine
sink down to peacetime.'

Here, Murphy moved his hand from the door to Purefoy's shoulder and whispered, *'But I will stick to me fear.'* Purefoy shuddered.

He knew it was possible for people to go mad with starvation or dehydration *...but Murphy had been a ding boy all day so why now was he all set and a blab?* Something in the corner of Murphy's mouth glistened. Murphy licked his lips. Suddenly he howled with laughter. 'Back to the pawnbrokers. Decision's done.' Purefoy was shaken. He'd heard about what madmen can do to people; things much worse than death. He followed, stunned; again aware of his precarious position.

Before they entered, Murphy paused once more at the door to the pawnbrokers. Inset in the door was a small, oval window with three red balls painted on the glass. With his back to Purefoy, he spoke simply, at a normal level, 'Behold the monster with the pointed tail who cleaves the hills and breaks the quiet worlds in twain, behold these things that infect the world.' He opened the door.

The contents of the pawnbrokers betrayed its size. Trinkets and troves hanging from beams meeting stacks of crockery and dolls made for maze-like aisles. The contents of a whole house, of hundreds of whole houses, could have been there. Only a little light shone in through the window, the only source except for a small candle at the desk.

The small man behind the cramped desk seemed unreachable. When the bell on the door had rung, he'd looked up from his newspaper, smiled, and beckoned them in with his hand before returning to his reading. Purefoy had only been to one pawnbroker before: that particular broker was in the West End, on Drury Lane, and was much smaller than this. He'd entered that one bearing all the scripts and scrolls he had left when he and BB ran out of money, out of hope. The clerks had sniggered but he'd left with enough money for them to last in London two more months. That day had been the first BB had smiled in some time.

A great deal of dust and hair settled between the stacks and the piles of people's pawned possessions. Purefoy was once told that dust in a pawnbroker's is the snakeskin shed when the owner fleeces. These trails led back to the man. The man's desk was surrounded by books. The books piled as high as the room, making a castle of worded bricks around him. Three lay on the desk, open, on top of each other. A strangely shaped mirror sat on the desk's top.

They'd made their way around the borders to the heart of the shop. Murphy spoke to the man, 'Are you the pawn?'

'I am the man who buys and sells things, yes, but I'd rather not be called a pawn, or a broker, or a fleece because I do none of that here.' The man's voice had a slight Welsh lilt on his pronunciation of 'yes'. He hadn't stopped reading.

'Well, we've a ring if you'd like to see it.' Murphy was gruffer than Purefoy had expected.

'I would like to, yes.' The man folded his paper, put it down, and stood. He took another candle from beneath the desk and lit it from the smaller, dimmer one. He put this candle next to the mirror and their section of the room illuminated. Purefoy stepped back from the intensity of the light.

'This is a parabolic mirror. A fascinating thing, really, the ancient Greeks thought of...but, well, you're here to trade not to—'

'No, we're here to pawn. I might come back for this.'

'Ah.'

The man's voice had been immediately recognisable as Welsh on his pronunciation of 'fascinating'; irresistible to immigrants, Purefoy wanted to know more about his fellow countryman but the man had stopped talking. They waited.

'There's a slight problem there. You see, I've stopped offering tickets and charging interest because I know that no one can pay it back. I've had enough people in here getting in more and more debt that I've had to stop it all. Now I'm only a trader but I will pay you a better price than any pawnbroker I know so long as it's mine and that's the end of our business.'

'Tha's not how pawnbrokers wor—' Murphy spoke quickly.

'No. It isn't. I'm sorry if you feel you've been misled but those are my conditions.' The trader was quicker.

'Esgusodwch fi ond beth ydy dy enw di?' [*Excuse me but what's your name?*] Purefoy had to ask.

'Geyron Nadir ydw i.' [*I'm Geyron Nadir.*] A smile. The recognition.

'ap...?' [*son of...?*]

'Does dim tad.' [*There's no father.*] Geyron said this without recrimination or sadness. Purefoy stepped closer to see Geyron properly.

Geyron looked as Purefoy looked.

The two men evaluated each other and realised they could be brothers.

Though Geyron had fewer lines on his face, their structure was almost the same; the only obvious differences, the colour of their eyes and the size of their stomachs. Geyron had the small paunch of the comfortable and his shoulders stooped a little. Geyron spoke with a hushed tone, 'I once saw something in the theatre where there were two mirrors on stage, reflecting the other; one had its back to us but the other, bigger mirror could be seen and the reflection in the reflection made a tunnel headed by a medieval arch that confused the eyes and went on forever.' They looked at each other again. Then at the ring.

Purefoy attempted the beginning of a discussion about it. 'Yr modrwy ydy...yr modrwy ydy fy nghodrwy. Dwi—' [*The ring...the ring's my ring. I—*]

'Dwi gwybod...[*I know...*] and I should say that I honestly think you gentlemen would be less well paid elsewhere. I'm no tallyman nor money lender and, like I said, I'll not try to give you an unfair price.'

'Think yaself a cut above, do ya?' Murphy was defensive again, perhaps he always was.

'I'm no better or worse than anything but I try my best not to take the advantage unlike the lenders or the credit unions or the tallymen who'll have your shirt and your child before you've woken...I have a wife and two children myself, I...well, there are levels of fraud I'll not permit myself to commit though I am thought of as a creature of fraud. I cannot be more honest with you than that.'

'Sut ydych chi'n yma, Geyron? Yma, mewn East End o LLundain?' [*How are you here, Geyron? Here in the East End of London?*]

'Rydw i wedi anghofio Cymru, Cymro. [*I've forgotten Wales, Welshman.*] I've been in London long enough to settle and to gather things around me. What I lack in freedom to move, I make up for in capital. When she was alive, I sent what I could back to my mam but I am a London trader now, I'm no longer a Welshman...it's possible I never truly was...but it doesn't matter because I'm happy here.'

'Beth am eich cartref? Eich craidd?' [*What about your home?*

Your centre?]

'Mae'n yma...ond mae *ddim* craidd. [*It's here...but there is no centre.*] There is no centre to hold, Cymro. By the look of your boots, you should know. There's only change, adaptation, and remaking. You look like a sweeper or a cleaner. You should know.'

'Murphy, I – I think he's being honest. We should trade it.'

'...aye, I suppose you'd know. Alright trader, take a look.'

Geyron's hands came up from the desk, into the light; he handled the ring gently; the backs of his hands were covered in thick, dark hair that you knew covered his back also. As Geyron looked over the ring, Purefoy thought over what had been said. He wondered whether he would have done better in London if he'd not tried to hold on to his home and the hope to return. If he too was a fraud for not attempting to settle more but then, he thought, *I'm not a fraud...no one truly is...they're, they're just afraid for what they'll lose.* He closed his eyes again. He felt the last of the opium wishing him well as the sight of BB faded.

'This is an impressive ring...' Geyron lied.

'I'd say it's worth at least a guinea.' Murphy replied.

'A guinea's a lot of money, sir. No, I can't offer that but I can offer sixteen shillings. That's the truth of it and all I can say.'

'What about a quid, then?'

'As I said, sir, I don't pawn or broker – sixteen shillings is a fine offer and I'll only make four more on it, if I'm lucky. That's the truth of it. I make a little more out of everything I acquire, that's all there is to it and all my business does.'

'Eighteen shillings.'

Geyron looked at Murphy paternally and opened his mouth but didn't say anything. Instead, he sat back down then said, 'Sixteen shillings, sir. That's all. Take it or take your leave.'

'Fine then.' Murphy grumbled.

The transaction done, Geyron wrapped the ring in a little cloth and put it in his pocket. Their thirsts building, they made to leave the shop. Murphy was already at the door when Geyron spoke, 'Esgusodwch fi, Cymro, ond…' [*Excuse me, Welshman, but…*]

'Ond…' [*But…*]

'Bydd yn ofalus, heddiw. Dwi'n un…twyll, i chi, ond – ond dwi'n un twyll onest. Eich Gwyddel ydy gwag.' [*Be careful today. I'm a…fraud, to you, but – but I'm an honest fraud. Your Irishman is just empty.*]

The bell rang as the door closed behind them.

'Tryin'a get ya to come back, was he?'

'Yes…yes he was. As well as asking me to say hello to Wales when I saw it next.' Murphy laughed. The sardonic edge to it had returned.

Chapter 18

They'll ask us why we're there. Why we should even come out this far. I'll tell 'em. If they don't listen, my fistesez'll tell 'em. They've told a few, they'll tell a few more that needs it.

But that isn't the way of it, only the way it offs.

He's still behind. Doesn't even realize he needs to catch up. That's the fate of the prodigal immigrant – prodigrant, hah – unless he's wealth of his own. Hah. From there to here. Here when he's seen enough, when he's had enough. He's nowhere near there, nowhere near here. The prodigrunt. We Irish haven't trusted the Welsh since that business with their giant king and we threw our lot in the pot to bring 'em back. Bring 'em back, like they wouldn't leave. Leave like anyone else in need of money, of something, of safety more than bringin' 'em back can. The bulge, the bolge; the basins, the canals, the canards; canin canali. And they wonder where we get it from. Us, the dogs; the surplus. The surplus population. 'The surplus' as if there's not enough of the lonely and too many gathered. Fine, I say then, fine. I've an alternative...but my alternative's ineffable. If I had it my way, there'd have to be a hanging the whole world could see just to cleanse the memory of me. Not that that would be enough, the bitter end. Never bitter enough for the bitter. The wheel turns, they spanner it. Those left leave and push on.

The push, the great push, great brotherly push – 'We're in this together' he said. Paul's a poor liar and he lied to me. Still, I lie more. 'We are.'

Poor Purefoy. Still, it's gotta be done. He'll get it; all in time. Good time – especially if he's a good man. He's hardly proven himself today. Kills a lamb to all eyes, loses his check, and sells his last. Pitiable lully prig. Don't matter if he did or nay, he's on now and this is the last of it. 'Want a pair?' I asked him but I suppose he had the sense after I got bottle-head over those billy bilkers by St Paul's. Sense. As if he was all sense and no fun. We'll see what the black cove dubbers think. You've been buggy enough with him. Aye, I have. He's had his quota. You can trust him, mind. Can I now? With the basins all around and what school butter they bring into play, I might. Aye, he's a lamb himself – 'plagas, sicut Thomas, non intueor' – no, I don't but he's ovine enough…but I can't know him. To touch him is struggle, to know him is death. Knowing can sprout trusting and trusting only leads to trouble. Why is it so difficult? I don't have to explain my own actions to him or her or all their hims. The memories, this derail, it's all self-justifice—

It endures is why. We struggle…and we're lost in not knowing when we're calm…and we're lost when we're happy is why – says he, asking himself, with shillings in his cly. 'Oh, no – the apprehension of the good gives but the greater feeling to the worse.' There'll be enough at the basins who'll touch me now alright. Hardly true though…but about the only thing that is is what's good for what ails ya. And that a poison, they say.

A true poison.

Well that's trust for ya. Means well and good 'til the time comes. The time it takes…30 annums in my case. Damn you, Paul – you coulda stood by me, ya wo-ball sop. I hear you're in The Academy now. The one Bryn thinks he might get to if he's lucky. He won't be. Half as lucky as you and we'd all be scuppered.

Bryn must know I'm mad by now.

I've done enough. I hope I've done enough. He has to know, he'll know. All in time. Good time. I should have been quicker to go by him but no matter, he should be shaken now. I've done enough. If he's to get it, to get at it, and to get at that last, he'll have to know the bitter and the bitter wrapped in the sweet. Though that's on the wheel already – it's an oil, it rises and it falls with the wheel but God is it light. Its own economy of light. Lighter to carry than to turn.

I turned it on though, that was enough. I've been keeping it on all day, on and off. All day's enough – that's as long as he's known me and that's the rub. A song and a dog too.

It's the nuances in the song, not the dog. Forget any notions of the dogs. 'Shillings in the cly oh my oh my.' You should treat him to a show. Aye and a play – they'll be plenty of a hunting at play. Mustn't give it away though, mustn't give it away.

I didn't care much for that pawn. That 'trader'. Trader, my glim. I can't keep going adding good notches ignoring my own seizes so I glim that 'trader'...my glim.

So my seize was a patterer was he? Poor sop...

Poor sop probably tried to sell paper to the poor and that with Welsh on it or worse. Scriptures. What was it he said earlier? 'Scripture should bring us together.' Evidently he wasn't paying attention in school. The school, the shoal, the gaol: fitting in its way. At least mine won't fill him with what bean trapper dreams he didn't have, can't have, won't have. Or was that the women? What was it he lost? Two women? His mother, his sister. Welcome to it, Bryn – you're one of us now. At least he had no brother to betray him. It wasn't him that...

What does 'prifardd' mean anyway? Why's he so picky about it? Not that it matters, not that any name matters. Or anything for that matter. A struggle's a struggle's the struggle. Maybe it was my own fault but...

Tallymen, credit unions, moneylenders, pawns, what would they know of the weight's wait? The wait's weight, aye. They're too busy curling dust. It all comes back to that though – Imalone [sic] and sick in it. If I'd not been, Paul would have and I would have...

There's no end to it. You'll have to answer it. There's no end to it.

Alright, Paul, so here it is: you were right, I was wrong. You still did me in though—

Ah, your brother didn't, you did yourself in.

Aye. Aye I did.

At least I never had any women involved. Aye but he did and that was that, that was his – always was – and never yours. No, he didn't. I was the work and he was the Pippin. Aye. A couple of star-eyes, if we couldn't pander riches I figured what was the harm in a little star-catching? Plenty it seems and he was always the quicker of us. That'd be the dad in him. Not that we knew ours, not even knew or renewed. Not once. Aye, there's the snub. The great white – doesn't matter. All of them, all of the elder not carers not doing one thing while saying another whatever they will and doing the other. Father or not, doesn't matter. Goodly thing Mam took to the God too or we'd have been buffered for life. 'For want of a good man' 'goes there a gone soul' 'gone to everyone' but meself. Heh. For want of a strong woman go wayward men. They all do. We all do. Oh the Lords forbid any woman should find herself in such a place – I'd be surprised if they don't try it soon enough.

Their ghosts, they're witches – aye but for their butts and but can they?

Always three, they say, but they've never met a wall of mothers on washday. Nor any of the dock mothers either – poor wretches; every port in every town in every sea facing quimmery. Aye but there's a see [sic] in there too, whether or not I admit it every time; there's a wash and a rush and a hurl of her loves, her worries, dailies, dallies, crinkums, crankums, *wap and wash 'ems, what for her, eh? Eh? Eh eh? You need to calm them then and slow them some then turn again and see the faces blossom. It's all there for the breathing.*

What manner of breeding is this? Heh. You'll do what your dad did, 'What your dad did, you'll do' 'Aye Ma, we'll fuck off.' I got a clip for that one...and rightly so. Still, didn't stop us. We still left. We waited 'til she'd died, mind. God, she'd clip us. For this for that, for talking back, for not knowing how much she loved us, for thinking about going over and coming back, she'd still, aye she'd still, when Paul looked at that picking girl and she knew what he was thinking – 'Thick heads,' she said, 'You'll need a thick one in this world won't ye? I'm just givin' ye a head start.' Aye she thought she was velvet for that. Ah, Ma, your memory's a killer. Memory is. Like you said you would, 'If anyone touched you or hurt you, I'd kill 'em' – God, she was fierce. I fear for ya if you're up there. She'd clip her way outta there to back down here.

But that's that and that's all.

She's no more and soon he'll...know. More, I suppose.

It's a good thing I fogled in the opium in the opium fog as we'll need that for what's to come. The more fog the better – 'A regular pea-souper', aye, but not water. Not the mist he'll have known from his climbs. Not even the soup of the West End's the same as his climbs. Aye there it's less worse but it ain't clean either. The 'West End' like it's any better or no from the East End. At least here we're a little-freer from the swells. Course, you would think that. 'Ya tribal doctor, ya'. What was it now? 'It ain't the Chinamen...nor yet the Bengalees as would hurt you;' no guest does but the problem comes when we're thought as invaders. 'But there is an uncommon rough crew of English nationalists hangin' in and about there.' Always is, constable, always is. Wherever you've immigrants you've opposition. The worst is the opposition from the just settled – that file trader – as if we'll replace 'em. If we've not the skills? Doesn't matter. If we've not the intent? Doesn't matter. Not the intent – Lords forbid & they will – of settlin'? Doesn't matter even more – so much so. Then you've really somethin' to fear. I say fear me. Who killed all those husbands? Me. Once you've given those answers or answers to those answers, then they'll put you in The Academy...right Paul?

And why did you kill those buttock and files on the steps of St Paul's? Because you lost the old earth again, didn't ya? Came clear off it and sacrificed another to the fiery cousin of Cuthbert. Aye well, all that's done and done with and won't be, shouldn't be, ah it might be done again. Heh. Just once. In the end at the end. Wouldn't be the first nancy for it.

What's to be done after. Fine, fine. That's a fine one. You tell me. I'm you. Aye...

What's to be done is what's to be done.

Aye. Mustn't give it away though, mustn't give it away.

Aye aye!

Mustn't.

Won't.

Aye.

Won't eye, either. Not unless, aye. What to give? What's what is what. Mmm...but how much to share there, in between there and now to, too? The sun'll be off soon and that'll start us. Aye. It's only fair...Heh. Fair on 'the lahhd' that poor Bristol boat was and I'll have to be just a little less so. Heh. Just a little. Still he liked the suck and I'll not deny him simple pleasures. Necessary pleasures. Nece – no, no such thing. Voluptatem nece, maybe. We'll get to that – if a narc's would have me. We'll get to murder pleasure. All in good time.

CHAPTER 19

Purefoy was sure.

Murphy – criminal, intelligent, vicious before – was now driven beyond sanity by the combination of drink and opium. Hesitantly friendly as they once were, Purefoy felt Murphy's mood changing dramatically. With it, the status quo. His throat had dried. He found himself making small noises to try and ease some fluid into it.

A little north of them water flowed openly toward the Monster Soup but paused and waited a while in the Basin. No king can control the tide but the people had built a container and a stopgap for the water. Purefoy wanted to see it but didn't dare ask. He'd not known Queen Street crossed over the release where the water was finally let into the Thames. Briefly, he glimpsed small boats chained to the side, pressing into each other as if forever stationed, *Forever damned* never to move.

They'd taken the small street from Queen onto Narrow and soon it would become Fore. North of where Narrow became Fore Street, there too engineers had trapped the flow of water. The area had been known as Limehouse Dock for some time now, whether a warehouse stocking lime stood near or not. Men were everywhere on Narrow Street. In balconies, men with the same hat as Murphy sat smoking and shouting down. On the barrels that had slowly begun to fill the side of the streets, men sat or stood around playing. Some stacked barrels into pyramids, some lifted them from the top of those pyramids to the men in the balconies. Ladders and ropes supported, hoisted, and hung men and barrels and baskets.

Salt, dirt, lime, tobacco and a hundred others filled the senses. Purefoy looked up to see men caught in ropes and chains underneath small bridges. Men stood on the bridges and yanked at the ropes and chains. The men below screamed. The further in they got, the more screams Purefoy heard. From the bridges to inside warehouses and back again, screams echoed.

The bridges, the joins, the very configurations of the buildings made him dizzy. It seemed as if the hanging men and the rope-pullers went on, forever repeating, into the distance. Purefoy felt a tiredness coming over him that he knew would make him drop to the floor if he gave into it. He didn't want to respond to the screams or the smells. Yet the instinctual part of him, the one too dead to tell him to run or plead for help, still flinched at the screams. He couldn't hear the sound of the canals or the Thames now.

He heard a terrible screeching like nothing he'd ever heard before.

When Murphy looked back, he saw Purefoy standing stone still with wide eyes fixed on a northern point. Purefoy's breathing was fast, shallow. Looking where Purefoy looked, between buildings, Murphy saw steam. Murphy laughed and clutched at Purefoy's shoulder. 'Hydraulics, Mr Llewes. I mustn't have noticed. The sound, was that it?'

Purefoy nodded and the steam fired again. Purefoy flinched and looked at Murphy. 'Don't worry yourself, Purefoy. It's man-made. It's the science that operates the cranes and keeps the docks workin'.' Another magic Purefoy hadn't known. Wouldn't ever know.

The sounds of moving chains followed the steam and the screams. The hisses and thuds of mechanics began, hidden from sight. Some of the men whistled, some smoked, some even sang. The cacophony built.

A faint howl of music drifted in between the men's songs and their work sounds. If he closed his eyes, the noise of it all was too much. Purefoy tried to keep them wide to pinpoint the origins of sounds. There were many he couldn't. The composition built.

Purefoy was surprised to see so many women on the street. Some were white, some black, and many Mussulwomen. They all wore headscarves. The Mussulwomen covered all their face except for their eyes. They watched the men and muttered to each other or to themselves making a background of tweets to which some of the men replied. It wasn't yet afternoon. The women waited. Some of their eyes fixed on a man and grew hungry and strong; some of their eyes roamed all of the men, not settling until recognition came. Some of their eyes were wet with tears; some of them held children. All of them watched the men.

Will a whistle blow? Will there be a clock chime? I was told once, 'The Isle of Dogs runs on time.' Purefoy knew he'd lost his sense of time a lot that day. He hoped for some noise to emerge from the others to give him something to make sense of it.

Through buildings to the right, they could see the Thames and glimpses of ships. Purefoy knew these ships could take you away forever if you could live with a life at sea. He knew they brought new life into London, to Britain, every time they came in. Today they held no interest for him, only the understanding that he might finish this day in the chains of one. The rigging sounds of the Thames came closer the further they walked.

They passed an open door. The steam hiss that scared Purefoy before was the only sound emitted. Purefoy looked in and saw great black machines. Large metal columns thrust up and down as steam filled the space around the workers. The men wore only trousers and gloves. They shovelled coal from the black piles behind them into the furnaces. Behind one shovelling man, a column thrust up and down with each action he took controlling his pace, drilling into his neck. The steam ran down their backs and mingled with sweat. Their feet, just visible, were bare. The feet of the man closest to the door were as pink as if he'd trodden on the hot coals. The man behind, his souls were black. To Purefoy's eyes, the machines they fuelled seemed to action nothing and feed no one. They continued steaming and hissing for an unfathomable reason. *Is this the hell that seems 'normal', the one Murphy talked about earlier? Surely these machines must do something and surely they do something someone wants. There must be machines in heaven too – it can't be the machines at fault.* Purefoy's thoughts went unheard by heaven's machinations. The clamour built.

Nearing the end of the built-up, closely bridged warehouses on the street, Purefoy could smell a cesspit or a sewer opening. He looked ahead – a gathering of what looked like flushers or nightmen in their large, heavy overalls. Another figure stood near them dressed in black. He heard the figure chanting before he saw the white strip around his neck. A priest. Murphy'd dropped back to walk next to Purefoy, Murphy must have seen him too because he jeered, 'Need a dying confession, Purefoy?'

'...?' He'd considered a show of strength, it dried with his throat.

'Nothin'? No sin, no hubris – no man is entirely pure, Bryn.'

Purefoy knew of only one thing he was guilty of, he'd only had today to consider it. It was something Murphy had said earlier.

They were near the priest now. The smell was strongest here, coating the insides of their nostrils. The priest still chanted, the flushers held onto a pipe. The sounds of human movement through thick water bubbled up. One flusher held the other end of the pipe as he stood, neck-deep, in the cesspit. The priest stopped his chant and asked the flushers for his payment because, 'I have blessed this ground and this work. '

'We never arsked ya to.'

'For this work, would you men rather you went to heaven or hell? Your payment decides.'

The man in the cesspit shouted, 'Someone pay the autem bawler, will ya?' He'd had enough of hell. The faint music that Purefoy'd heard earlier was prominent now. Extended notes and drone haunted Purefoy – it was like nothing he'd ever heard before. A clatter of metal accompanied its rhythm. At the point just after the cesspit, there stood a bear on its two hind feet. It danced. A man stood by it, turning the handle of a hurdy gurdy.

He yanked the chain if the bear got too far away from him.

Fore Street widened. The bridges fell away to be replaced by the shuffling carriages on the road below. They could see the sky without impediment. When Purefoy looked up ahead and into the sky, he saw a steel tower with a steel pyramid for a roof. It was bigger than anything he'd seen. It cut through the sky – *A monument…a vicious monument*, it was like nothing he'd seen before. It filled him with terror and awe.

He closed his eyes and shook his head.

He looked back up. It was gone.

He knew he hadn't spoken in some time but he didn't know until then that he was so thirsty. He felt a fever scrawl up his neck and into his lymph glands. From there it climbed to his cheeks. It choked his throat. He clenched his teeth. A poisonous taste gathered at the back of his mouth. He removed his hat to relieve the heat building in him. He breathed deeper to stop the vomit he could feel brewing in his stomach. All the while they continued walking.

It was a few hours since his last drink. He wanted another. He wanted something – anything – to fill his stomach. To calm him. He kept his breathing long and deep. He felt his lungs push on his diaphragm to constrain his stomach. He clenched his teeth and kept breathing this way until his lymph glands shrank. His fever receded into some rough marker in his throat.

Soon they were on the corner of Fore that swung back north to take them around the Limehouse Dock. That particular corner faced both the Thames and the dock – though the rotting smell of the river increased, the cool air off both waters helped. Purefoy paused at the corner; Murphy weighed him with a look. 'You're all green again, Llewes.'

'Water.' Speaking hurt.

'Aye there's plenty of it; that must be why ya stopped.' Even Murphy sounded dry now.

Purefoy looked out at the river.

At that corner the river turned to the south. That corner's where the Isle of Dogs begins. From there, he saw the grand southern sweep of the river in all its wrath. The river has been called many things: Monster Soup; Father Thames; Mother Death; Time-Teller & Life-Taker; Life-Bringer & Cuckold-Maker. Purefoy closed his eyes. He imagined the whole stretch he could see and all its occupant banks as frozen over. Since Murphy's earlier remembrance, Purefoy'd wished for the magic of a frost fayre.

On his last day, when he opened his eyes, it was there. The sulphur sky remained but a frozen valley lay in front of him. He looked over the part of the Isle he could see and that too gleamed as if frozen. He smiled a tight smile. His jaw hurt. He closed his eyes and knew that when they opened again, the frost would be gone. He turned to his left. He didn't let himself look back.

To his left, the dock was a valley of its own with a life all its own.

Chapter 20

The street ahead of them shrank. The carriages previously filling the widening of the street gave way to people in their place. There were still warehouses but these were thinner and opened directly onto the dock. You could see straight through them. In these, the activity was less ceasing; no one sat around; even if they weren't carrying anything, no one stood still. Purefoy hoped their breaks were restful.

Larger gaps sat between these warehouses. Traders, entertainers, and their custom filled the spaces. The street performers knew that no one gave them attention in the morning or too much attention in the afternoon so they saved themselves for the evening, going through their acts with deliberate slowness in preparation for the showmanship they'd need later. Near them, the eel & lamb's feet sellers did a small trade. They hoped the after-work crowd would stop to watch a small show and buy a number of small eats. Purefoy had considered food selling before becoming a purefinder, *If only the risks and the initial cost weren't so high.*

But the entertainers and the food sellers were nowhere near so prominent as the fortune-tellers.

Around them, they'd hung sheets of bright fabrics interwoven with feathers and small, reflective shards of glass. Bold type stated CHANGE YOUR LIFE – FIND YOUR HEART'S DESIRE – ACQUIRE YOUR SPIRIT GUIDE. Purefoy saw people come from where they sat, silently weeping and walking away. Occasionally, a smile.

Murphy soon edged them into one of the gaps between the warehouses. Here he took out a pipe. He winked at Purefoy. 'You liked that Chine pipe from the place earlier, didn't ya?' 'Yes...and no.'

'Well do ya want something to calm ya or not?'

'Yes. Please. I need a drink though Murphy, just something.

Without one, you'll be carrying me to wherever we're going.'

'...aye. Alright, we'll get to that. Until then, we'll smoke.'

As Purefoy waited for his turn on the pipe, he looked around. The fortune-teller's advertising covered the walls. Their direct questions were both intriguing and preposterous to him. They intrigued him for how they worked. Purefoy didn't believe in fortune telling; he'd always believed in God and always would but it wasn't that belief that kept him from agreeing with Spiritualists, it was their methods.

The advertising read:

ARE YOU A SPIRITUAL SIREN?
YOUNG LADIES, DO YOU HAVE YOUR LOVE ALTER?
LOST ONES ARE NEVER LOST – HAVE YOU BEEN
POSSESSED? – RID THE STAINS OF EVIL
HERBAL TWIGS TO HEAL YOUR CESSATION & REVITALISE
YOUR YOUTH
YOUR LOST LOVED ONES COULD BE HELPING THE
LIVING

Murphy passed the pipe and, with a slight chuckle, indicated a fortune-teller. Purefoy smoked, remembering to inhale slowly and slightly. A well-dressed woman, all in black, approached the teller. Purefoy was sure Murphy thought of the woman as a potential client and a potential pocket. Her veil was patterned with black snowflakes, letting light in. She lifted it as she sat down in front of the teller. The teller was a chameleonic mix. Her hair was light at the roots but became black at half an inch up and stayed black going on, back into the gypsy red cloth she tied it up into; she had few lines on her face but a dark, dirty complexion that had many small moles and one great one on her left cheek. The clothes she wore included many colourful items beneath a black ragged jacket-top and loose blue dress; she wore brown boots that looked cleaner than all the other parts of her and, near the heel, the outsides of these boots had buttons from the sole right to the top. As the woman sat, the teller spoke with an old voice, 'You have lost someone? Someone dear to you?'

'It's…it's my daughter.' Hesitant, the woman spoke.

'Let us chat. It is fate that you have come here. What do you need to find?'

'I want to know that she's safe, that's all. That…that she's crossed over and all is well.'

'Hmm…this is a difficult thing you ask.' The teller's accent was faintly European, faintly Russian.

'Can it be done? …please.' The woman's accent soft, middle-class Estuary.

'Oh yes, of course, but I must consult the spirits.'

The teller-woman rose from her seat. She stroked the fabrics and feathers. She whispered to them as she did so. She inspected pieces of glass, held them, looking through them – each for a longer spell than the last. The woman watched and her mouth opened. Purefoy couldn't see exactly what her facial expression was. When the teller sat back down, she asked, 'Do you own a china doll? Or a bisque doll?'

'Why yes…'

'Yes, the other spirits have told me so. I can see much emotion in this doll. It is there that the spirit of your dearly deceased daughter lives. Look into its eyes and you will be looking into hers; listen to it and it will speak to you.'

The teller and the woman went on talking for a short while after Purefoy stopped listening and focused on smoking. He'd already passed the pipe back to Murphy during his listening and now Murphy had passed it back to him.

When the woman left, she looked neither aggrieved nor calmed. She pulled down her veil after a few yards.

Purefoy looked at the advertising again. Below it, the teller also had Spiritualist literature on sale. All of these signs played on human weaknesses. It gave them false hope – he knew hope to be important but knew, *There is enough hope in real life and truth…if you've enough to look for it. They don't argue the truth of God or attempt to be a part of God.*

'Alright, Sal.'

'Alright, Murph!' She jumped up from the chair, definitely not an old woman. She kissed him on the cheek. With her arms around his neck asked, 'What you down this way for?'

'Ahh, ya know. I got business. See ya got ya full make up on this week.'

'Yeah, wewl, there's only gone and been a mass burial out in Greenwich, ain't there? An' I'm not one to miss business. Though I do miss you, Murph. When you gonna take me out on the town again?'

Murphy only smiled in reply. The teller's accent had changed as quickly as her age had. Purefoy'd been left holding the pipe as Murphy had walked over. He laughed to himself at the great change the teller had undergone. She was an old woman, experienced and haunched but now she was a young girl, all loose limbed and attention-seeking from the older man. The girl was wrapped around Murphy's left shoulder, he signalled Purefoy with his free arm. Purefoy approached and handed him back his pipe. Murphy removed himself from the girl's grip, winking at Purefoy with his right eye in thanks. To Purefoy who'd been with him all day, Murphy sounded cold when he said, 'I'll be away for a while. I've business with this purefinder and I may not be coming back after it.'

'Oh.' The girl looked at Purefoy, smiled and swivelled her hips toward him, then turned back.

'If ya've anything to say, you should say it now.'

'Oh, I'm sure we'll see 'ch'other again – won't we?'

'No. I don't think we will, Sally.'

'Well where you going then?'

'Away. For a while.' Purefoy heard a desire for something else in Murphy's short sentences.

'So no words for me then, Sal?'

'I think we'll see 'ch'other again. Tha's all.'

'Well then.' Purefoy looked back at Murphy, he was smiling the same smile he had when the girl put her arms around him just a short while earlier; Purefoy saw now that it wasn't a smile but a grimace that came close enough to be indistinguishable from a smile.

In the silence, the girl hugged Murphy again and kissed him on the lips. She turned to Purefoy, came toward him and kissed his cheek. Purefoy didn't know the girl nor had he motioned toward her at all. He looked at her as her face drew away from his. He saw in her the china doll that she'd told the woman of; he noticed how under the dirt and dark make-up, were brush strokes of red dust; how around her eyes some blue paint sat under the black. *She's made of make-up.* Murphy and Purefoy moved on and the girl returned to her chair, turning back into the old woman teller.

Purefoy's throat was no less painful but his awareness of it had become distant.

Back on the street, a young woman in plain, clean dress walked ahead of an old bearded blind man in rags; the old man held onto the woman's shoulder, she held onto his hand. A small trail of dried blood ran down the sides of his nose. A very short man with a tall top hat and a brisk gait walked past them, stopped, and returned to the girl. He took her spare hand, without word, and put a coin into it. He walked back in his original direction as briskly as before.

Another gap in the warehouses, another reminder of what he was missing. Water. A vast field of it in the dock alone. Purefoy saw men in the dock, swimming or trudging. Their heads faced him but they went further into the dock as if walking backwards. They spluttered and tried not to let any water into their mouths. Purefoy envied them bitterly for an instant but remembered the Thames is undrinkable. These men shouted, to each other and to unseen figures on the bank, 'It's going this way.' Each one contested the other.

Purefoy could see a crossroads ahead. They were almost at the point where Colt Street met Emmet Street, Fore Street, and Limehouse Court Approach. Another old man and his daughter aid; this pair were stood on the street but, like the other, didn't beg. Though the old man's eyes were closed they looked up and to the West; she had strong, dark olive features unblemished by cosmetics; he had soft, pale features, woman-like in his fair complexion; though she held his one hand on her shoulder, he needed a staff to stand. Though Purefoy'd seen what he thought to be many, he'd never seen a walking-stick like it – three inter-woven branches, all gnarled and lost but for the singular guiding branch through the middle around which they'd grown; his haziness saw a number eight in the branches and, where the branches finally stopped meeting, two mouths at the top, communicating. Purefoy felt like a sponge, absorbing the life of the street as the opium had quietened his own.

Purefoy didn't yet know the importance of crossroads but this one struck him as remarkable because it may be the last he'd see.

'Have ya ever been to Dublin, Bryn?'

'No. No I haven't. I'd like to…'

'In English, it means 'Black Pool'. As if we were moors or Mussulmen; and there's never been a less Mussulmen country than Ireland…or as if we all practiced some black magic.' Though Murphy mostly kept his usual, controlled monotone, certain words had flecks of anger, Purefoy questioned, *Why would he be angry about the name of a place?*

'I'll tell ya what it is Bryn,' on this, Murphy stopped and turned to Purefoy, 'Don't let anyone tell ya it's because Dublin's the name of some ancient, Irish, sacred site – it's because there was a lake nearby that was deep and people are afraid of the deep. That's all. D'ya hear me?'

'Yes, Murphy. Yes, I think so.' Purefoy felt no need to ask why he was telling him or to remind Murphy that it wouldn't matter after today. Instead, he simply remained in his opiate distance trying not to think about the future.

A city, a sea, and a country away, an old composer grew fat in a city that wasn't his own: in 1858, he sat for a dangerous photographer – Félix Nadar. Three years prior and every year since, Nadar had photographed Gustave Doré. The composer Franz Liszt stood for Nadar too. Though neither parties would fully realise it, all of these men were linked to Purefoy.

CHAPTER 21

They came to the crossroads. The southern road would take them on to The Isle of Dogs and past the docks; the west to the West India Docks; east back the way they came; north to Whitechapel, Hackney, The North and distance from The City.

When Murphy reached the crossroads, he looked south. His arm came out to stop Purefoy walking further. He muttered under his breath. He looked around. He pushed them both to crouch behind some crates nearby. Purefoy chuckled at his cumbersome movements, not fully realizing the damage his body laboured under. Murphy covered Purefoy's mouth.

The hand was clammy. Mucus ran from Murphy's nose into his mouth as his breathing became heavier. Purefoy glanced at Murphy – he'd turned his ear to the south, listening intently. Purefoy thought *Maybe I should be afraid,* but chuckled lightly into Murphy's hand. Murphy increased his grip, put another hand around Purefoy's throat. Immediately, breathing was difficult.

From one sense of euphoria to another – fear unwound in him, the tight grip on his throat made him panic and paw at Murphy's arm – Murphy only increased his grip; Purefoy kicked uselessly. 'Hush Purefoy or I'll rip out your tongue and sell it'. Purefoy knew he'd die today but *Not here, not now, not…yet.* Murphy released his throat.

Purefoy heaved in breath but in a split second Murphy's hand was back at Purefoy's throat – something metal pressed against his neck just under the Adam's apple.

Purefoy tried to steady his breathing as he sweated profusely. He wanted to shout one last time. He closed his eyes, preparing himself. All things seemed marvellously dark then, all felt warm but the metal at his throat. For a moment, his heart and his breath met at the top of their arches and time stilled.

A rush. The metal had gone from his throat.

He opened his eyes. He was still alive. Everything seemed

brighter for a second. He blinked. As his heart rate dropped, he looked around for Murphy. He motioned to turn and look over the crates – his side ached. Once the pain in his side was evident, his lower back pained him. A sharp twist of muscle and a shooting pain struck him.

His lower back pain intensified the more he tried to move. He doubled over, his head onto his knees. There he hurt less. When he'd numbed his lower back, he turned his head to the street.

Murphy had jumped up behind a man and the knife was at this new man's throat. Murphy'd pulled the man's right arm behind him. Murphy smiled and shouted into the ear of the man, 'Well if it isn't the Right 'N'onourable Vinny Babel, the arch doxey.'

The man Vinny swung himself under the reach of the knife and right, around Murphy, grabbing the knife as he did – placing it on Murphy's neck.

The man asked the group gathered around them, 'What do we reckon then?' The demons, under cover of their hat brims, replied, ''Ere, the Seamus has no place!'

'Be none of ya malignant! Because you all owes me a thing or two, you know you do.' Murphy had shouted his reply. The group and their leader measured the situation. Murphy continued, 'And if ya think ya don't, then I won't be buying a drop when we get to the next window.' Murphy smiled as best he could. His movement caused the knife to cut into his throat and a drop of blood appeared. At this, the group laughed. Their captain let Murphy go.

The leader, Vinny, handed Murphy back his knife as he said, 'That was slick, Murphy. I didn't think we'd see you again.' He had a nasally voice but a flat accent that to Purefoy sounded occasionally Northern. His face looked older than the rest of the group; Purefoy thought he might be sixty-nine. His broad flat cap couldn't hide the fact that he'd been bald for some time.

'Aye. Well I thought I owed *you* a drink, Vinny.'

'That you do, Irish – and a lot more besides – but now you owe all these sods a drink as well.' The group members chuckled lightly then looked at each other, grinning. Vinny obviously noticed and continued, 'You're lucky though, we're already on some business this afternoon. Alright you lot, now strike him not.'

'I've an associate that needs safe passage. Purefoy, come over here.'

While they'd talked, Purefoy'd moved from being doubled over to lying on his side. He'd found the closer he was to the ground, the better; he pushed himself up with his arms in the only position that didn't harm him. After pulling his feet into him, he raised himself to standing with the help of the crates. As he stood, his lower back pained him again. He put his hand to it. He walked over and stood close to Murphy.

The group whistled and cawed at Purefoy. In an alarmingly clownish Northern accent, one of them shouted to the others, 'Wilt thou have me hit him on the rump?'

'Yes! See that thou nick him of it!' The whole crowd replied in unison. The effect disoriented Purefoy. He didn't know if it was the opium and the pain or if the last of his understanding of people in the city – of the little he knew of The City – had been left behind in the centre. The grotesque faces of this new company threw him.

'Quiet, Billy Vague. Murphy, do the introductions will you?'

'Surely, Badtail. Purefoy, the man you just heard is the Right Honourable Vinny Babel, a friend to any in need and the leader of this, The Mighty Cabinet Troupe – so called because if you cross 'em, you'll end up in a cabinet. So don't, understood?' Purefoy nodded, shaking slightly.

'Good. The white-haired northerner who wants your arse is the Right Honourable Billy Vague, your man for foreigners. The buck with the massive forehead, that's Crag Loliver and he's your man if ever anyone needs a speaking to.' The Cabinet Troupe occasionally spat at Murphy as he indicated each of them but little more.

'The young ginger Scot is the Right Honourable Dabby Hander, buz extraordinaire and your man for any loan advice. The big-cheeked bulldog next to him is the Right Honourable Ken Snark, the justice man. The less said the better when Ken's in a bad mood. It may surprise you to know that the person in the hat there next to Ken is a woman.' The woman quickly displayed her middle finger and raised it toward Murphy. Some of the Troupe cackled and Murphy went on, 'That's the Right Honourable Tessy Lay and scarecrow hair or not, she protects the territories. The old bow mow mutton over there is the Right Honourable Pip Gammonfond, an Essex boy with a proclivity for weapons and commercial endeavours. Then there's the Right Honourable Davy Pickpockets – ironically named because he's the man to go to if ya need to give anyone a school butterin' and I believe he's also an Academican with his hands in a few scholars at an academy, if ya know what I mean. Then we've the Right Honourable Iam Bunckum-Smith [also known as IBS], the Right Honourable Sandy Slanty, the Right Honourable Weasley Roves, and your big fella there is Ernie Trickles. May they find themselves in their rightful place in heaven in the year of our lord, twenty-eleven. Behind them —'

'That's enough, Irish. They'll go with you and the rest will go with me.'

'Who'll go with me?'

'The Cabinet you just introduced. You'll be buying them drinks. Alright?'

'Alright. Yeah. Yeah, of course, Bad Tail. Then we'll be all squares...won't we?'

At that Vinny Babel signalled the group. All but those intro-duced, left. Murphy walked on a little but the introduced Cabinet Troupe didn't move to follow him. Vinny Babel must have noticed. From behind them, Purefoy heard a nasally shout of,

'Fuck off then, you ingrate pleb-quims. Go get sucked.' The Troupe followed orders. Some even rubbed their hands.

They headed south on Emmet Street. To their right, the dock briefly suffered a strong wind. The waters around the ships pitched and boiled. Men fell into the water. Some cries for help were silenced by the turn of the tide.

It was on Emmet Street they found an appropriate window to serve them. Murphy didn't ask what they wanted but ordered heavy-brown ales all round. Purefoy relished the chance, his last chance, to have a drink in the street. Though it was frowned upon by so many, to him and the people that he'd been close to in London, it was the preferred option – on the street you can interact with everything, even have a dance or a sing should you want, but inside a place everyone sits and everyone stares.

The Troupe mumbled between themselves, jostling for power even within their small group. The money from Purefoy's wedding ring would serve them well.

As he accepted his drink, Purefoy silently thanked BB and Geyron. As he thanked him, he thought on him again. What was it he'd meant by '…there are levels of fraud I'll not permit myself to commit though I am thought of as a creature of fraud' and '…there *is* no centre'?

Before Purefoy had a chance to sip his drink, Weasley Roves had bumped into him spilling a little. Most of the Troupe were already half way through their drinks. Purefoy asked, 'Murphy, will we be having another drink?'

'I hope not but that may not be up to me.'

'Let me give you a little education,' Weasley offered. 'If you owe us something, then you're ours. *Twas ever thus.* Now I don't know you, taffy, but I do know this navvy owes Bad Tail a thing or two and Bad Tail told us to get sunk. So, rightly, we will. *O tempora, o mores.* You don't have to like it but that's just the way it is.' Weasley had a plummy accent but it was clipped to ensure he didn't give away too much. Purefoy thought he heard a soft

Scottish leftover softening in some of Weasley's words but wouldn't say so. He tried to catch up with the pace of drinking. His thirst ebbed, his fear too. His lower back pained him more the more he drank. His lips cracked but he didn't think on it because with each sip he got closer and closer to oblivion.

He didn't need to encourage conversation in the Cabinet Troupe. Murphy, for the first time, was also quiet in company. Purefoy thought back over the whole day. It raised something in his throat.

He'd lost his wife and his freedom that morning but not given up entirely, merely acquiesced with the intention of finding the right moment but then on his angered attempt at escape he had foolishly tried to trip a giant. He'd seen many giants that day. *Will I see more?* The more he thought about his losses, the more he realised there'd been no absolute structure to the way he reacted to loss. He'd flittered from inaction to action, acquiescing to anger, understanding to nothingness. All of these things had changed places in him throughout the day – there'd been no story in his chest of denial then rejection then acceptance; the feelings interwove, *Never resting, never finishing...today I'm the Monster Soup.* If he had the strength, he thought he might have used his drink to serve a bloody blow to Murphy's head. He knew he couldn't. His throat felt cool. His Adam's apple shot up to his jaw. He swallowed to control it. There's no universal for the grieving individual.

Murphy bought everyone another drink with the money from Purefoy's wedding ring. In mourning, we create. In others deaths, The Cabinet revelled.

Chapter 22

Comedic as The Cabinet Troupe were, Purefoy quickly tired of them. Without their leader, they fell into jabbering and jostling. They didn't speak of any opinions or definitive things, as such, but just spoke for the sake of speaking – going round and round, slowly defying what definition any other had given of anything. They made no sense at the end of all their talks. Each of them could see what they said had no sense in it because none of them agreed yet they continued saying it anyway.

The quicker they drank, the more they talked. By the time Purefoy and Murphy had finished their second drink, The Troupe had paid for two rounds of their own. They were then louder than any noise coming from the lock. They hadn't offered Murphy or Purefoy a drink. Purefoy savoured his second – all too quickly, he could feel it filling his stomach and erasing solid thoughts. He slowed his drinking, savouring each sip as best he could. Anytime he looked over at Murphy, Murphy stared either at the Troupe or into the bottom of his drink. Purefoy couldn't decipher if Murphy was sad at seeing so much money spent or if he watched for ways to pacify the Troupe and to know his debt with them was gone. *Is he afraid? He's bigger than them but there are more of them. What is it that's stopping him? Has my hangman joined me in the rope? No. He's waiting, I think.*

The evening began as the light quality blued. Murphy spoke quietly then, 'Have you ever noticed, Bryn, how here it's yellow in the afternoon, green between, and blue in the eve of the black?'

'I have Murphy, yes.'

'So we're agreed then?' Murphy's sentence ended higher than it started.

'…yes. I suppose.' Purefoy didn't understand Murphy's surprise or why they needed to agree again when they'd both confirmed it. *What else is there to agree on?* The Troupe erupted into laughter; both Murphy and Purefoy turned to see Ernie Trickles dancing a jig.

Murphy could see the confusion on Purefoy's face and inwardly smiled. Murphy thought, *He's still not with me. He will be soon enough.* He knew not to trust the troupe but felt he should at least try to get somewhere close to being back in their good graces. He didn't want to but he felt he had to. *Why bother? You're not one o'them, ya never were. They'll turn on ya as soon as ya've served your purpose. Aye, I know.* He thought on how this day had gotten much worse, much quicker than he'd predicted, *But it's always never how you thought it would. Ain't it?* He smiled inwardly again. *We'll be alright here a while. It's not even work-end yet. God I need a piss. I could make it around the corner so long as a peeler don't come along. 'Piss' – a great word for booze.*

'Bryn, you're coming with me. I need to relieve meself.'

'Now now, Irish. There's no need for that. We can look after your friend here.' Tessy Lay was already too friendly for Murphy's liking. Murphy walked off.

Murphy didn't attempt talking again for a while. Purefoy didn't know if he still tasted something odd in the beer or if he was drunk enough and weak enough not to care. He hoped for salt in it ...*somehow*. As time passed more people came to the window, ordered, and drank their drinks in the street. Purefoy watched them. He tried to capture the details of their features, the subtlety of their movements, to store in his last day's memories. Their clothes, mostly dark, each had their own variations caused by nature or intent; it didn't matter to Purefoy, he started to feel a warmth of understanding for all of the quiet drinkers. Apart from The Cabinet, most people seemed to want a sense of equal calm to the end of their day.

Murphy finished his drink and spoke again, 'Come on, Bryn. It's the tavern for the saints, the church for the gluttons, and the witching for us. Finish your drink.' Once Purefoy had finished, Murphy ushered him away toward the South.

The Mighty Cabinet Troupe weren't done with them yet.

Though they'd skirted around the Troupe members, when Murphy looked back he'd caught Ernie Trickles' eye. Trickles turned and danced once more like a large spit of meat or a manatee coming up for air, he stopped and shouted after them.

Murphy gripped Purefoy harder and pushed. Their pace sped to a run.

Excitement licked at Purefoy's sides as he ran – whatever they were doing, why there were running, he knew they shouldn't be. It felt good. He laughed as he ran and Murphy smiled. He whooped as he jumped between people. He felt they'd regained the small connection they'd had and – terrifyingly quickly – he felt glad at it. They ran to beat each other's speed as much as from whatever they ran from.

Purefoy would soon know, explicitly, what.

Trickles had alerted The Cabinet and they were on the hunt.

They too whooped but not in joy.

The Cabinet hunts for passing fair to make their own glory. Tessy Lay cackled and Sandy Slater sang:

There's no pleasures can compare
wi' the hunting o' the fair,
in the morning, in the morning,
in fine and pleasant weather.

Then the whole troupe shouted:

With our hosses and our wigs,
we'll scamps it over the gigs,
and sing traro, huzza!
And sing traro, brave boys, we will foller.

Many of the older, balder men slowed. They stopped hunting and returned north to drink at the window. Murphy and Purefoy had run all the way down Emmet Street already. Murphy signalled to cut into the West India Docks.

The docks were busy, the dockmen unhappy to see anyone unfamiliar running through. Steam driven cranes pulled crates filled with animals or cloth or foods or rarities from boats of all shapes and sizes. Ignoring the new sound of the steam cranes, Purefoy ran under their crates. The water in the dock slipped up the sides, slick with sick fish. The dockers shouted at the runners but Purefoy was behind Murphy and only paid attention to him.

His earlier excitement began to turn into anxiety that he felt in his neck. He wanted to look around, to see where The Cabinet were, but the shudder of movement in his neck when he moved it away was too painful. He felt the weight of his clothes as they began to stick to him. He'd gotten used to his heart racing today. His gut churned. He released a wheezed burp.

They could hear the madness of Sandy Slater singing again.

When poor navvy arise,
then away from us he flies;
and we'll gives him, boys, we'll gives him,
one thundering and loud collar!

Murphy ducked behind barrels and crates. As Murphy crouched, Purefoy put his hands on his knees trying to get his breath back. They waited briefly for Slanty's shouted chorus.

With our hosses and our wigs,
we'll scamps it over the gigs,
and sing traro, huzza!
And sing traro, brave boys, we will foller.

Between their breath, tiny clouds formed. They listened again for

Slanty's proximity. They couldn't hear anything well, their hearts were too loud. They tried to be quieter and listen. They couldn't hear any loud, running steps or singing, *So Slanty must have lowered his voice, stopped running*. They looked at each other. Between the warehouse and the dock din, Purefoy could see the fear in the contorted lines of Murphy's face. He couldn't think of anything to say. Even if he had, he wouldn't have been able to say it. He felt a coldness in his neck and in his throat. His stomach churned again and clenched.

Purefoy looked up and aside the crates on the barrels. The difficulty of spotting a person amidst the dockers at work made his eyes flick back and forth from moving thing to still thing until they were able to take it all in. He looked for anyone running their way: no one. He looked for someone walking: several but none he recognized. He looked for someone moving slowly, creeping: yes. There were two, Tessy Lay and Pip Gammonfond. They each advanced with lowered heads and arms outstretched looking into crevices. They looked practiced.

Purefoy whispered, 'We need to move, Murphy. They're close and they're looking for us. We need to get out of here – can't we get to your beak?'

'Not yet. I – I can't run much more. I…'

'Can we hide? Can we hide in these barrels or between them and under the crates?'

Murphy looked behind him. There weren't big enough gaps between the barrels but there were above them, between the crates. It meant climbing the barrels and risking being seen. Murphy looked into the street. He shot his head back in. Remaining crouched, he put his hands on a barrel and lifted himself onto it. He moved around the back of a crate. He signalled Purefoy to follow. Crouched, they made their way as quickly and soundlessly as they could. They shuffled between two crates. They sat with their knees at their chests.

A great noise came from above them. They craned their necks

at a painful forty-five degree angle to see – another crate lowered down on top of them. It stacked on the crates surrounding them: a deafening thud.

They sunk their heads into their chests.

They were imprisoned, top to bottom, by crates and barrels. The claustrophobia was clear in their trembling. Only the gap where they'd snuck in, between the wall and the crate, still remained empty.

They waited.

They held their breath to slow their hearts. They breathed as quietly, as slowly as they could.

A whisper—

They could hear a whispered song nearby.

And when poor navvy's killed
we'll retires from the field;
and we'll count boys, and we'll count
on the same good ren to-morrer.

With our hosses and our wigs,
we'll scamps it over the gigs,
and sing traro, huzza...
And sing traro, brave boys, we will foller.

The song passed them by but they waited.

They waited until Murphy's heart had returned to a normal rate. Purefoy got the feeling Murphy wouldn't be normal or well for the rest of the day. He asked, 'Are you alright to move?'

'Aye. Let's go.'

They moved out, back to where they'd come in.

Chapter 23

Silent, alone, they went; the one in front, the other after. They communicated only in signals as Purefoy led the way. He didn't know where he was going, only that wherever it was, he was the sharper of the two. Sharp enough to notice any of The Cabinet Troupe. They walked carefully, instinctively back west.

Purefoy thought about the situation. *What if Murphy only brought me along to offer me up to The Cabinet instead of him? This could all be a trick. Even the policeman could be a lie...* At this he looked back at Murphy but instead of the devious figure he'd seen throughout the day, Purefoy saw only a trembling child fumbling along as if in the dark.

They were reaching the end of the warehouses. The end of safe cover. Purefoy knew, *If The Cabinet sees us now, we're worse than dead*. He stopped, moved them further against the wall and asked Murphy, 'If we go back on to the streets, will they find us? And if they do find us, what...what will they do then?'

'...I don't know...Bryn, I don't know the answers to either of those.'

'Where should we go then? Where now?'

From staring at Purefoy's feet, Murphy looked up. He looked around and sighed. 'Come on, Prifardd. We'll go into the warehouse. If we can get through it to the other side, we'll be able to get to my man.' They looked at each other. Purefoy saw Murphy's uncertainty. Murphy saw that Purefoy's hunted eyes needed to move. They slipped into the nearest warehouse through the vast doors.

The smell hit them first.

Then the sight.

Though the warehouse wasn't populated, it was full: full of tall, stone vats. The vats stood on large constructions that held them up at the sides; by the sides of the walls were box-crates, like those outside, piled high but not in pyramids. Though mostly silent, there was a sound they didn't recognise repeating itself. Above the vats, labyrinthine walkways stretched from both sides of the building. Giant black stairwells reached up to them from the ground level. Small doors were at the end of each of the walkways.

'Bryn, take off your boots.' Murphy began taking off his.

'What? No. Why?'

'If we are to die, let's do it with our souls on the ground.'

Purefoy hadn't thought that they'd die yet. At the hands of The Cabinet, he'd thought there'd be worse but he hadn't yet put them as killers. He'd thought that they'd survive with a debt and dark scars but not dead. The thought shook his drunken nerves a little freer of their stupor. Suddenly he vomited. He didn't think he had it in him. 'Good thing you weren't looking at me.' Murphy offered a friendly smile. He'd been facing away from Murphy and now stood to the side, with his hands on his knees getting his breath back, controlling the contortions in his gut.

Out of the corner of his eye, he saw Murphy take off his second boot. He stepped away from his vomit and took his own off. The cooling of his feet from the floor calmed his untempered nerves slightly. He tied his laces together and hung the boots around his neck. The mud smell was preferable to whatever the smell was in the warehouse. It overpowered the vomit; Purefoy bent down, with his right hand he wiped the vomit under the construction holding a vat up. He wiped his hand on his trousers. *Always the right hand for the right job...*

A metal clacking sound came from the far corner of the warehouse. Both their heads jolted to its direction. Their eyes flicked to each other, back to the sound. Murphy grabbed Purefoy's arm and pulled him flush with the construction holding the vat. Their backs to the danger, they only had sounds to go on. With his focus on them, Purefoy could hear the blood beating in his ears.

'So what do you reckon?'

'Na, it'll never work.'

The sounds of danger were two voices he didn't recognize, speaking loudly of nothing he recognized. They made their way around the warehouse in Purefoy's direction. Their voices growing louder with each sentence.

'Works in town though, dunnit?'

'Yeah but if you put the police on the docks, you might as well put 'em in docks up and down the 'ole country.'

'And why not? There's more police in cities all the time. I 'eard they 'ad 'em in Liverpool.'

'Why not? Why not?! They'll not be a proper force for long enough is why not. Soon enough it'll be back to the way it was. You'll see.'

'What do you mean?'

The faceless men were easily four yards away. Purefoy felt an urge to look around the vat, to see them. Murphy tugged on Purefoy's left shoulder pulling his attention away. Murphy silently moved around the vat to their left. Purefoy followed.

'We'll 'ave separate police for separate bits and they'll do as they like, as they used to. They'll charge what they like and if you don't pay 'em, they won't 'elp. Just. Like. They used to.'

'Na. Sorry but na. The toffs like 'em too much to get rid of 'em now and—'

'Alright, maybe. Maybe they'll keep 'em but if they come onto the docks there'll be one 'ell of a game. Would they 'ave our jobs, is that it?'

As the men talked, Purefoy skirted around the whole vat. They were close. Too close. Their volume stayed the same. He moved as carefully as he could, quieter than he thought he could. He held his breath just in case. Everything in him heightened. He suppressed the need to vomit again.

'I never thought of that.'

'Well, that's it innit. We gotta think about it.'

The men had walked all round the warehouse, all around the

vat Purefoy hid behind, and back to the place they'd come in. Murphy and Purefoy were back where they'd started. They were safe. They were unseen.

The two guards talked more as they left but closed and locked the entrance they came in.

A wave of dopamine flowed over Purefoy and he smiled. A wave of oestrogen went over Murphy – he spoke with more than his usual monotone, 'Bryn. Do you remember the teller, the fortune-teller, from earlier?'

'Just about, I think. Yes.' Purefoy knew it best to let Murphy speak of his own accord, without pushing.

'I loved the teller once and she'd said she loved me too...'

A silence. Still Purefoy knew to let Murphy speak in his own time.

'But after she'd told me, she slept with a dozen sailors – I'm not even exaggerating, I often wish it was exaggeration. No, she'd slept with a dozen. I was told about it an' practically killed a man for sayin' it but, I heard more people say it – and ya can't kill everyone – so I asked her. She told me it was true. It wasn't for money either; that I could've understood. She just stood there lookin' at me, smilin' like rain couldn't touch 'er.'

'Her': it remained a lump in his throat, another break in his speech. Purefoy had never loved any woman but BB. He felt for Murphy as a brother feels when he sees his family in a pain he can do nothing about. Purefoy placed his hand on Murphy's shoulder.

'She had the widest eyes, ya know? There was everythin' in those eyes and I coulda forgiven 'er if she'd known what she'd done...but she couldn't see it at all.' On 'all', his voice cracked. Purefoy saw Murphy clench his jaw.

It pained Purefoy to see his executioner in such pain. He squeezed Murphy's shoulder gently.

Murphy smiled. 'I thought...I thought that was it, ya know. I thought that was The Mighty Cabinet Troupe gang come to finally take me away and beat me into mud and the worst part is, I wished I'd told her more.' He wiped his eyes and rubbed his face. He removed his hat briefly and stroked his hair back, over his head.

How easily we become children again. I wish I'd known. Purefoy's thought was first for Murphy, then a reproach for himself.

Had he never wanted to be a father? Why had he and BB never truly talked about it? *It would have made me a stronger man; a man who knows how to act now.* He remembered the children he'd seen that morning, sat with their feet in the dirt. He imagined their scramble to the coin he dropped. *Not all of us have enough to be fathers.*

'Come on, Purefoy, we best get our boots back on and get moving.' Murphy was pulling himself back to being the man Purefoy had known. Now he knew there sat inside Murphy a mountain neither he nor Murphy would climb in this lifetime. As they sat putting their boots back on, Purefoy watched Murphy and wondered, *Will this be the last time I see the real Murphy?* Murphy noticed him watching and smiled. 'You're slowin' down, lad. Keep up.'

Murphy stood and stretched. He laughed a laugh of relief, a laugh at himself. 'We'll have to find another way out. Let's try…' He walked over to the stairs. 'Aye.'

Purefoy joined him and they went up.

The air felt thicker. The smell of the warehouse increased. They had been there long enough for Purefoy to realise it was a smell similar to one he'd smelt before. There was something animal about it.

They'd taken the stairs with slow steps but they were still too loud. They'd have to be slower and their footfall gentler still if they were to avoid the men checking the warehouses.

He coughed and cleared his throat. Murphy hushed him wordlessly. He coughed again and continued coughing. They reached the top of the stairs and Murphy began coughing too.

Murphy took one of his handkerchiefs and wrapped it around, covering half his face. He offered another to Purefoy. As soon as their faces were masked, the coughing stopped. They didn't stop to find out what it was.

They walked to the end of the walkway they were on, their difficult breathing audible through the handkerchiefs. The door at the end looked made for a child. Murphy tried it. Locked. They looked out over the other walkways. There were seven more doors on their side of the warehouse, some small, some double-sized. Some of the walkways looked sturdy, some far less sturdy than they should be. Purefoy knew one thing about metalwork, *Look for rust.* His eyes searched the frames of the walkways and their various wall-connections.

Rust crept out from under most of the walkways.

The connections in the walls were strained but not rusted. Murphy moved to pass Purefoy – Purefoy stuck out his arm. 'Wait, Murphy. Look. Rust.' Murphy looked. He thought for a second.

'We've little choice, Purefoy. Come on.'

At the smaller connecting walkway, they heard a sound coming from beneath them; it was coming from where they'd entered. They had no time to hide. They had nowhere to hide. They ran along the connecting walkway to the next that lead to a door. The door was locked.

'Oi! Navvy! You still owe The Cabinet some fun.'

Chapter 24

The Cabinet had found them.

Panic hit.

There were three of The Cabinet members chasing them, Hander, Loliver, and Gammonfond.

Before Purefoy could know what he should do, Murphy'd ran forward on the walkway, crossing to the adjacent one. He shouted to Purefoy, 'Come on!'

The Cabinet made their way up the stairs in leaps.

Purefoy moved as quickly as he could. He got to Murphy's new walkway as Murphy shouldered the door – it wouldn't budge.

The Cabinet were close. At the top of the stairs, they'd stopped running. They whistled and laughed as they walked, taunting Murphy. Crag Loliver shouted, 'Look, Murphy; we just want to talk. You're a little…off-message and Bad Tail knows that you're a good sort – we just want to talk. You know the sort of thing. Come over here and we'll all talk about what the right thing to do is.' The other Cabinet members laughed.

Murphy's head moved, hawk-like, to every corner of the warehouse, seeking a way out. He looked at Purefoy. He looked down. Purefoy looked at The Cabinet, each of them held gleaming, long knives.

He felt metal at his throat.

Purefoy's arm was behind his back. He knew it was Murphy – only Murphy could have gotten to him that quickly. For a second, he was tempted to plead but he knew it pointless. He was tempted to fight but he didn't know where he'd go – he knew that all of the weight on the walkway was bad for the rust he'd seen, he didn't want to make it any worse.

'Stay where you are – d'ya hear me?!' Murphy's shout was all the more fearsome coming from directly behind Purefoy's ear.

Hander's dark, slow Scottish accent was clear, 'Murphy, we

don't care if your friend goes through the mill. We just want you to play with.'

'Shut up, Dabby – if I kill 'im here, you'll get the touch for it. I'm on my way to see a peeler and 'e knows I've something good for 'im.'

The Cabinet looked at each other. Gammonfond nodded his head. The other two smiled. There were two walkways between the two groups. The Cabinet advanced on Murphy and Purefoy.

Murphy backed onto the furthest walkway he could, Purefoy still in front of him – shielding him from anything The Cabinet could throw at them – the knife still at Purefoy's throat. Through Murphy, Purefoy felt them bump into the wall behind.

Purefoy blinked and felt himself falling.

His throat hurt. His chest hurt. When he opened his eyes, he was still on the walkway but lying flat on it, near one of the warehouse doors.

Murphy was running at The Cabinet.

Murphy threw his knife at the first, Gammonfond – it sunk into the middle of his forehead. Gammonfond took a step forward and his hand came up toward the knife; his eyes crossed trying to see it; blood seeped out from under the knife as his hand missed the hilt – he fell forward. Murphy stepped on his back. Roaring, he leaped into the air.

Mid-air, Murphy leant all his weight forward and punched Hander. Hander reeled back a step, shaking his head – Murphy already had control of Hander's right wrist and, with it, Hander's knife. He grabbed Hander's neck and pushed him toward Loliver. Loliver shouted but froze.

A scream.

Loliver looked down – his knife had cut through Hander's ribs and gut. Even Purefoy could see a knife came through Hander's side. Murphy wrenched Hander's wrist and arm up and back, plunging the knife into Loliver's shoulder. A guttural cry.

With the railing to the walkway, Purefoy lifted himself up.

Once he stood, he saw the two men Murphy had hold of – interwoven by the cuts they'd given each other – halfway over the railing. Murphy was pushing them over the railing and down to the ground level.

In three seconds, they were over. They were falling.

Bones cracking. Damned screams.

Purefoy moved over to the walkway where Murphy stood and looked down. The screams continued. The men hadn't fallen onto the floor – they'd fallen into a vat. The repetitive sound they'd heard before was a boiling sound. The animal smell suddenly made sense.

This was a bone boiling factory.

Hander and Loliver strained upward. They screamed to get out. Intercut as they were, they only did more damage. Their hair grew slick and fell off in chunks. Their skin was the second quickest to go, sluicing from them with each attempted reach for freedom.

The sight made Purefoy wish he still had something to vomit. He wretched. His eyes watered. Murphy's shoulders heaved with the deep breath and the effort of fighting. He worked his jaw, he ground his teeth as his breathing slowed.

The screaming had stopped.

Purefoy looked down again. He saw the muscles of a hand melt off the bones.

The last things he saw above the line of the boiling liquid were the white bones of the hand falling into themselves, gripping at the air, only to find nothing and to flex again – leaving the tips of the stripped-fingers pointed and sinking.

CHAPTER 25

The two men stood on the walkway above the vat, holding their handkerchiefs, ensuring their noses were covered. The stench of the members of The Cabinet boiling was partly chemical, partly animal. Even holding their noses, it got in. Purefoy'd known what to expect since Murphy killed those men on the steps of St. Pauls but this smell was by far the worse.

They stood there a while, in silence. In shock.

One of them finally spoke, 'The City's a digestive system, Purefoy.'

Murphy had finally calmed his heaving, his shaking, and his heavy breathing. His hands gripped the railing. His knuckles were white. Purefoy moved to the closest wall. He slid down against it. 'You're better not to sit down, Bryn. If ya sit down, ya may never get up again.' Murphy raised his bottom lip after he'd said it. A gesture of indifference.

'Won't more be coming?' A question of indifference.

'Maybe...but I doubt it. They usually only send out one last group if they've lost someone...I should know, I was one of them f'ra while.'

Murphy walked over to Purefoy and offered his hand.

'Why should I get up, Murphy? Hmm? Can you tell me a good reason for me to get up? Is it so I can die? Face the end with you pushing me over the railway into it – is that it?'

'Aye, something like that or you could think of it as your release – a release from all this. 'The end' as you call it would be welcomed by some. You might count yourself lucky that you know yours'll come at the end of today. Until then, you're under my keeping.'

Purefoy took his hand. He'd seen what Murphy was truly capable of. He knew that if Murphy meant to kill him, he could have at any point in the day. He looked down again. The light on the ground level was becoming too dark and too thick to see through.

They tried another door. Locked.

They tried each of the doors. They were all locked. They chose a small door and began kicking. They developed a rhythm. Purefoy felt that day's nerves ebb with each kick. The alcohol still in his system gave him warmth. He laughed when he felt it. The laugh threw his rhythm off and he stopped kicking. Murphy stopped too but began shoulder barging. The door was too small for them both. Purefoy stepped behind and, when Murphy prepared to barge again, Purefoy put his arm around Murphy's back and his head to Murphy's side. Instinctively, Murphy put his right arm around Purefoy and they pushed. They pushed again and again until the door moved an inch. With this, they broke apart. They kicked the door furiously. It cracked. It cracked again. They kicked until it opened.The light outside, a vernal change, had quickly faded from the blue they saw earlier to black. The streets of the Isle of Dogs were hardly lit but from their elevated position, Purefoy could just make out the end of the line of warehouses. The whistle of trains was near and calm. He looked around for others but the docks were deserted. His stomach reminded him, it must be six. Time to eat.

Once over the crates and down from the barrels, Purefoy's modicum of strength returned. He asked, 'Murphy, I've never heard of any police coming to the Isle of Dogs – if…if you plan to give me to The Cabinet, I'd like to know. I'd like to hear it from you and then I'll be silent until what…what must happen happens.'

'Don't worry, Bryn, The Cabinet won't touch you. It's like I said, until the end of the day you're under my keeping so 'for the modest asking ought to be followed by the deed in silence'.'

'Sorry?'

'So what I mean is don't worry, Bryn. You won't be hurt further until the end of the day so let's be quiet, eh?'

'Oh…right.'

They walked west toward the end of the warehouses. The further they got, the louder a hissing sound grew. The foam from the dock spilled up at its regular pace. The hissing grew.

Murphy held them still. His hand on Purefoy's arm, they listened. Purefoy couldn't see much of anything. He felt the wind off the water. He saw the end of the warehouses, the dock to their left, and the crates stacked next to the warehouses but beyond that, only black.

A false alarm; they walked on. They both walked much slower in comparison to how they'd walked that day. Each muscle began to make its tiredness known, the lactic acid building up in them. They reached the end of the warehouses. There was little activity. They could still hear the trains going by, just north of the dock; the water in the dock still foamed and struck against its sides; far off sounds of early evening entertainment came from their left, from the south. Purefoy thought he could still hear the hissing. He didn't say anything.

Instead, the image of the first railway station he'd arrived at in London came to him. Its giant walls and glass roof; its pristine clock and the clean-pressed people; the glass arches at the exit, as big as thirty men; the light that filled the whole; the railway bookstall; for a second, standing in that place, he'd thought, *I could stay here, just here*; the traders outside creating almost as much noise as the steam engines inside. In his mind, the station became the site of the mine near Wrexham – its towering construction, pulling things up from the ground. That became the fields nearby and those fields took on the station, on top of them. He imagined the train station with all walls removed, open to the birds and with trees lining the ends of the tracks; pigeon messengers guiding passengers without need of guards or ticket stamps while stall owners paid their dues with handshakes that exchanged invisible money. He rubbed his eyes. His right eye hurt.

The hissing hadn't stopped.

Murphy knew it too.

They took the left, south, around the dock past more warehouses. Once passed, they got back to the road they'd left. Back on Mill Wall Street, all the previous unsettling sounds ceased. They only heard their steps and a door or two close. The air in the street was surprisingly crisp. Their breath turned to condensation in front of them. Purefoy was glad of his ears feeling the cold, glad of the normalcy. A full day and nothing normal had happened. He asked himself *But isn't all this normal? …what was it Murphy said about going through hell?*

South, ever southward, past The Basin. Onto the Mill Wall Street, South Dock Bridge – here they stopped. Murphy spoke as he looked down into the small channel flowing beneath them, 'D'you ever think about it, Bryn? I mean, did you ever think about what's down there? What's beneath all that black.'

'I can't say I did, no.'

'For a while, I wasn't just with The Cabinet. No. I was with The Forty Thieves too. They used to store stuff here, under this bridge – nothin' valuable, no, just…just messages, ya know.'

The slush of the water flow beneath them filled the silence.

They could see light from much further south on the road. They went toward it. They should have left the soft sounds behind with the water but it followed them. The hissing grew again.

Ahead of them, mid-air, a flame burst from nowhere.

With it, a grimacing face.

In the flash, Purefoy saw something slithering between his boots.

The flame was gone again in an instant and they heard a guttural caw. Something constricted Purefoy's left leg.

Another burst of flame – another different face. It appeared that way until the flames settled and illuminated a box around it. The box of the lamp and the face of the lamplighter. All over London, men must have done the same – welcoming in the night.

Beneath and above ground, the hissing flowed. They walked toward the flame. Another flame lit, lamped, and stayed burning, closer to them. With a few more steps Purefoy's cramp left and another lamp lit.

They met the lamplighter at his work, his short ladder propped and his hand lamp readied. Murphy called out, 'Good evening to ya, sir.'

'Good evenin' to you an' all. What can I do for ya?' The old man rounded the sound of the letter 'l' to sound like a 'w'.

'My friend and I are looking for a little illumination.'

''Illumination', very good – well, I'm your man for that. What, in particular, are you lookin' to put into your gas then?' The old man had a kindly, deep resonation to his cockney accent.

'Ah, ya know. A good quart o' the usual.' Murphy sounded friendly too.

'Well, help is at hand.' The old man turned a nozzle Purefoy couldn't see. There was a hiss and a slight movement from the man before the lamp was easily lit. He fixed the lamp box and stepped down from the ladder. He had a thick, white beard trimmed close to his face.

'You're Irish, ain't ya?'

'I am that, sir, aye. Yes.'

'Well, you may understand the ducks' lingo better than I so you'll be alright. Round 'ere is mostly Scots narw. They're a good bunch, 'ard workin' you know. Course, in a locali'y so favoured by Scot children, there's a kirk, and a very comfortable little kirk i' is. I try to let my grandaugh'er play down this way when I gets a bi' a time wivver. S'difficult though, she comes back with the funniest sayings. Dunno what it means for 'ow she'll grow up, where she'll belong to...' He looked up at the light and took a deep breath before continuing, 'You know. Still, if iss drink you're after, drink you'll 'av. There's The Thistle, The Burns, and The Highland Mary further south. They'll be good for ya and I'm told they sing a fing or two.'

'You're very kind, Mr...?'

'Wells. T. Wells.'

'May all your lamps be lit, Mr Wells.'

'And may your gas be full.'

'A sting. A wit! Very good, sir.' Both men smiled. In the rapt gaslight, though it sputtered, the men acknowledged a knowing of the other without the need for a handshake or anything more. They went their ways. The hissing subsided.

Further on, further down, the population were well lit. From the far off music, they were in the process of becoming brighter. Purefoy thought back, *Have I known any lamplighters? Or any Scotsmen? I don't think I have. How odd. How odd that on my last day I should have so many firsts.* There would be many more. *I haven't thought about it yet. About the moment when it's with me...but I suppose I'm thinking about it now. Murphy said that it'll be at the end of the day but when is it? When exactly does he mean? And why has he let us drink? It must be to keep me drunk. Drunk and happy. Close to nothing.* Purefoy thought he'd ask, ask exactly what Murphy meant by 'the end of the day' and he went to. The right words failed to come to him. He put it out of his mind. He tried to stop thinking.

Behind them, they heard another guttural caw. They slowed. They looked at each other. Murphy jerked his head back and smiled.

A roar.

A scream.

A crack.

They both lurched round. They knew they'd have to run to the lamplighter. They could see flames rolling, flicking on the ground. They heard more guttural caws. They sounded like pleas.

Purefoy had no idea what to do but ran toward the flames anyway. The screams confused him but he looked around for water, in the hope that it was close. He found none. He thought about running to the South Dock but *it's too far.*

Murphy removed his jacket and threw it on the man's head. Purefoy shouted, 'Murphy what are you doing?' Murphy didn't respond, he wrapped the jacket tightly around and suffocated the flame. The old man's screams stopped. He could be heard breathing through Murphy's jacket. 'Up ya come, Mr Wells. I'm goin'a take the jacket off ya now.'

'No! Please. Don't. Just…just get me to the river.' He hadn't shouted but the pain in his voice was sharp.

They shuffled to the Regent Dock Inlet nearby. It fed straight into The Thames. They made sure the old man got safely to the river. Purefoy heard him rapidly sucking in air through his teeth beneath the jacket. Murphy spoke quietly, 'Mr Wells, I have to take the jacket off ya now. Alright?'

'Before you do, I just need to parlay this.' He held his hands up, palms facing out and continued speaking though it sounded exhausting to him, and muffled, 'Did anyone ever tell you we came from water? My ol' gran did. She said it wipes you down, dusts you off, ready for the next…she said we could return…anytime we needed…

'Alright, you can take it.' Murphy removed the jacket as delicately as he could.

The old man ran into The Thames.

'Wait!' Murphy's shout was lost. Purefoy thought he saw Mr Wells bob up and down a while before he sank as the current took him. He couldn't be sure. The Monster Soup was too black.

Murphy stared south, along the path of the river. He put his jacket back on. He turned to the road. 'What do ya think, Purefoy?'

'I…I don't know. I've been trying not to think…today.'
'How were you raised, Llewes? Is what he just did not the coward's way out? Practically inexcusable.'

'I think he didn't scream more than was necessary. He harmed no one. In his death, even when in extreme pain, he controlled himself. He didn't let anyone else suffer for his…accident. I think he was very brave.'

'Ah what would you know anyway.'

Back on the Deptford Greenwich Road, people had started to walk further north. They walked happily past the site where an accident had taken a man's life just moments before. Southward, Murphy and Purefoy walked, guilt between them; it wasn't deserved but neither of them could help it. Murphy muttered, 'I need a drink.'

They came to The Thistle pub. Murphy motioned to go in. 'Stop, Murphy. Stop.'

'What is it Purefoy? I'm not in much of a mood to talk.'

'I've had enough, Murphy. I want you to finish all this. I want you to take me to your police constable.'

'What? You wanna go to limbo before your time, do ya?'

'I just want it done with, Murphy – whatever the cost. I'm done now. I'm ready now.'

'You're far from ready…'

'Can't we just go on and not stop in another pub?'

'Ah, but you're in luck. The man we need is in here.'

CHAPTER 26

Standing outside The Thistle, Murphy paused and moved to the side of the entrance. He leaned against the wall, took out his pipe. 'Care to join me for one last Chine dream, Bryn?' Purefoy did. Murphy stood smoking, Purefoy waited.

'I know I was tough on ya this morning, Purefoy, but you have to admit that I was relatively nice to ya for the rest of the day.'

'Were you being nice on the first or the second time you held a knife to my throat?'

'Now the wit? Well good as that was, I didn't kill ya did I? And here we are. Safe and sound.'

'Would you have used it, Murphy? If things had got worse with The Cabinet?'

'No. Come on. Ah, don't be a raw muff; if I had, I couldn'a brought ya here – could I? I had no reason to do ya in. I just had to make a show, ya know. We all have to make shows, Bryn.'

Murphy passed the pipe. As he inhaled, Purefoy closed his eyes and saw the smoke travelling down his throat, into his gut – to his imagination, it coloured his insides. It poked at his thoughts. He smiled. He thought, *Whatever it is doing, it's a funny illusion.* He felt suddenly exhausted and elated at the same time. When he opened his eyes again, they'd only open to squint. The world looked lob-sided and fuzzy around the edges. 'I've probably had enough opium now.' He'd said it aloud, he hadn't meant to. He laughed.

'You're a stranger man than I, Bryn Prifardd Llewes ap Llwyn. I couldn't meet my end laughing.'

Purefoy abruptly stopped laughing. 'How do you know that name, Murphy?' His anger began to rise.

Murphy knew he'd touched on something he shouldn't. As he watched Purefoy he thought, *Sorrow is a desperate thing: it's all nothingness for one then all fury for none but I'll be damned if I can figure out this man. No wonder I wander.*

Will he like it, I wonder? Why's he angry now? He knows I know. How could he not know? Maybe...this could be it; this isn't it; it's close. I should, I can't, I will.

'It's your name isn't it? I saw it on your letter. I ah...I'm sorry about your mam. I didn't know you were... I didn't know you'd lost...well, lost your family.'

Purefoy's anger subsided. He unconsciously smoked the pipe once more. He passed it back. He knew it was the opium, the day, and all the days spent hoping it would change now coming to meet him – to build his defeat onto him. He knew all of these were the cause of the clashes in him.

'Right, Bryn; ready yourself to meet your maker.'

'Finally.' Purefoy said, deadpan. Murphy guffawed.

'You've a fine wit, Bryn.' The two men smiled. They entered The Thistle.

Inside was expansive. There was room enough for children to play between tables. Even then people stood around in groups. Purefoy couldn't see one top hat. He also couldn't see a policeman. He thought he might like the place if he'd found it of his own accord. Murphy trod predictably to the bar. He ordered two drinks, paid, and walked with them both back to the side of the entrance where Purefoy stood. Purefoy didn't take it from him. The world was still fuzzy. He knew anything other than food would make it more so. Murphy's extended arm remained so until Purefoy took the drink.The effect of the drink wasn't good. Purefoy felt the alcohol in it burn the back of his throat. He burped immediately after his first sip. He looked at the liquid: it was brown like earlier and nothing could be seen to be different about it but Purefoy felt as if the world had gotten heavier – pushing down on his head, pushing his shoulders into the ground. 'I need to sit down, Murphy.' Murphy, mid-sip, saw Purefoy's pallor become green again. He recognized the process from earlier. He guided him to a seat. Once down, Purefoy took another sip – his guts hurt. The pressure on his head lessened as the pain in his gut increased. He propped his head up with his hand. He hoped the world would right itself after a few more sips. He wouldn't have chance to notice.

'Ladies and gentlemen! Your attention a moment.'

A voice Purefoy recognized but couldn't put a face to spoke. It had a measured rhythm with a rubbery jollity to the word 'gentle'. Purefoy's eyes and his mouth remained closed. He breathed into his gut to calm it and supped on his drink in the vain hope that it would calm him. The voice continued, 'Some people say that to succeed in this world, we need to be more like China or India or other far off places, I say we need to be more like Britain – the Great Britain! Hard working, pioneering, adaptable Britons – no matter what country you're from within Britain, you still have the opportunity to be great for our country.'

Ah yes, play to the patriots. Purefoy's thoughts were turning as bitter as his drink. He knew it but he didn't care; he drank more, the voice continued, 'You all know me. I am not Mr Brunel but I'm also not as much of a slave driver as he is. I want to give you all the opportunity to get things done. I want to give you jobs. I know the critics will say 'what about workers' rights?' Well let me assure you that I have them at the forefront of my mind and something that's always on my mind is the most important right of all, the right to have a job in the first place.' With this, the pub cheered.

The rowdiness opened Purefoy's eyes. The voice was too familiar not to pay attention but he couldn't put a face to it at all. Even in the fog of his exhausted synapses, he knew that he'd heard this man recently. He looked up.

There stood the man named Flash from Ludgate Hill.

He stood by the bar but men had cleared a space around him so others could see. When Purefoy saw Flash, he looked as if he had six arms and each arm held an ale. When Flash put up his front two arms to calm the cheering, the other four lowered behind him. Purefoy felt dizzier. He put his hand under his chin so he could keep watching. To him, Flash had six arms.

'As a final piece, let me say this: some people will tell you we're too far from where we should be and there's not enough being done to get the jobs to the people who need them but I say that nothing worthwhile is easily won. I am working on making more jobs. I'm a normal man and I'm in it with you. Let this time of challenge for us be turned into a time of opportunity. If you want a job, come talk to me. We can make things up together. If I can, I will always help. Let us show the world some fight! Let us work together, let us pull together and let us, together, lead Britain to better days ahead.' The pub roused for Flash again. His arms went out to his sides with his palms tilted upwards. Purefoy saw four more arms behind him do the same. Where the drinks in those arms were before, now there were knives. He coughed. He rubbed his eyes. The extra arms were gone.

The cheering and back patting slowed. For a second, Purefoy felt uncontrollably drunk. It was an intense warmth that filled his face and burnt at his throat – he'd never felt that way before. He knew his drunk mixed with the opium; he questioned his vision, he questioned his thoughts. *Has Murphy got me washed just to make sure I can't resist? He's done well…if that's it.* He tried to ignore everything moving in the periphery of what he could see. He squinted. The world sat fuzzy again.

'Bryn? Meet Mr Flash.' Purefoy moved from his hunched place at the table, looked up and over his left shoulder. Murphy stood there with Flash; Flash smiled a wide, jagged-toothed smile. His cheeks were red. *If you ignore his teeth, he looks nice.*

Flash spoke, 'Call me Flash, please. Hello Bryn. Lovely to meet you.'

'Flash has a job proposal for us, Bryn.'

'Yes, but it is of a rather sensitive nature. Could we speak outside?'

'Yes. Outside would be good.' Purefoy stood and the chair fell over behind him.

Outside, Purefoy removed his cap to feel the cool air and to calm his drunk head. Flash put his top hat on to keep him warm. Purefoy was still reeling from his drunken confusion, *Where was the harness? Why are we outside? At least it's cool outside. God, I feel—*

'Can I offer you gentlemen a *cigarette*? I don't smoke myself but I've been given some Ottoman types by way of France.'

'Aye, I'll have one. Thanks.'

'No thank you.' The cold was helping Purefoy gather his senses.

'You should, Bryn. You never know when it'll be ya last.' Murphy smiled at his own gallows humour. Purefoy took a cigarette. Murphy lit them both. Purefoy inhaled as slowly as he could.

The thing tasted awful. Purefoy coughed and coughed again. He wretched. He doubled over and vomited. He vomited on Flash's boots – Flash hit him on the shoulder, knocking Purefoy onto his knees. Murphy told him, 'Take another small inhalation on the *cigarette*, Bryn – it'll help.' Purefoy didn't, the vomiting had helped. He dropped the cigarette and let it stay where it was. He wiped his mouth with his sleeve. He tasted pure. He spat and stood. 'S-sorry about that, Mr Flash. I've never had a cigarette before.' Purefoy remained confused.

'Call me Flash. Well, shall we get onto business?'

'Aye. Please.'

'Gentlemen, I'm involved in many works and most of them work but sometimes, something doesn't go right in the plan: either someone doesn't do their share of the work or someone doesn't keep their word. In this particular case, lots of people haven't kept their word. There are houses on this isle that belong to me – other people may disagree with that but, trust me, they belong to me and the problem with them is that they're not paying what they cost. I've my own creditors and they need to be paid so when I'm not being paid, they're not being paid and this leads to a bit of a stink. Do you understand so far?'

'You're an upstanding businessman who expects professional behaviour. Some of the people you've entered into business with have proven themselves less than upstanding and entirely unprofessional.' Murphy had adapted his voice to suit the situation again but this time he spoke with the rubbery jollity that Flash did. The two voices were so alike as to be melded. Even his Irish accent waned. Flash looked at Murphy as Murphy smoked – to Purefoy, Flash seemed to stare at Murphy like a lizard; the more Murphy smoked, the more he became like a dragon. The smoke intermingled with the condensation from Flash's breath.

'Exactly...I'm glad to see that you're a professional—'

'Exactly that. What element of the business would we be involved in?'

'Well the real problem is that the prime foundations have become sub-so and so they're sinking into toxic, unpaid assets which, of course, means foreclosures. I need you to wade through those toxic parts and remove the foundations so that they can be rebuilt.'

'All very reasonable.'

'...quite. I'm glad you understand.'

'Business is business, Flash.'

'Exactly. Now—'

'Sorry, Flash. Could Murphy and I have a word for a moment, please?' Purefoy had to.

'Of course, take your time. I'll be here.'

They only needed to take a few steps away for the light to be fainter. They spoke quietly. Purefoy thought there might be oil in his skull, it was his only explanation for the pain. His head pained him like nothing he'd felt before. 'Murphy, what's going on? What does any of what he just said really mean? And where's the policeman?'

'The plan's difficult to explain, Bryn. He's the peeler. He

just—'

'There never was any peeler, was there?' Purefoy's voice raised.

'Calm yourself, Purefoy. Remember what I can do.' Murphy sounded pained to say it but continued, 'Do this job, do this job and you can choose what ya want – you can go where ya want…don't do the job and I know that Flash can afford to raise a cab to come here and take ya straight to a station. I'll gladly go with ya both to explain your crimes to the constables.'

Murphy smiled another flash of his black teeth. It ate the last link in their delicate connection. Acid gathered at the back of Purefoy's throat.

'Fine. So what does any of what you and Flash just said actually mean then?' He spat.

'It means he wants us to go beneath some of the houses here on the isle and – and correct some things.'

'That's all?'

'That's it succinctly, aye.'

'Fine. I agree.'

'Good.' Before he turned to go back, Murphy said, 'Take heed that thy tongue restrain itself. Whatever happens, leave me to speak because I've conceived that which you wish.'

Purefoy didn't believe that Murphy would let him go when the job was done. He felt that anything to quicken the end, the end to the pain in his head, was better than fighting.

It was five years before his death that Søren Kierkegaard published his last whole book. Five years after his capture, Jean-Paul Sartre first used the term 'existentialism'. It had taken Purefoy five years to realise he would die in that city.

CHAPTER 27

'The City rejoices when Great Britain's name is spread abroad. Since it is so great that over sea and land it should beat its wings – hell's teeth, it should beat its name everywhere!'

Flash had taken on his role of prime-speaker. With each sentence end, he looked to Murphy then to Purefoy. Murphy'd given Flash the opportunity by asking him what he thought of the India situation. Purefoy remained mute, as Murphy'd advised. Murphy invited him to speak more when he asked, 'Have you business in India, Flash? Would you have work for professional men like us over there?'

'There's always a revelation happening there but we'd have to talk about that at some other time. I think one of the marvellous things about—'

'Flash!'

The call came from behind them. They turned. They saw the man Gideon who'd been on Ludgate Hill. He walked briskly toward them. 'Gideon, you made it.' Flash was pleased.

'Of course. I couldn't miss this.' Gideon shook Flash's hand.

'Well, I'm glad you could be here. These are our new associates.'

'Ah so you're the men for the job. Good to meet you, I'm Gideon.' Gideon didn't ask for names. He didn't excuse him and Flash, either, but they walked away from the group to discuss something.

Purefoy'd never felt more sick.

He took the opportunity to ask Murphy something he'd wanted to since he saw him talk to Charlotte. 'What brought you to London?'

'Me? Some work…opportunity mostly. It might've been an illusion though for all it's gotten me.'

'What was an illusion?'

'The great promise of progress – industrial endeavours,

Purefoy. Like the Flash says, 'there's always a revelation' and he probably meant revolution because the wheel turns and nowhere moreso than London...it's just possible that my wheel isn't here. It's possible I was told wrong.'

'No family brought you here then?'

'Ya nozzlin' blab.' Murphy chuckled and spoke again. 'Before today, I thought London was where I'm meant to be...I – I guess we'll see.'

Gideon and Flash returned. On second consideration, Purefoy saw that they were wearing slightly different suits to those they'd worn earlier. They looked very happy. Flash spoke first. 'Gentlemen, before we can pay you, we need to meet another two associates of mine.' Purefoy hadn't thought about money but on hearing it, he knew he wouldn't see any of it. Remaining as silent as he could, he looked over at Murphy. Murphy's lips were pursed. He ground his teeth. He spat and the light briefly showed its black-blood colour.

In their expansion, the blood vessels in Purefoy's head continued to pain him. With each movement, he felt a little nausea. He scratched his scalp and put his cap back on, hoping it would help. He observed Gideon to try to remember the man's face. *If only to remember the faces of the men I've worked for. If I go to the clink and...if I get out...I'll be able to ask them for work if I see them.* From death to work; his hopes flitted, caged. Gideon's face was difficult for Purefoy to understand. Not only because his head hurt but Gideon's face changed in shape with every movement: once Purefoy thought it fixed, it shifted to another. He knew this much, Gideon's flabby jowls reminded him of the bulldog that had bitten him earlier. His face, like that of Flash, had no work lines. His eyes seemed green at one moment then brown the next. His smile turned to a sneer as easily as he smiled. His face reminded Purefoy of a man he'd met when he was a boy – the man had said he'd come from a country away; when Purefoy asked him how far, the adults had laughed. What he hadn't known was that the country was England. That man, Gideon, and Flash had trouble fitting into their waistcoat bands.

Murphy replied to Flash, 'Will your associates be meeting us here?'

'No I'm afraid not, old man, but don't worry, they are close.'

'And how close would that be, please? I'm keen to settle before the work is done. I'm sure you can understand my position.'

'Oh I do. I do. You're a professional, after all. They're quite close though. Both are on the isle and both have assured me that we'll be able to find them easily. They're supporting us with supplies and we can rely on them—'

'Well, we're all in this together,' Gideon said firmly.

'And some of us even more than others,' Flash replied.

'We'll make a strong team, advancing to revitalize the Isle of Dogs, eh Flash? We'll give it new freedoms while we'll also ensure that it's a fairer, more just place.' When they were talking with each other, Purefoy saw their exaggerated gestures confirm their meaning. He wasn't sure he fully understood. They'd gotten so deeply into conversation that they needed to readjust their hats. Standing with Gideon, Murphy, and Flash, Purefoy thought there was more depth in The Thistle than in any of these men. They liked talking, Purefoy's head hurt from hearing it. The cold was sobering.

As Flash and Gideon planned, Purefoy and Murphy remained in silence. Purefoy looked back at The Thistle. They could hear a fiddle being played, Purefoy tried to savour it. It hurt his head to do so but he attempted to hum along to the tune. There's no greater testament to strength than savouring joy in times of wretchedness.

'So which street, gentlemen?' Murphy's questions were getting shorter, his tone curter.

'Ah yes, let me think…Gideon, do you remember?'

'No, Flash. I thought you would.'

'Ah yes, I'm sure I do. Give me a minute and it will come back to me.'

They waited. Purefoy chuckled inwardly.

'Ah, yes it was Leeds Street…yes, Leeds. I was eating on Leeds just last week.'

'That street doesn't exist here. Here you've got Robert, Alfred, Gideon, Byng, Stafford, Thomas, Tooke, Charles, Maria, John, Melish, or Glengall. It's either that or we walk all the way south and find ourselves at the British School or eventually the Greenwich and Blackwall Road.'

'Right…er, Gideon?'

'I think it was Gideon Street, Flash, yes.'

'Gideon Street is north from here.' Murphy's interjection was met with bluster.

'Oh. Ah.'

'Erm, er'

'Are you sure?'

'Well…well, we – er —'

'If we need to head north, we should but I was under the impression that our business was a little south of here.' Murphy controlled his tone, only Purefoy knew he was irritated.

'Yes, quite.' Flash recovered first.

'I agree.' Gideon second.

Nothing happened. Murphy looked to Flash who looked to Gideon who looked to Flash. Purefoy chuckled again and focused on the voice he'd heard accompanying the fiddle. It was a woman's voice but not a high pitched one. Instead it sounded to him like an older woman's voice. He heard it as it finished one verse and began another.

…he that cultivates the land
Should sow it in due season,
he handles well his threshing flail
Whene'er there is occasion;

> *If he does this I promise him*
> *I ne'er for rent will call, Sir;*
> *But if he fails I will expect*
> *Him out of Sportsman's Hall, Sir.*

He wished he knew the song. The pub cheered when she finished. He heard a few happy squeals. The song reminded him of those his dad had taught him when he was young. He couldn't recall them at that moment, his head hurt. He shed a tear.

Murphy had cocked his head and Purefoy noticed him listening to the song. '"Not tho' the soldier knew, someone had blunder'd... Charging an army, while all the world wonder'd." That's the Laureate for ya, Bryn. Adept at all situations.'

Without any clear leadership, Murphy took it. 'Should we walk a little south, slowly, and see if your associate is present, gentlemen?'

'Ah, yes, I was just about to say so.' Flash smiled. Gideon smiled. Murphy didn't. Purefoy thought their smiles looked painful. They walked. The road had flat stones in it that Purefoy recognized beneath him – he slowed his pace and kicked lightly at the collected stone. He saw it glint in the light – he knew he recognized it. It was flint. Stretched out ahead of them were flinty steps. 'Flint', the very word reminded him of home. He asked himself, *What would life be like if I'd never left? Would BB and I have been married? Would we have kept the small money we made? What work would I have done?* Another tear. He wiped it quickly away. It hurt to think too hard. He put it out of his mind.

As soon as they started walking, Murphy asked, 'From what you said in The Thistle, Flash, will you be building a warehouse near here?'

'No, no, I...I don't think so.'

'Oh ho! What did you say, you knight of the lush?' Gideon scoffed.

'Oh I don't think Mr Flash was drunk, Mr Gideon. He was

saying how he wants to give people jobs but we didn't have time to get around to discussing how so. Would you care to expand, Flash?' Murphy, the gracious mediator.

'Ah yes. Of course…well, let's not say that I won't create jobs because I'd love to – I love jobs – but the truth is that we need to create in people a spirit of creating their own job even if there's none there. Even if they've never thought of making something before, I want them to make something up and it's this that will sustain them. My job is letting others create their own jobs but by doing so, I'm creating jobs.'

'So you won't be an employer to them directly then?'

'No, no. That isn't my job. Is it Gideon?'

'No, no. That's no one's job.'

'Quite right. No, we want to give people back their dignity by letting them make something up out of themselves. You see?'

'I do. You're an astute businessman so I understand clearly.' Murphy's tone was agreeable.

'Good. Good.'

'And don't mind me, I'm just the accountant.' Gideon was chipper. It gave Flash a smile.

An evening fire was lit inside one of the houses nearby; the light came out onto the path. Had it been a normal day, Purefoy would have walked east in the morning but over Bermondsey by sundown and halfway back again by now. Usually he knew he'd feel a warm ache in his legs. He was starting to get cold and the ache was his head, his throat, and his lower back.

'I say, Flash, do you remember going to Deripaska?'

'Of course, Gideon. Thank God it wasn't as cold as this. Why do you ask?'

'Well, I don't know if you remember all the details but we had a bit of a problem that didn't find a resolution.'

'Oh?'

'That is, until today. I managed to give it away.'

'What about the scraper problem, how's that merger going?'

'Well, it's no longer a real problem for us. Their accountant assures me that there's no limit on it and I've passed all the problematic paperwork onto your man.'

'Someone's had a busy day. Did you kill off that wolf that was stalking on your lands?'

'I didn't need to, someone did it for me.' They both chortled.

'Are you still in touch with the people in Bilderberg by any chance?'

'I fear I may have tripped up there by toeing the mark. I didn't think—'

'Ah well, it's not really a problem. Are you still in line for that ascendancy thing?'

'Of course.'

'Then everything's swell.'

Murphy continued in silence but Purefoy thought he saw Murphy moved his jaw some. Murphy spat. To Purefoy, Flash and Gideon may as well have talked in a foreign tongue. He briefly wished he knew what it was they discussed so that he might join in and offer an important point, as he'd done with Neshus, but the memory jarred in his head and he squinted at the pain. While regretting thinking it, he remembered that he promised Murphy he'd be silent and let him do all the talking.

CHAPTER 28

No sooner had they gone ten steps than a bell rang. Purefoy thought it six, perhaps seven at the latest. The further south they walked, the louder it became. Within twenty steps, the chapel of its origin sat to their left. The ringing continued – a shout came from behind the chapel. They slowed their progress. Another cry came but this one was drawn out as if in an effort to lift a great a weight. It attracted Flash's attention. 'Maybe we should see if we can be of assistance?'

'Or clean up what's necessary.' Gideon's hands must have been cold. He rubbed them together. They went left onto Charles Street.

The street was unpopulated but a shout came again from the lightless end. They hastened. Murphy stopped them all. 'It's only marsh after this.'

Purefoy let his eyes adjust to the dark. The bell finished. It rang nine times. Were there a war, and all the horrors of war left there, it could be covered with the mud and the dark of the marsh at that ninth bell. They heard a faint cry – Murphy waded into the mud. He shouted back, 'Purefoy, I need your help, please.' Purefoy wasn't sure if Murphy had asked him with a 'please' before. He walked out and put his hand on Murphy's shoulder. 'About five yards ahead of us, Bryn.'

The man they found looked half-dead. They dragged him back to the road. His stomach was either bloated or had already been too large for him, his whole body showed signs of scars, and his tongue lolled. He was dressed in a smart fashion with a bright yellow cravat. The mud had made short work of his colours. They laid him on the road and tried to wake him.

When Flash and Gideon approached, Murphy had cleaned his face. 'Holy ghost, Gideon, it's Legg.' Gideon and Flash knelt either side of the man. Flash punched the man in the side, Gideon punched the other. The man woke, coughing. Gideon and Flash smiled.

They all helped him stand. He brushed mud off his arms but it only muddied his clothes more. Even his cravat had a splattering. Legg continued coughing. Purefoy stepped back. He saw so much condensation come out, he thought it might be smoke trapped in the man's lungs. 'Legg, how the bloody hell did you manage to get into the marsh, you moke?'

'Sorry, Flash.' Legg continued coughing. He bent over and put his hands on his knees. A sack swung down from a shoulder strap and touched the floor. Flash and Gideon stepped back. Legg coughed blood and earth onto the floor. He finished coughing with a scraping sound, clearing his throat. He stood again and his back cracked. Purefoy instinctively looked away.

Legg only had one eye.

He was more scarred than any man Purefoy had seen. After only that glimpse, he could see a deep scar ran directly down from under his chin, over his Adam's apple, and into his clothes; red cuts were visible from behind his ears that joined to two more dark, red lines that ran under his whole face following the contours of his chin and joining the deep scar under the chin. Purefoy looked again. He saw black burn-lines surrounded Legg's nose that reminded him of branding he'd seen on a bull's hide. Purefoy had seen more cripples and returned soldiers in London than he'd seen anywhere but none were so bad as Legg. Purefoy'd tried to get used to seeing it but his instinct was always to look away, in case he caused offence.

'Gentlemen,' Gideon spoke, 'This is our fine associate.'

'And a bloody gump he is too. Is that it? In the sack?' Flash added.

'Yes.' Legg managed.

After having stepped back, Murphy had his arms folded. He stared at Legg. Purefoy looked at Murphy to try to make him stop staring. He tried a small lie, 'Murphy do you see what I see in the marsh?' Murphy didn't flinch.

'Will they still work, Legg?'

'Yes, yes. They were the reason I had to go in the marsh in the first place but I kept them dry.' Legg sounded exhausted but didn't flinch at Gideon's harsh tone.

'What do you mean 'the reason you had to go in'?'

'Some children tried to kid me and take the sack. They pulled on it and I held onto it but it flew out of both our grips and in it went. I ran after it to stop it from —'

'Alright, alright. Enough, the two of you.' Flash covered his mouth with the palm of his hand and, while holding his hat up, stroked his hair back. Purefoy thought he was sweating unnecessarily.

'Introductions. Legg, this is Mr Murphy and Mr Purefoy. They're our employees for the sub-prime problem. Gentlemen, this is Mr Legg, our associate.' Purefoy shook his hand. Murphy raised his in acknowledgement. Flash continued, 'Mr Legg has the necessary equipment you'll need for the job. Legg, hand over the bag to Mr Murphy.'

Slowly, carefully, Legg handed it over.

Murphy looked in the bag and laughed. Flash asked, 'Have you experience with the equipment Mr Murphy?'

'Aye, enough.'

'Good. Good. Now —'

'About payment, Mr Flash —'

'Please, call me Flash.'

'Aye, about payment, Flash.'

'Yes. We wouldn't have it any other way to pay you properly but we do insist on a quarter now and the rest when it's done.'

'A half now or we won't do it. There are two of us and I'm sure you can understand that, from a business perspective, if you're not pleased with our work we'll still have to split what we have.'

'I can offer a third now —'

'A half, Flash.'

'You're not seeing this from my viewpoint. We —'

'We agreed a half, Flash. I won't do it for any less. Mr Purefoy and I still have some business to attend to which will earn me a good deal.'

'Wait – yes…half is fine. Legg, pay the man.' Legg looked at Flash then at Gideon.

'I – I don't have any…I mean, I just have…I didn't bring more than…'

'Oh, Gideon, just do it, would you?'

'Here you are, Mr Murphy. Twenty pounds – a great deal of money, I'm sure you can agree.'

'Yes. Thank you, Gideon. A pleasure doing business with you, gentlemen. I'll look forward to the other twenty.'

'So long as the work's fulfilled to a satisfactory…design.'

'Don't worry yourselves, gentlemen, it'll be more than satisfactory.' The men laughed and Murphy smiled. Purefoy, still unsure of his role, kept quiet. He let his head lean a little forward to ease the pressure.

After the payment, they all headed further south. Purefoy didn't quite know why they all walked together when only he and Murphy would do the job. Then he remembered that he still didn't know where the job was. Legg asked, 'Are you Welsh, Mr Purefoy? You have the face of a Welshman.' Purefoy looked to Murphy. Murphy nodded.

'I am Mr Legg.'

'Yes, I've never seen a more Welsh face. I've family in Wales.'

'You've family everywhere, Leggy.' Gideon teased with the comment. Flash blurted a laugh. Legg, though visibly made anxious by it, continued, 'What's the feeling there? What are people talking about? Are they happy?'

What a question. Are they happy? It's been so long I… Purefoy thought for a while. Before beginning, he considered how whatever he said would impress on Flash, Gideon, and Legg the last thing that he might say to another human being other than Murphy. *Murphy, my jailer.* He wanted to give a well-rounded summation and a hopeful picture of his home even through the rising pain in his head. He cleared his throat. When he spoke, though it was still his pitched Wrexham accent, he spoke with a strength he'd thought lost that day.

'We're a proud people, Mr Legg. Sometimes too proud...but we've been let down by many things over my lifetime. It's only when a common goal, a common richness comes along that we gather a sense of possibility again. I can't speak for all of Wales because each part is very different. There are masses of the country that seem unpopulated and rightly so. I can only speak for my part of the north and Flintshire.

'There was much ado about The Treachery of The Blue Books and I think that that went over all of Wales. Before that, we heard tales about the Rebeccas making trouble in the mid. Even before that my mam told me about a Chartist uprising. We're a proud people.

'But people aren't talking about that. They're talking about betterment and fairness. Fairness for all.

'Unfortunately, sometimes that means they're talking about leaving. Like me. They're not always right...and some return...but they want more than what's there.

'There are tramways coming now and canals to take coal or flint or more – in parts, there's great amounts of work. In my home town, Wrexham, there's a fine leathering industry and other mining gets bigger by the day. We can't compete with our Southern cousins but I'm told that there, they have just as much hope and even more talk of change.

'To your questions then, the feeling is of change unlike any we've known before, the talk – the talk is of the change and what shape it should take. Are they happy is not a question I can answer, Mr Legg, because change is both hopeful and dangerous. So long as it's guided well, it is hopeful but if it's given to unruly men...well, I cannot say, Mr Legg.'

'That is a fine answer, Mr Purefoy. Thank you.' Mr Legg didn't ask anything more.

Purefoy felt he'd made a good answer – certainly the clearest answer he could give considering his current situation and how long he'd lived away from home – but he felt the pain in his head increase. He felt the difference in pressure between what was in his head and the cool, free air outside. The effort to answer had taken his balance from him.

Occasionally, Murphy looked over at Legg but he would quickly move his gaze if anyone noticed. Murphy didn't like Legg; he thought *is his nose burnt on or burnt off? If he can't smell, he can't smell that he's in trouble with his 'associates' – to me it stinks to high heaven. I should've known he'd try to get on side with Purefoy. I should protect him but then we've not far to go. From here to here – Legg's ear to ear. A true poison. 'And death unto thy race'. I know I think I know but I wish he hadn't. The nose, the face, the modern seat of beauty – aye, the seat. He'll not sit right for weeks after tonight...if he sits at all. Bryn must have figured me by now but maybe not. He's a strong one, you were wrong about him. Aye, maybe. We'll see. Hardly able to take a drop though. He spoke well enough to drop that though – aye, well enough. 'Betterment and fairness, fairness for all,' he says – as if Charlotte or Angie or even an amen curler. 'And death unto thy race'. If I'm tired, he must be far more then and I'm tired. Tired of the mawmouth twins, tired of the Legg and his sow and his sowing. 'And death unto thy race'. What's he had in that skin? What's got under it? What was under it? What was he when he was just he? His chin juts with it. He's not as fair a band about him as the other two but he's as swell; he's quieter and fairer than the whiddler Flash but he's still an associate; likes them or not, they pay and they'll pay again. A pretty penny too, I'll be no scroof now and can finally do what needs be done. Maybe I'll go. I was wrong about it here. I was wrong about him and here and his her. Poor lad. He'll come by...when he comes back. But that's another thing and nothing of mine. 'And death unto thy race'.*

Chapter 29

The pressure rose. The pain in his head couldn't be ignored any longer. Purefoy'd started to see sharp flashes of light where there were none; his tongue had become loose and difficult to control; he started to falter in his steps.

His mouth felt drier from speaking – he laughed inwardly as he realized how little energy he had – as if the last of him had been pulled from him. Behind his eyes, a dryness elided into the top of his throat. When he closed his eyes, he began to see himself from above: his faltering, silly walk, and his bobbing head drifting away from him as if separating. The pressure inside his skull continued to rise. He tried to remain constant.

He had to keep his head up and his eyes open. His thoughts began to blur languages. He'd never been this way before. He breathed deeply. With each breath, he began to feel a little more back inside himself. He kept his eyes open for longer stretches and kept breathing. The pressure still rose.

'What are you thinking on, Purefoy?' Murphy had interrupted Purefoy's focus.

'I – I was thinking on…what…I said, what I said about Wales.' He lied, his tongue hurt.

'Fairness for all, you say?' Flash and Gideon laughed. To Purefoy, Murphy sounded scornful.

'Y – yes, I think I did. Yes, I did.'

'Aye, well. Good luck but remember this, there's no point looking back at something thinking it better than it was.' Flash and Gideon laughed again.

To his right, Purefoy could see the adjacent road they'd been on when they'd met Flash. Ahead, they were coming to the end of the makeshift road. They turned on to Mellish Street. Purefoy didn't see the 'M' on the sign. Though the back street had been unpopulated, this part of the main road was busy. He could hear a dock nearby and further south, a pub glowed. When he paused, the others walked on and down the Deptford and Greenwich Road. Purefoy clearly thought, 'D-A-G-R, if only I'd had one this morning.' It was the last clear thought he'd try to remember until the end of his day. He wanted to remember it because it reminded him of BB – how she'd loved him for not carrying, and refusing to carry, a weapon.

He walked, trying to catch up with the group. Of the people on the street, some were aware enough to give him a good space in which to walk, some were too busy. Several barged into him. Each time he apologized but each time he'd thought he'd been maintaining a straight line. On the third time, he looked back to excuse himself when the girl – no more than 14 – spat at him. The spit landed in his right eye. The fourth time, he looked back and the man had a growth covering his right eye – Purefoy realised he'd walked into the man because he walked to the right of him. The last time he looked back, he saw a man whose entire skin had small, cream mushrooms growing out of it. He rejoined the pack.

Apart from Murphy, all in the pack were laughing when he caught up with them. He hadn't felt up to running, he'd tried to steady himself as he walked but the laughing was too loud, too offhand, to ignore. It hit his tympanic membrane and it let out a high-pitched resonation, it caught in his cochlea and went back into his ear's semi-circular canal. It echoed inside his head until it felt like an offensive on him and his waning strength. With every blink, he began to see new shapes form behind his eyes. The Freisian faced man he'd seen at The George earlier became a bull and horns grew from his head. The bull charged at him and Purefoy, half-delirious, gasped – the bull ran straight through him. He told himself to blink less. He was glad to be at the back of the group.

More people walked by as they got closer to the pub. The sound of the docks grew louder. They'd taken a few steps.

Purefoy blinked and the bull faced him again. The bull jerked his head back twice, in quick succession. His horns shrank first and then his whole shape. As the mass shrank, the skin transmuted from black and white patches to brown fur all over. The hooves became paws and they flexed out claws. The beast stretched its back by lifting itself onto two legs – it was taller than Purefoy, taller than Murphy. Purefoy stepped back.

The others walked on.

Convinced the beast would disappear if he could just keep his eyes open for long enough, Purefoy stood still to make sure his eyes stayed open. Soon he could see the beast in the street. His eyes were open.

He finally realized what it was – it was the bear he'd seen earlier but free from dancing, free from his chains, and wishing only to rid himself of any obstacles to his freedom. Purefoy continued walking. He maintained his line of sight directly ahead of him. The bear only sniffed at the air. When Purefoy and it were side by side, it whispered to him in Murphy's voice, 'The City is a diseased lover, the only way to know it is in breaching taboo, in fucking puss.' Purefoy clenched his jaw as he walked past. He closed his eyes once past it completely. He turned and looked back, the bear walked north three steps then cocked its leg – it pissed blood and made the noises Neshus had made. It stopped, shook, and walked on.

Purefoy turned to face the pack. They'd taken one step.

Purefoy looked back to the bear. His head felt too hot, he removed his cap. The bear had gone but where there'd been blood there were the bones of a hand emerging out of it – as the bones reached further up, nerves began to apply themselves in drips from the blood-pool onto the skeletal frame. The streams running upwards grew a second and third – those were blood red, wrapping around the first like snakes, like the staff he'd seen the old man carry that day. Slugs of meat fleshed the bones and the process gave life to an arm, a torso, a whole naked white body. Purefoy thought it must have been the light but when the body stepped forward, he saw that no, he was wrong – the man's head wasn't on his neck, he held it in his left hand by the hair.

Another trick – another opium dream. Just the ale and the opium – just Murphy – just the day…just keep walking and end it. It'll go away now. In a minute now. The others had taken two more steps ahead of him.

The headless man advanced toward him. Purefoy knew they didn't but he thought he saw people walk around the man. The man reminded him of someone. The closer the man got, the more Purefoy froze – he wanted to walk, he tried to walk, but his legs wouldn't. He couldn't look away from the man's naked skin – it was already beginning to peel and expose the flesh underneath. The man scratched at his right side. Blood dripped behind him, leaving a trail from his neck to where the bear had made him.

A whimper escaped Purefoy's throat. He'd been trying to control himself but – however imagined he knew it all to be – the fear got the better of him. It crept up from his gut, over his chest and into his throat – the amygdala inside his head throbbed and made him sweat a cold sweat. He began to plead quietly with the man, 'Os gwelwch – please – sir, don't. Don't come any closer. I don't—'

The others hadn't noticed Purefoy stop. They were four steps ahead of him.

The headless man's skin on his right side came off in his hand as he scratched at it. He continued scratching into the flesh where the skin had stripped away.

When blood dripped from his side down his fingers to the ground and his intestines began to bulge through the hole, he winced. He moved his hand to scratch at the stump of his neck. Purefoy made a sound deep in his throat he couldn't control. It sounded intermittently. The headless man lifted the head in his left hand up to shoulder-height. Purefoy screamed.

The others stopped.

Purefoy was murmuring. The face of the headless man was his father, Mr Llwyn.

Both men asked the other to stop but neither could. The closer Mr Llwyn got, the louder Purefoy became. He gabbled and shook. Mr Llwyn took another step. Purefoy shrieked and tore at his head. Another step. Purefoy screamed again, shouted and punched and—

Murphy's arms were around Purefoy, dragging him away from the headless man. Purefoy twitched and kicked. Mr Llwyn stopped, spoke something Purefoy couldn't make out and walked away.

Murphy lay him down on the ground. Around them, Flash, George, and Legg questioned, 'What's this all about, Murphy?'

'He's a madman, a—'

'We can't be expected to pay for this sort of—' Murphy spun his neck round and growled at the men. At the tail end of his gut reaction he said, 'Shut up you never-used fags.' Though they blustered, the three quickly silenced.

Murphy tried to help Purefoy recover. Purefoy moaned and spat, breathing in contorted rhythms. 'Slow down, Bryn – it's just the dark. It's nothing more. What are you looking at?' Murphy looked up in the direction of Purefoy's wide stare. Murphy nodded. 'Aye, Bryn. It was back there.' Murphy put his left hand at the back of Purefoy's head and the other over his eyes. 'Peace now, lad. You've work to do when you're ready.'

Murphy counted thirty seconds.

When he removed his hand, Purefoy's eyes were closed. He trembled less. Murphy pulled his torso upright. Purefoy let out a little sound that could have been a 'v'. Murphy took something from his jacket. He held Purefoy's chin. 'Open your mouth, Bryn Prifardd Llewes ap Llwyn.' Purefoy did as his true name told him. Murphy put something in Purefoy's mouth and said, 'Swallow that, quickly, before the taste sits on your tongue too long.' Purefoy did. Within a matter of seconds, he felt calmer and warmer. Calm enough to speak. 'Fy tad…'

Murphy lifted him up from under his shoulders. He held him

while he regained his footing. 'Y'alright now, Bryn?'

'I – I think so.'

'We've further to go ya know…'

'Yes, I know.' Murphy nodded and scratched his chin.

'Well gentlemen. Have we any other associates of yours we need to meet or should we call this a good time to part ways and let us get on with our work?'

'Actually, Murphy,' Flash smiled. 'We do have one more associate and she needs to give her blessing on all this before we can let you go.'

'You didn't say anything about a woman, Flash.'

'Didn't I? Oh, it must have slipped my mind. She's the one with the detailed map and plan of what must be done, you see. Don't worry, she's nearby.'

'How nearby?' Murphy's speech was becoming even curter.

'Glengall Street, she likes Scottish things so said we should meet her there.'

'Fine. After that, will we begin the work?'

'Oh yes, I should imagine so.' Gideon sniggered. Legg smiled. Murphy tried not to scowl as he looked round all three. Murphy stretched his hands from their balled position. He moved his neck against, then away from the strap on his shoulder. He looked at Purefoy. Purefoy stared at the ground. Murphy stood beside him and said, 'After you, gentlemen.'

Purefoy hated the idea that his dad hated him. *Was it that?* Too much swam in his head for him to think past it. *It couldn't be. What was it I thought earlier…some people shouldn't be…? No. I don't know. This still hurts. Some people aren't made to be fathers, though there are many that try. Was that…'* Murphy held onto Purefoy's shoulder as they followed Flash, Gideon, and Legg.

Chapter 30

People thronged around the King's Arms. Purefoy wanted the warmth of their thick, clean, black clothes and the warmth of a fire. It was just fifteen yards away but Glengall Street was four.

When they took the street, they all raised their handkerchiefs to their noses. Purefoy silently thanked Murphy then thanked God he wasn't hallucinating again. His ability to function had returned. He was calm enough to feel a great finality, a sense that he finally knew how low we all stand when we're against time. It didn't help relieve the pain in his head but it didn't add to it. He was dehydrated. He still couldn't quite get his footing to be true. He rubbed his eyes more and more with each few steps – his right was too painful not to.

For all the blurring in his eyes, the madness of what he saw couldn't be unseen.

Bodies upon bodies lay at the sides of the streets, festering. Some were still alive and moving. Some were too sick to move. Most were too far beyond recognition to be anywhere near living. The fungal skin and the growths that Purefoy had seen on the main street populace were nothing when compared with this. This was what caused the stench. Murphy looked at him and winked. Purefoy couldn't gather the mirth to return it. He thought Murphy meant to remind him of St Paul's.

Flash spoke with a voice clipped in its attempt to control, 'The end of the street, friends.' Murphy laughed.

They progressed at a cautious pace. Purefoy was happy to walk slower still. Even looking mostly down he saw limbs sprawled out, into the road. Arms were purple; feet, green; some hands told of a smoker through their yellow fingers, some hands were unidentifiable as people because of what grew on them – worse were the hands that looked like they'd been cut open on the palm and maggots ate at the inside. Murphy whispered, 'All the glues men've ever known are here. Don't touch – don't even kick anythin'.'

Purefoy's eyes, as is the wont of jaded eyes, drifted to the centre of the pile of bodies. He counted at least ten bodies on top of each other at the centre and, looking up the street, this number shrunk then rose again ahead of them. Some of the bodies were no thicker than sapling-wood with paper skin but those lay on top of bloated, gout-covered lipid-beasts. On top of the starved-dead were the distended and the infected. Purefoy wanted to feel indignant and passionate for them but only a spark of empathy presented itself in a tear he quickly wiped away. He was too exhausted to get angry.

He looked again. One man underneath reached his arm out toward Purefoy. It seemed to Purefoy that he was trying to get his attention, however soundlessly. The man squirmed out from under the other and looked at Purefoy. Purefoy didn't look away; the man had no flesh on his face, only bone, but behind the bone his eyes worked and the muscles lived but his tongue had been cut out.

'Hello your majesty!' Flash had raised his voice to say it and Gideon backed it up with a happy exclamation. A woman sat on a chair at the end of the street. She sat in profile with her legs to their left, looking at them. She was very still. She was young and had red cheeks. She wore black all over and even black gloves. The only white she wore was the white of pearl earrings. Her hair was held up at the back. Her red lips contrasted with her blue-grey eyes. Her face gave nothing away.

Closer, a tall man could be seen in half shadow. His skin was yellowing. He wore a red, army jacket. Though tall, his stomach bulged and sagged. Closer still, his features couldn't be said to be a man's or a woman's.

When the group reached her, Mr Legg kneeled but Gideon and Flash laughed. 'Don't be a fool, Legg. Get up.'

'Hello boys.' The woman spoke with a low, clear voice that never dropped a letter. As she said this she extended her hands –

Gideon and Flash kissed them, followed by Legg. She giggled as each did. The men made satisfied, snorting noises with each kiss. She smiled and her teeth were blacker and less numerous than Murphy's.

She stood and swiftly walked over to Purefoy. He looked up from the street and saw that she didn't have a spot of dirt on her. 'You look unwell, young man.'

'Young man – very good,' Gideon blurted out.

'Very good, Your Majesty,' Flash reiterated.

'Do you wish to kiss the royal hand?' Purefoy looked to Murphy and Murphy stepped away.

Purefoy said, 'I'm sorry miss, I don't know your name.'

'Of course, I'm Liza. These boys call me 'Majesty' because they want something, they always want something, but you can call me Liza.'

Purefoy took her hand and shook it as he said, 'Liza.'

She immediately retracted her hand and slapped him, grunting her disgust.

She looked at Murphy and Murphy nodded. They stared at each other a while. Murphy smiled a wide, black smile. Liza returned to her chair. Purefoy noticed that the three smartly dressed men bowed each time she walked by.

'What is it you want this time, Flash? Another leg?'

'No, your majesty, we need the map and the locations of the closures we discussed recently. If you remember we discussed social investment finance intermediaries seeking investment to complete the work for us. These gentlemen are they.'

'And there I was seeking him out among this squalid folk, although the circuit be eleven miles, and be not less than half a mile across.'

'Ah-hah, another good chaff, Your Majesty. What a wood-pecker you are.'

'Yes. Do shut up, Gideon. So these are they.'

'Yes, Your Majesty.'

'...they'll do if you trust them, Flash.' She inspected Murphy and Purefoy again. Purefoy noticed that the three smartly dressed men bowed each time they replied to her.

She removed her glove, finger by finger, and clicked her fingers. The tall man stepped out of the half shadow and to her side. In the light, his baldness and his smirk could be seen. 'Commander Pip, give these men what they want.'

'Thank you, Your Majesty. You've always been very accommodating to me and my parties.'

'I shall expect to be in control of a good few of your parties, Flash.' The man, Pip, was old and looked older than Purefoy. He was taller than Murphy and didn't wear a hat. His white gloves were obvious even in the darkened light of Glengall Street.

From behind Purefoy, a mad laughing was heard. He turned to face it and stumbled backward a step. When he looked up, two naked men were running toward them. Purefoy stepped back again. Murphy's outstretched, guiding hand met him. The men, one white, one black, bit into each other and spat the skin out onto the side as they ran. Both men were hairy and screamed as the other bit then laughed as the other would spit. They ran directly for the woman, Liza. She didn't move from her seat. She blinked once.

When the men were only a yard away, Flash and Gideon stepped too far back – they fell into the piles of bodies. They struggled and pushed each other further down into the rotting flesh so they could get a breath away from a reality they'd never faced before, would never have to face again.

The two mad men ran straight past Liza, into the marsh behind her. Laughing, howling; dying. Liza moved to the same way she was when they'd first seen her – she put her hands in her lap. Her face took on a stone quality.

The tall, slender man, Pip, walked over and pulled Flash and Gideon out of the bodies. He brushed their shoulders down. He signalled that they should follow him. They did so and walked into the shadows behind Liza. She didn't move. If she blinked, Purefoy didn't see it.

'Woman. Can we expedite the men's progress?' Murphy was curter to Liza than he was to Flash. Purefoy was too wrought to figure out why. She didn't answer except to move her head and look at Murphy. They held each other's gaze for all the time it took for Flash, Gideon, and Pip to return. Liza clicked her fingers, Pip returned to the half-shadows. She extended her ungloved hand. Gideon, Flash, and Legg kissed it. 'Good day, boys.'

'Good day, Your Majesty.'

'Liza,' Murphy said. 'Make account that I am, aye, beside thee if ever it come to pass that fortune bring thee where there are bodies in a like dispute – for a base wish it is to wish to hear it.' For a split-second, Liza looked troubled as she moved her jaw slightly and her nostrils flared. She returned to her held, icy look. The men walked back to the main street.

Who was it that said all kings and queens have a criminal lineage? I've a criminal lineage, just ask Paul just over in The Academy, I'll be a queen then and she'll be as brutish as a king if ever I see her again.

Back on the DAGR, the group stopped but didn't immediately speak. Something brewed. Murphy looked to the King's Arms. Purefoy looked at the ground while attempting to regain inward control. Legg looked at the blood and the vivi on Gideon's suit, Gideon looked to Flash.

Flash was the first to bite. 'Murphy did you really need to be so disrespectful to Her Majesty?'

'Aye.'

'"Aye?" "Aye?" That's all you've got to say for yourself? "Aye?"'

Gideon, the second.

'Aye.'

'Listen Murphy, Liza brings a lot of men to her court in this town. You'd best apologize.'

'Aye.'

'So you agree?' Flash, relieved at how easy Murphy changed his mind, flushed.

'When all's said and done, aye.'

'…good. Good.'

'Perhaps we should conclude our business so that Mr Murphy and Mr Purefoy can get to theirs?' Legg offered, trying to hurry away the awkwardness.

'One of the best things you've ever said, Legg.' Gideon returned Legg's gift.

The papers were given to Purefoy. Murphy had the sack. He wasn't given opportunity to read them or even look at them before the business was done. Flash said, 'You must follow these precisely. The locations of work have been circled by our friend Commander Pip with Gideon's watchful eye on it so do not stray from their exact path.'

'We understand, Flash. Thank you for your aid in facilitating this process. You've been a consummate professional.' Murphy smiled and offered his hand to Flash. Flash hesitated a second and then took it.

'Thank you, Murphy, for being a part of a bigger plan. Without men like you—'

'And you.' Murphy said.

'And me, quite right, then there'd be no hope for the future.'

'Aye. Yes, you're so very right – I'm glad we're in such good agreement and understanding.' Both Murphy and Flash smiled at each other as they shook hands. Murphy then shook hands with Gideon and even Legg. None of the men approached Purefoy to shake his hand. He neither minded nor attempted it. They said their goodbyes. The group finally divided to how they'd first met. Murphy and Purefoy walked south; the others, north. As they left, Gideon could be heard asking, 'Shall we get 'rum lock' then gentlemen?' A laugh from all three came next.

'Murphy, why did that woman, Liza, slap me? I can't figure it. Not at all. Not then, not now.'

'Because that's the privilege of the privileged, Purefoy. They can get away with it, so they do.' Purefoy thought Murphy was mocking him until he felt Murphy's hand gently squeeze his shoulder. The sights of the last hour wouldn't be relieved through gentle means.

Just over two hundred and eighty miles to the north, William Armstrong sang the song of 'D'ye ken John Peel?' He sang it to himself after he'd considered 'What must be done about the patents?' The guns he'd made had done their job and taken their place, he'd soon be knighted for what he'd made – when he'd finished singing, his stomach hurt and he felt cold. It passed and he continued.

CHAPTER 31

A pregnant quiet developed between them. Murphy saluted the King's Arms as they went past. Purefoy reasserted control over his innards, if only just his innards. The thrumming in his head wouldn't go away that day. That much he knew.

The road was soon uncluttered by buildings. Marsh surrounded them on either side.

Purefoy asked himself, *Am I mad? Have I finally gone the way of my father?* But couldn't give an answer. He didn't know how to stop the pain or the flashes of light. He realized his right eye now wept continuously as if his vision needed a constant reminder of what it is to see – a constant cleansing. *Will Murphy actually free me? I shouldn't hope for it but he might actually be true to his word...I should ask him about the job...but he'll tell me when it's time...in his time.* He would have tried to read the papers had it not been so dark. He would have asked to stop for food – a last supper – were the ache in his stomach distinguishable from his other aches. Now that he could walk without falling, Purefoy looked ahead.

No more people walked by. They were between populated locales. There was only a very light fog. Though they had no light themselves and the lights of the Isle of Dogs were too far away to light there, in the distance a faint orange glowed behind great swathes of shadow.

'Murphy, is – is that Deptford?'

'Aye, but behind a towering feat.'

What towers are there in Deptford? Purefoy was meant to go to Deptford today. He thought about the walk that would have taken him half a day. He'd hoped that a friendly cart would have come along or been open to a trade. He would have watched as London receded from view and he would've breathed the fresh air. Once there, the men on Tanner's Hill might have shouted, asking pleasantly, to see if he'd any pure to sell. He would've felt a small happiness in their requests, a sign of respect and a communal understanding. They were men like him.

'Well shalt thou see, if you arrive there, how much the sense deceives itself by distance; therefore, a little faster spur thee on,' Murphy intoned and walked faster. Purefoy hastened and kept pace. Though he had to swallow down acid, Purefoy felt he did well to stay on his feet. *This is the last time I'll see Deptford...unless Murphy lets me go...or if I can get away...yes. I can get away. I just need to stay strong. Don't fall. Don't be dragged down.* The encroaching dark increased the flashes when he closed his eyes.

To steady himself, he asked, 'What tower is that?'

'Know that what you see are not towers but giants – giant ships – and they are in the well, around the bank from the navel downward. One and all of them.'

'Do they have names?'

'Nimrod; Ephialtes; Briateus, which has fire burning in fifty furnaces to keep it moving ; Tityus, which is never finished due to some vulture or another; and Typhon. There are more but those the ones I remember. I should warn you though, they're...surprisingly easy to get along with.' Murphy chuckled and said, 'I know a good few people who enjoy the life and the giants themselves? Well the giant-ships do actual trade and get things from one place to another. Like all tall tales that become real, they're necessary.' Purefoy absorbed these words through another bout of a high-pitched squeal from his inner ear. He let them sink in and hoped they'd rid him of the noise.

From the ships came a sound neither of the men had ever heard before.

It wasn't a steam whistle, a horn, or a pipe; it wasn't the bagpipes they'd both been lucky enough to hear somewhere on the streets of London; they both stopped moving. Purefoy tilted his head so his left ear was higher than his right. It wasn't the orchestra music he'd heard but to him it sounded close. To Murphy it was only mechanical noise, to Purefoy it was dumbfounding.

He knew it was a language but one he didn't know – he didn't understand it but he thought that sometimes you didn't need to understand the music of a language to know its musicality was beautiful. He only spoke Welsh and English but when he heard other languages, he appreciated their qualities. To him, the giants' communication was an expression of intent – the giant-ships would travel, see the world, and they would live lives as beautiful as they could, connecting as many as they could. 'Be not afraid, Bryn. It's just the machines.'

'Oh, no. I'm not afraid. I think it's...I think it's beautiful.'

'You're an odd man, Purefoy. I'm beginning to see how you could be liked.'

What the bear had said to Purefoy – what he knew he'd said to himself – came back to him.

'Murphy, if I told you that The City is a diseased lover, the only way to talk about it is in breaching taboo...what would you say?'

'...I'd say you're right. ...aye.' The men looked at each other and could only make out each other's shape. Murphy said, 'We're almost there. Come on.'

As they walked, Murphy felt inside the sack. Purefoy couldn't see it but he heard the familiar sounds of skin on canvas. 'Bryn, take this.' Murphy guided something to Purefoy's hand. It was large and round – large enough that he couldn't get his fingers to meet his thumb and ensure he had the best grip on it. It wasn't metal or glass; it took him a moment but he thought it might be wax. Murphy lit a match. Their faces were briefly illuminated. Purefoy saw some stubble on Murphy's face then only the flame of the match as it touched on the wick of the large candle he held. 'Walk slower and put your hand in front to guard the flame. We're close.' Murphy didn't light a candle of his own. The light from Purefoy's candle only lit a couple of yards around him and little in front of him. Murphy moved to Purefoy's right and frequently looked over to the side of the road.

'We're here, Bryn.'

At the side of the road an enormous door sat where he was sure there hadn't been one before. Even in the faint candlelight, he could see the door was blue and taller than two men. It had some words written across it. He lifted up the candle. Murphy busied himself. He moved the candle slowly from left to right and read what he could: ANTI-INCENDIARIES MUST BE USED BEYOND THIS POINT. He said the word aloud, 'Anti-in-ken-die-aries…Murphy, do you know what this word is?'

'Aye Bryn, I do.'

'Do…do you know what it means?'

'Aye, I do.'

'Well…? Will you tell me, please?'

'…aye, ya deserve that much. It means that we should be using lanterns for our candles – 'anti' means against and 'in-sin-dee-ah-rees' means fire or open flames.'

'What happens if we don't?'

'We'll find out.' Murphy swallowed the word 'out'. 'But I'll need ya to help me get the damn door open before we do.'

The door's crossbar showed no signs of ever being opened. Murphy tried on his own. He failed. Purefoy put his candle on the ground. Murphy put his sack down, away from them. They pushed. Together they moved it but only an inch. They pushed again and gained a foot. Once more and the bar was loose. They collected their items, Murphy pulled at the crossbar ring. He couldn't move the door. The ring was big enough for three men to hold it – Purefoy put his candle down again and pulled. With each exertion, the flashes of light came more frequently; the pain spread from inside his head to the surface skin on the right side. His shoulders burnt with the effort. The door pulled back by just a foot. When they went to enter, Purefoy saw that the door itself was a foot deep.

They entered. The door closed behind them of its own accord.

The candle gave little solace in the thickness of the dark. The damp, mould smell slowly filled them. Murphy lit another match and with it, a candle for himself.

The two men observed each other in the candlelight. Though both had visibly aged that day, Purefoy knew he was the worse. His eye still wept, he felt his head tilted to the right without conscious choice, and he knew his core balance was lost – so long as they kept moving, he would be fine. He couldn't look Murphy in the eye. Murphy looked less and less like the swell, healthy giant he'd been when they first met, when Murphy first attacked him. In the candlelight that only uncovered the space between them, he looked more like the child Purefoy'd seen shivering amidst the crates and barrels.

'It's time, Bryn. Have ya any questions?'

'Yes. Yes I do. What's the job, Murphy? What are we actually doing?'

Chapter 32

'We've a long way to go before we even start the job. Any other questions?'

'Yes – what. Is. The job, Murphy?'

The two men stared at the broken man in front of them – Purefoy, half blind with even the candlelight illuminating his trauma-emphasized lines, saw Murphy drooling blood and hunching like an oversized child just to fit into the space. Murphy, afraid at what he might do and knowing what he must do, saw Purefoy weeping from one eye and staring back more resolute than he'd been before.

They stood in an unknown darkness, only Murphy's hunching indicated the size of the room. The damp mottled their skin. The moss smell grew further into them. Murphy turned away from Purefoy's gaze and took the papers from Purefoy's hand. 'We need to know where we're going before we can be sure of what we're doing.'

'What's the job, Murphy?' Purefoy's volume increased – with it, the difficulty in keeping his head held up. He gritted his teeth. Murphy unrolled the papers.

'Now, we need to follow —'

'What's the job?!' Purefoy shouted. It echoed and he twitched with each repetition. He looked into the darkness to his right. His anger died with the revelation, *This isn't a room* '...it's a tunnel.'

'Aye, Bryn. We're in a tunnel. Or, at least, we will be when we go down the steps.'

Purefoy slowly moved his candle from between them to as far right as he could. Only darkness. He turned around and put the candle directly in front of him – brickwork. He took a step toward it but felt something near his head. He took a half step back and lifted the candle higher – the bricks arched to fit the door.

'This is just an antechamber, Bryn. This leads to the steps which lead to the tunnels.'

'Tunnels…? You mean there's more than one?'

'Yes. I've no idea how many…but there'll be more soon and they'll be bigger.' Murphy raised the map between them. 'If we're able, we've got to navigate Tunnel Magog before the Camicion de' Pazzi. Then we've work to do. After that, tunnel Gog. From there it's a long way but there's more to be done on it when we cane – can, when we can.'

A strong breath of wind flooded the antechamber. Their candles snuffed.

He spoke softly, 'Murphy, tell me what the job is.'

Murphy lit a match and lit the candles. Purefoy, unblinking, stared at Murphy. Murphy nodded.

After placing his candle on the floor, Murphy stayed knelt and held up the map.

'This map shows us where we are above ground. See the circles? Well…' He put that first map down and held up a second. 'Those circles are where we do the work and this Cocytus map shows us how to get there. When we put them on top of each other, we can see where we put the charges.' He put the two maps together and traced his finger along a line. 'See there's the Iron Cable Manufacturers, there's the Napier's Works, and there's the British School.'

'Charges?'

'Aye. Charges.'

'What do you mean, 'charges'?'

'The…the explosives, Bryn.'

'Explosives? What does *that* mean? What are 'explosives'?'

'Gunpowder, Bryn.' Purefoy's procerus muscles pulled together, ridging his brow.

'Why are we putting gunpowder in tunnels? That doesn't make any…'

'That's the job, Bryn. Take or leave it…though I think you'll have a hard time of it getting back up through that door. You're down here now.'

That's the job, brother, and that's the way it is if you accept it. I accept it as we all accept it, but...here's how we live and how we must. Here's what we must...the purefinder's are eaten up, they're not sustainable. We survive in losing, we survive in loss. You'd be better knowing it now – from me – when I'm trying to do you a kindness. Take it, Bryn, take it – go on, I dare you. Prove me wrong. Please prove me wrong. No one has so far – I've logic enough to win the argument – but no accord to make it clear. 'Make it clear, Mal. Make it clean.' Can't believe he said that – to me, when he was the brother with all the star-eyed lies. This brother doesn't know but he will know once he's chosen. One day a moneyman will be forced to pick up dog shit to make into something else – in an age of austerity, we're all purefinders. That month I was cartman was the first month I'd been happy and happy on my own until Paul came back, back with a blue boar. Thick shit. Hah – thick shit here, aye. We'll see won't we?

Purefoy knew what the job meant then. It meant destroying buildings from underneath. It meant risking their lives to destroy what wasn't theirs.

'What if there's people in these buildings? Sorry, above these 'charges'?'

'There shouldn't be, it's night and they're all—'

'Shouldn't be anyone there, Murphy? *Shouldn't?!* Will there or won't there? And how can you even know?' Each question growled.

'I don't know and it's not my business to know.'

Purefoy looked away from the maps, into the darkness. He remembered his headless father walking toward him. What his father whispered to him, on the last time he saw him, came to him. His heart skipped and increased pace. Looking at Murphy again as he inspected the maps, Purefoy took a step backward, toward the door.

He snuffed out his candle with a pinch. His nostrils flared. His jaw clenched.

He grabbed the back of Murphy's head and slammed it into the wall.

Murphy fell, stunned. He unconsciously knocked the candle over and onto the maps. His hat came off as he flicked his head and gasped – Purefoy grabbed Murphy's head by a tuft of hair and slammed it into the wall again. Twice, three times – he saw blood – four times, hair came away in Purefoy's hand. Murphy groaned and fell to the ground holding his head. *Run, get away from him.*

Purefoy remembered the steps.

With only the light from the burning maps and nothing to guide him but his hands, he put his left hand on the wall and walked as quickly as he could. He found the steps and descended quickly. At the bottom, he stepped into water. The smell was overwhelming. He ran.

Murphy's groan languished.

That buck's faced burner. That Cainite – who knew? Not you, you fool. When were you gonna get him? When were you gonna pull him aside and kill him with it? The man's half your size and he just threw you against a wall – hah! I knew it. That's who – I knew. Hah! You're more Abel than you are able. And how 'bout you Paul, you here too? Sure you are, somewhere. Perhaps that's the trick – you walk with a man, you drink with a man for long enough and they become your brother whether you like it or not. So this is it then, so he's your brother now is he? Aye, I'd say he is. Aye. We know he is. Aye...time to do what brothers do.

Murphy's groan turned into laughter. It echoed through the tunnels, chasing Purefoy.

Purefoy's chest was tight, his breathing erratic. The water at his feet got deeper but patches made crisp, frost-crushing sounds beneath him. He didn't know where he was going. He could feel his left hand bleeding but he couldn't stop. He knew the laughter meant he'd soon be chased by Murphy. He kept his eyes open, trying to adjust, but there was nothing. No light to help – the absolute black picked at the base of his neck and – he didn't dare stop. *There'll be light, there'll be light somewhere. There always is.* Both his eyes were wet from the exertion of running.

The pressure in his ears grew. The high-pitched scream returned to his right ear. He tripped. His mouth and nostrils filled with water – he coughed it out, he knew it was full of pure. The moisture in his lungs weighed him down as he scrambled to his feet. He coughed again and put out his left hand – it felt nothing. *Oh God*. He feared an immediate drop that would kill him; he put out his right – it found brickwork. In those quiet seconds, he thought he heard noises coming from behind him. He walked trying to regain control, to not lose his footing. He followed the feeling of the wall and felt that it curved around to join another straight wall. He ran again.

As he was running, he remembered that earlier today he'd felt a calm in the face of his impending death. Now all that was gone, it only served to increase his fear.

And the word was 'I am'. In here I'm not – in here 'I am' alone. Imalone Imaloné Imalone. 'I am' negated, you old deaf bastard – but then what was it the little Bryn said? 'I think it's us who need to listen more.' I am listening now, Bryn. I'm listening for you and I can hear you. I am a star of silence absorbing every sound you make. I fear what's inside me.

The tunnel curved again but Purefoy's hand felt it out. A relief. He kept running. The dark was doing odd things to his thoughts, to his eyes. He heard tiny squeaks and scurrying. The flashes of light he'd seen earlier came again but came with more than just light.

His chest hurt, his heart strained. The faces of his mother, of his sister, flashed at him. The water was half way up to his knees and made too much noise for him to know if anything was nearby. His first employer laughed at his mistakes as his plantar interosseus muscles cramped. BB – 'strong, sweet BB' – cried. George, Bristol George, died smoking a pipe in front of him. He ran as best he could.

His lower back winced, his rectus femoris muscle burnt and the child he'd seen that morning thanked him. The photograph of two women bound became him and BB sewn together at the back, unable to kiss. Their sewn form became an unknown man but Purefoy knew his name was Paolo – in the way of dreams and visions – and the bound Francesca came to Paulo and was sewed to his back. He could feel himself being flooded with terror and elation – he wanted sex as much as he wanted to survive – and it only made him run faster. He couldn't control his breathing. He coughed as he ran. The damp air flooded his throat.

A sudden blow to his lower back knocked him off his feet. His vision went entirely white. He curled in on himself before he hit the water. This was it, *Murphy will kill me now.*

Chapter 33

No water hit his face.

A sharp jerk of his neck into his chest and an arm around him, yes, but he didn't feel any water on his face. He waited for another blow or the feeling of metal in his side and under every stretch of skin, his nerves trembled.

Murphy made sure both Purefoy's arms were held in front of him. Murphy stood behind Purefoy with his teeth rested on Purefoy's skull.

But he didn't bite. He waited until Purefoy's breathing had calmed.

Purefoy breathed through the mucous in his nose and spoke through the grinder in his throat, 'It's fine. You can…you can do it. I wish I could…well, it's up to you. I – I'm ready.'

'Don't worry Bryn, I truly am here to deliver you from all evil.' Murphy uplifted his mouth from its grim position.

'Truly Bryn, I'm not here to hurt you – I promise I won't. I know that today seems an odd proof of it, but were you to look back over what I've said today and what I've done, it's all been only to test you. I mean you no harm and now your breathing has calmed, I'll let you go.'

Murphy let Purefoy go. Purefoy slowly turned around. In the dark, he couldn't see Murphy. He waited for the second punch. He waited for the lie to be broken.

Nothing came.

He waited. Purefoy's instinct was to run again but he felt too much intrigue at why Murphy hadn't already killed him. He didn't trust Murphy but asked, 'Do you mean it, Murphy?'

'Aye, I do. I won't touch you now unless it's to save you from harm. I was only half-sent by that woman in the church. The rest was my own choice. I came to find you, Bryn, for more than just a reward.' Something had changed in Murphy's voice. The monotone had gone, replaced with a soft lilt.

'I don't understand. You're... were you acting today?'

'I had to, Bryn. Sometimes I wasn't and sometimes you were too – remember that you saved me twice. I'm a tall man with few teeth. No matter how I dress myself, I know how I look. I know how strong I am too but I never meant to truly hurt you, just test ya.'

If only I could see him. I might actually be able to tell. Purefoy wiped his eyes and his face. His right eye stung, his right ear pained him but the ringing had disappeared along with his fast heart rate. He was stuck, unable to think clearly. He could feel a chemical release running down his spine, flooding his aches, but this couldn't help him know whether Murphy was truthful. Now that they'd stopped, he wanted a release. He wanted to sit down, to be warmed. He wanted the reality of the comfort Murphy's words promised. 'I think we should keep moving, Murphy. Our legs might get hurt otherwise. Is there a way out?'

'Aye, it's the way you were going. Turn back around and we'll do as we've done all day. We'll walk and I'll guide you.'

Half expecting to be punched again, Purefoy turned around.

He walked. He could hear Murphy behind him. 'Will you tell me why, Murphy? Why all this? Why today?'

'When we get a little further along and when we get to some light, yes. I'll tell you. The water may get deeper. Be careful.'

'...are these sewers?'

'Aye. Before I was professional, I was a cartman, and before that I was a ratcatcher in the sewers and sewers much like this one. The man we met today, Legg; I gave him the opportunity to work in the sewers with me once but he turned his back on us and, instead, told a police-beak on the nose where he could find us. He got paid enough to work his way into Flash's lot and that was that. I don't think he could even tell ya what a rat looks like.'

'So you weren't going to destroy those buildings?'

'I might have, if you hadn't stopped me.'

'But—'

'I needed to test you, Bryn, but I needed you to stop me just as much. I came to find you because I needed someone like you. Earlier today, you mentioned The Reserve and I had to test – I had to see – how much of a reserve you have in you.'

Purefoy couldn't accept everything Murphy was saying but Murphy still hadn't hit him. They'd walked twenty paces. *'Someone like me?' What does he mean? A poor man...a tired man...a Welshman. What did Geyron say? 'There is no'...*

Purefoy put out his left hand and felt the tunnel. His hands didn't fully understand what his feet were doing but they didn't falter. Now he'd stopped running, he felt the intensity of the smell again. He coughed and searched his pockets for his handkerchief. He found it, put it to his nose.

A gust of cold, clean air came to them. 'Did you feel that?' Purefoy couldn't trust it.

'Aye, I did.'

'Where's it coming from?'

'All in good time, Bryn. You'll know it when you see it.'

The water had risen to their waists. Purefoy could feel water trickle through the brickwork. The cuts that Murphy had kicked into him stung. 'Murphy, why did Flash want to destroy the buildings like The British School?'

'For lots of reasons really, but the most important is that they've laid the foundations poorly. One day The City won't know how to act because their forefathers have set up a system so built on shit that their sons will believe it's the only system that works. Flash isn't even his real name – like I was today, the man's an actor. The difference between him and me is that he's always acting. No matter what. I'm sure today you've thought that I'm heartless – gutless, even – and you'd be right to that opinion considering what you've seen of me but unlike Flash, I stop acting. I despise that man because I can tell there's nothing behind his eyes. Sure there's anger behind mine but at least there's something. That's why I wanted you to stop me. So that I wouldn't fall into the shit with him.'

'So all of the land behind the tunnel walls is made up of pure?'

'Not exactly. It's marsh and there's some human shit there but when you said you were 'a cleaner' earlier, you underestimated yourself. You're more than that. Ya see, Bryn, I needed to know about you before today so I watched ya for a week. I knew all about ya before today and none of the pure that you collected ever ended up making a foundation. It only made things cleaner, better. I needed you to come with me today because...because I think the real world cannot be true. I needed you to see what I see – to feel what I've felt. All the shit, the grimace-smiles, and the semen – do you ever notice how some people look at you as if they're disgusted with you just for living?'

'...yes...'

They had to bend down. The water continued to rise. The roof of the tunnel continued to lower. Purefoy felt more water trickle through the brickwork. There was no more than half a foot between the water and the tunnel roof. 'We'll have to swim through it, Bryn – can you swim?'

'Yes but it's sewer water.'

'Aye. We have to do it. Dive down and swim for five seconds. After that, you should be fine to come up.'

Is this it? Is this when Murphy takes his chance and drowns me? As he took a deep breath, Purefoy played a song his father had taught him in his inner ear. He dived.

Purefoy emerged out of the water and breathed again.

He coughed and cleared his nostrils. He laughed. He'd thought Murphy might grab his ankle as he had that morning. He stepped forward. *I'm alive.* He laughed again. The sound of Murphy rising out of the water followed him. Purefoy was still laughing. 'What's the gig?'

'You – you didn't drown me.'

'Ah, Bryn, I know ya can't let yourself trust me yet but know this – I will not harm you. Not ever. Like today I may pretend to, but I never will. Not even if we lived to be two hundred years old – two thousand years old. We've not far now, let's keep walking.'

The water was still at their waists but lowered as they progressed. Purefoy kept his right hand out, less water trickled on to it. He could only trust his hands. The rest of him was cold. The air was getting colder. The tunnel took another curve. At the end of the new tunnel they came to, there was light. A small fraction of grey light. Purefoy hurried toward it. The light only showed more tunnel but he didn't care.

A desire for revenge came over Purefoy. He thought that here, *he* could drown *Murphy. For once, I could be the one in control…*but he asked himself, *Why? Why would I need that? Even if Murphy's still lying – why would I need that at all?'* He walked on but noted how unlike him are the thoughts that grief causes. How unlike anyone.

All that day, Purefoy had thought himself half-dead. His body still felt things out, he still thought, but at a half-removed state. Waiting on the end, walking toward it, he'd been himself but he'd lost himself. Sometimes limbs hadn't felt like his. He couldn't trust his vision. Now he wasn't sure he could trust thoughts. In the moment he'd received the news of his mother and his sister, he'd given up on himself. He'd felt dead. Dead or no longer his own.

But now he was returning to himself – the cold, the water, the exhaustion. The tunnel, the light, and the struggle gave him something to focus on. In the kindling of possibility, he began to feel reconnected to himself.

CHAPTER 34

The tunnel illuminated. Though the light was faint and all it revealed was the water at their feet and the cramped tunnel around them, Purefoy thanked it. He finally knew that Murphy wasn't lying. From the absolute black they'd come from, he felt saved.

Can I trust him now? Perhaps…it's too quick a change…but then, perhaps all change is. As he'd reconnected to himself, he'd begun to feel all the aches again. His left hand rubbed the wall to guide him. Ahead he could see a circle that differed from the tunnel but he couldn't tell what it was. He walked faster toward it, if only to be out of the tunnel.

'Go easy, Bryn. We're there. We've reached the end – the way out – but the tunnel pours out into the Monster Soup. Don't go too far toward it. Lean against the left side and look to our right.' Purefoy did. It felt good to lean against something.

He couldn't understand what he saw. *Is it…* 'Is it all of London, Murphy?'

'All except The City.' He saw a series of low black bricks spiked only by towers. He tried to think what each could be – he knew St Paul's from its roundness and the unfinished tower of Westminster Palace but the rest were nameless spires. *Sometimes it looks as though it's Westminster which makes the fog.*

'*Vexilla regis prodeunt capitalis.* Look at it, Bryn. It's beautiful isn't it?'

'…yes. Yes it is.' Purefoy was beginning to feel sleepy.

'Aye. The place itself's very beautiful. Can you see Westminster Palace?'

'Yes. Why?' He yawned.

'Behold this and behold the place where thou with fortitude must arm thyself. I always wondered why it's called a 'palace', I—'

'Murphy, I'm sorry but I'm tired and if I fall asleep, I know it's too cold for me to sleep and that could mean the worst. If you truly mean what you say and you don't want to hurt me, keep me awake – tell me…why have you done everything you've done today? Why me and why all of this?'

'All of this – all of today – was, as I've said, a test but…but it wasn't a test of you, it was a test of me *and* you.

Did you believe me when I said I'd watched you? Because ya should've. I saw you one day, walkin' in the centre, and you had a smile on your face. It was raining hard and you had a smile on your face – your feet were covered in mud and ya had shit on your hands yet ya kept on smiling. I thought, "There's an odd fella. Might be an idiot." And I walked on. Forgot about ya. Then Angie – the church woman – she set me to find ya, gave me ten days. Her ten days chimed with the offer of work from Flash. I kept him on the rope to see what he was up to. When it came to you, all I knew was your name's Bryn Prifardd Llewes, you go by Purefoy because you're a purefinder and you're often found round Dean Street. To some people that might not be much but to me, it was plenty. I found you in a day and I was gonna get my reward but…but I recognized ya and you were smiling again. I thought maybe you were on the laudanum or maybe you were just an idiot but either way, I thought I better watch ya for a day or two to find out if you're trouble. Course, I only found the opposite. I found out you're a rare breed, Bryn – you're a good man…'

'So you thought you best beat me half to death. Well forgive me for saying so, Murphy, but…but…' He sighed then spoke, again, 'Oh I'm too tired to get angry. I'm freezing too.'

'It's not just that, Bryn. I had to show you other worlds – worlds you didn't know.'

'You've shown me hell.'

'Yes. It *is* hell but it's not of our making and you needed to know that. Anywhere can be hell, I've just shown you one of them. I saw you trudge through days on end following the fat women with their fat dogs, cleaning up after them, and even be apologetic to them if they approached you. I saw you when you thought you were alone and you looked at the ring around your neck – I knew you were lonely, Bryn. After I'd realized all this, I still had to get you to Angie but I knew – I just knew – that I had to know you.'

'I – I don't understand, Murphy, why you couldn't just have come to me...'

'Because...because I'm alone.' Murphy laughed then continued, 'Aye, Malone – that's my real name, ya know. My real name's Malone. Only Charlotte, and now you, know it.'

I know I can trust him with it but I wish it was easier.

Through his tiredness and the dark, Purefoy tried to see Malone, to understand him. 'Murphy...Malone, could you come closer, please.' Malone came to the edge of the tunnel and leant on the side, opposite. Purefoy looked at him. What he saw touched him. Malone was trying not to cry. To Purefoy, he looked like a child once more. He knew then that all Malone wanted was a brother.

'You wanted a brother.'

'I have a brother. I wanted a friend. I want someone to help me make a choice I have to make but one I can't seem to make...though I know it'll make it for me soon enough. Will you help me, Bryn? Please?'

'Was that all it was? Is that everything?'

'No, there's much more to it...before today, when was the last time you'd been to The City? A year? Two?'

'Four. The four years since my wedding.'

'I had to show you The City and everything it is – the warehouse, today. One day it could be under Flash's control. Imagine how many people's lives would be ruined by how he handles it and what kind of thing would he be, would it be, that could destroy so many so easily? You said it yourself, Bryn – it's hell...and you must never return to hell once you've seen inside it.'

A memory, a strong memory struggled through the cold and his tiredness. First, Purefoy remembered the forehead touching his own, then the whispered voice – his father's voice – and '...you must never return to hell once you've seen inside it' and the tear that fell from his father's cheek. The hairs on his forearms bristled in the cold realization. His own tears mixed with the effluvium from his eyes. 'So...what's the choice you've got to make, friend?'

'Today, you've seen what I see every day. Now you know how we all live and what we live through and—'

'I knew it before, Mu – Malone. I know what people live through.'

'So how come you can smile? You said it yourself, they look at us in disgust. How can you smile at that?'

'Because – because that is my lot in life. I have nothing but...I had nothing but my wife and in a way, I lost her before she died. She died this morning...'

'I'm sorry, Bryn.'

'But she went in the workhouse a long time before. We said it was for her health but we knew it wasn't just that. When you've nothing, Malone, you can smile so long as the one you love is safe.'

'And if you've no one to love?'

'...then you need a friend.'

A silence.

The air seemed warmer. Purefoy understood. 'My choice is like a choice between you and me. Do I go through hell every day or do I somehow ignore it?'

'I don't ignore it, Malone. I just can't help it.'

'Then my choice is this. Do I go back into the city, knowing what I know – what you now know – or do I leave London completely but as a free man? This is your choice too, ya know. Unless, of course, you want to go back into hell?' *Help me, Bryn*

– make your choice and I'll follow. Rise up upon thy feet; the way is long, and difficult the road, and soon the sun to middle tierce returns. Choose and I'll follow.

His eyes were so tired. He leaned back his head and shut them. His father's song he'd remembered before diving through the sewer came to him again. He sang it:

Diolch i chi Wraig Llwyd.
Diolch i chi Wraig o'r Llwyn.
Diolch i chi am yr amser.
Diolch i chi am fy cartref.

Roeddwn i'n fachgen ond nawr dwi'n dyn;
roeddwn i'n fachgen ond nawr dwi'n hen...

Diolch i chi Wraig Llwyd.
Diolch i chi Wraig o'r Llwyn.
Diolch i chi am yr amser.
Diolch i chi am fy gartref.

Nawr dwi'n mewn breichiau â marwolaeth,
dwi'n heddychol.

[Thanks to you, Grey Lady.
Thanks to you, Lady of the Bush.
Thanks to you for the time.
Thanks to you for my home.

I was a boy but now I'm a man.
I was a boy but now I'm old...

Thanks to you, Grey Lady.
Thanks to you, Lady of the Bush.
Thanks to you for the time.

Thanks to you for my home.

Now I'm in arms with death,
now I'm at peace.]

When he'd finished, he stood and stepped to the edge of the tunnel. 'Bryn? Have you chosen?'

'I have.'

He jumped.

Purefoy chose the river.

How dare he? Why would he give up? It's cowardice. It's giving...is it giving up? What did he say earlier? 'I would say to lie down in your own place, in your own way, is a beautiful thing.' But suicide is an unpardonable offence...unless...unless you've already been through hell. From hell to purgatory, maybe...clever. Clever little bastard. If it isn't that and all that's ended then at least it's an end. The other option. Absolute exit. Bones and maw maw. No mew for this maw. Hah. He took you on in the end then? Aye. In all ways – he went from mewling newt to tailor for my last suit. Tricky little bastard. From prisoner to leader in a day, so's the way – so's always been the way – so should it always be if I have my way. The bearded, old Wells, 'Did anyone ever tell you we came from water? My ol' gran did. She said we could return...anytime we needed...' The water washes us clean – always has. Even in the old church, the older churches. The water washes us clean – always has. Always will.

Purefoy chose the river. Malone followed.

Eventually the tide brought the two bodies together again. As they lay in the river, walking out once more beneath the stars, a small flicker of Malone's consciousness knew that they'd done this before, that they'd do all this again – that all the hell they'd seen and the demons they'd met would be there but in new guises and under different names – in a hundred and fifty years.

Epilogue

...after a while of living in London you stop seeing the signs.
Purefinder, **Chapter 5 – The Lovers, 2013**

Purefoy looked back at The George Tavern, its external features were in the revival Gothic and even Purefoy knew that Gothic was considered a good, Christian style. Before today, he'd heard the gothic talked about as a 'morally superior time'. He laughed.
Purefinder, **Chapter 12 – Phlegethon, 2013.**

* * *

But first let us ask ourselves why the demand for an intellectual deliverance arises in such an age as the present, and in what the deliverance itself consists? The demand arises, because our present age has around it a copious and complex present, and behind it a copious and complex past; it arises, because the present age exhibits to the individual man who contemplates it the spectacle of a vast multitude of facts awaiting and inviting his comprehension. The deliverance consists of man's comprehension of this present and past. It begins when our mind begins to enter into possession of the general ideas, which are the law of this vast multitude of facts. It is perfect when we have acquired that harmonious acquiescence of mind, which we feel in contemplating a grand spectacle that is intelligible to us; when we have lost that impatient irritation of mind which we feel in the presence of an immense, moving, confused spectacle which, while it perpetually excites our curiosity, perpetually baffles our comprehension.

* * *

What facts, then, let us ask ourselves, what elements of the spectacle before us, will naturally be most interesting to a highly developed age like our own, to an age making the demand which we have described for an intellectual deliverance by means of the complete intelligence of its own situation? Evidently, the other ages similarly developed, making the same demand. And what past literature will naturally be most interesting to such an age as our own? Evidently, the literatures which have most successfully solved for *their* ages the problem which occupies ours: the literatures which in their day and for their own nation have adequately comprehended, have adequately represented, the spectacle before them. A significant, a highly developed, a culminating epoch, on the one hand, – a comprehensive, a commensurate an adequate literature, on the other, – these will naturally be the objects of deepest interest to our modern age. Such an epoch and such a literature are, in fact, *modern*, in the same sense in which our own age and literature are modern; they are founded upon a rich past and upon an instructive fullness of experience.

Matthew Arnold
On the Modern Element in Literature, **1857**

* * *

'When an antigen-presenting cell ingests an antigen, such as a virus, it is broken down in an endosome. An MHC II molecule may bind to one of the fragments and carry it to the cell surface, where it is presented to a T(H) cell.'

Purves, Sadava, Orians and Heller, Life: The Science of Biology

The white blood cell wears the head of its enemy. A murder-swagger undiminished by micro-ontology. Berserker, *viro-serkr*, it flaunts itself, draped in the trophy skin of dead prey.

China Mieville
rejectamentalist manifesto, **2010**
http://chinamieville.net/post/1713592672/when-an-antigen-

presenting-cell-ingests-an

* * *

Why are we, in the 21st Century fetishizing the Victorian?

Why am I, as a writer aware of said fetishization, writing in the historical form?

See the white-blood cell above. See me dressed like a Victorian on the street but with more chains.

Know that I know my enemy.

* * *

Rich and Poor: Disparities, Perceptions, Concomitants

'The poverty of our century is unlike that of any other. It is not, as poverty was before, the result of natural scarcity, but of a set of priorities imposed upon the rest of the world by the rich.'
John Berger
Springer **2003**

* * *

'Money has often been the cause of the delusions of multitudes. Sober nations have all at once become desperate gamblers and risked almost their existence upon the turn of a piece of paper.'
Charles Mackay
Extraordinary Popular Delusions and the Madness of Crowds,
1841

ADDENDUM

Original chapter titles:
1. The Poet / A leopard, a lion, a she-wolf
2. The Plea / Rhys Llwyn ap Llwyd / the deal of the deck
3. The Beggar / '...just the ones without shoes' / Charon
4. The Wheel / 'So the wheel turns'
5. The Lovers / Sontag's Photography / Francesca Bound
6. Temperance, Reversed
7. The Devil / Ludgate Hill / The Leader / *Papé Satàn, papé Satàn aleppe*
8. The Tower / Phlegyas / The Opiate / 'Now art thou arrived'
9. Styx / The Kindly Ones / *après* Lizst, 1849
10. The Walls of Dis / May you live in interesting times... / masseter muscle
11. Heretics / May you find what you're looking for / 'How quickly sweetness...'
12. Phlegethon / The star, the friend, his whore & her leaving / Asterios & The Centaurs
13. The Forest of Suicides / Crimps / Camus
14. The Trade / The gulf / Charlottan [sic]
15. A desert of sleeping pilgrims / The Cruel Mother / '...only hold you at a distance'
16. I likes a drop of good beer, I do / an economy of souls / must soon reveal itself
17. Geyron / *Success to the war in fear!* / And what rough beast, its hour come round at last
18. The crux, his crux, whore's crux, you crux / *What's what is what* / The Unnameable
19. Onto Narrow and soon...Fore / the hanging men and the rope-pullers / *machina caelestis*
20. HERBAL TWIGS / Oedipus, Antigone / Tiresias, Manto
21. The Cabinet / The Malebranche / *twas ever thus*
22. Is he afraid? / *our hosses and our wigs* / slick with sick fish

23. Labyrinthine walkways / our souls on the ground / children again
24. Hander, Loliver, and Gammonfond
25. For the modest asking ought to be followed by the deed in silence
26. Between his boots / welcoming in the night / thy tongue restrain itself
27. All animals are equal / *Sportsman's Hall*
28. Tweedle-Dumb & Tweedle-Deed / *'And death unto thy race'*
29. To peel and expose / Boch / up to shoulder-height
30. Bulls, Bears, Fiscal naysayers & hucksters / Descartes loves his dad / Two do disease
31. One does diseases / spur thee on / *Raphèl maí amèche zabí almi*
32. The Giants / Antaeus
33. Caina / the real world cannot be true
34. St Joan / *Vexilla regis prodeunt capitalis.*
35. The Lightbringer

Diolch i Gareth Jones am 21st Chwerfror, 2013.
Diolch i Elfyn Jones am pob.

If you think you're in this, you already are.

Thank you, you who've made this with me and been here then seen it there.

Thank you more to those who want to change it.